# The Mezzo Wore Mink

## A Liturgical Mystery

# by Mark Schweizer

# Liturgical Mysteries
## by Mark Schweizer

Why do people keep dying in the little town of St. Germaine, North Carolina? It's hard to say. Maybe there's something in the water. Whatever the reason, it certainly has *nothing* to do with St. Barnabas Episcopal Church!

### Murder in the choirloft. A choir-director detective. It's not what you expect...it's even funnier!

The Alto Wore Tweed
The Baritone Wore Chiffon
The Tenor Wore Tapshoes
The Soprano Wore Falsettos
The Bass Wore Scales
The Mezzo Wore Mink

**ALL SIX now available at
your favorite mystery bookseller or sjmpbooks.com.**

*"It's like Mitford meets Jurassic Park, only without the wisteria and the dinosaurs..."*

# Advance Praise for *The Mezzo Wore Mink*

"A hard-bitten tale of love and hate, of mystery and non-mystery, of hotness and coldness, niceness and crankiness..."
*Carol McClure, Harpist*

"Like Chicken Soup for the Medulla Oblongata."
*Dr. Karen Dougherty, Physician*

"A penetrating, impertinent, and finally amusing little mystery that dares to ask the question: How much are you willing to pay for cheap fiction?"
*Dr. Richard Shephard, Chamberlain, Yorkminster*

"Kids, your new textbook is here—welcome to home school!"
*Stephanie Nelson, Sister*

"I've found that if Schweizer's books are administered with sufficient force at just the right angle, they can actually correct a patient's overbite."
*John Rutter, Orthodontist, Great Falls, Montana*

"As a mezzo, I'm deeply offended. As a choir member, I'm horrified. As a reader, I'm appalled. But as a law-abiding citizen and a court-ordered member of an anger management group, I won't be camping outside Schweizer's house until the restraining order is lifted."
*Jane Wells, Choirmember*

"Pushes too much on the playground."
*First grade report card*

"A book that finally answers the question—What Would Jesus Read?"
*His Grace, Lord Horatio "Wiggles" Biggerstaff, Archbishop (Retired)*

"These books just fly off the shelves...like they're possessed or something."
*David Thompson, Assistant Bookstore Manager*

"A winding labyrinth of a mystery that contains many ingredients of really good fiction, although not in any particular order."
*Jan Mitchell, Insurance Claims Manager*

For Mom

"M" IS FOR THE MANY THINGS SHE GAVE ME..."

# The Mezzo Wore Mink
### A Liturgical Mystery
Copyright ©2008 by Mark Schweizer

Illustrations by Jim Hunt
www.jimhuntillustration.com

Published by
**St. James Music Press**
www.sjmpbooks.com
P.O. Box 1009
Hopkinsville, KY 42241-1009

ISBN 978-0-9721211-9-4

1st Printing February, 2008

**Acknowledgements**
Holly Derickson, Beverly Easterling, Marty Hatteberg, Elaine Hicks,
Kristen Linduff, Patricia Nakamura, Donis Schweizer,
Richard Shephard and Rebecca Watts

# Prelude

First of all, Meg was gone. Not gone for good. Just gone for a couple of weeks.

As a highly trained detective, I had two clues that Meg was gone. The first was that she told me.

"I'm going to Myrtle Beach tomorrow," she said.

"Yikes. I hate Myrtle Beach."

"That's too bad. I was going to ask you to go with me."

"Why are you going to Myrtle Beach?" I asked.

"Investment seminar."

"Teaching or taking?"

"Teaching."

"So there won't be any playing hooky and skipping classes in favor of more interesting pursuits?"

"I'm afraid not," said Meg.

"I hope you don't mind terribly if I decline the invitation," I said.

Meg sighed. "I don't blame you. I hate Myrtle Beach, too. I don't know why I said I'd do it, but now I'm stuck."

The second clue was that I was about to smoke a cigar, something I'd given up a few months ago. Meg never actually asked me to, and never said anything once I did, but I could tell she appreciated the gesture. Today I figured that I could light up in the den, smoke my stogie, then open the windows, let the room air out for the rest of the week and I'd be home free. No harm, no foul.

I rolled the cigar between my thumb and forefinger and ran the length of it under my nose, taking in the aroma of delicious illegal Cuban tobacco. This was not just any cigar. This was a *Romeo et Julietta*, smuggled into the country by my friend Pete Moss, returning from his Cuban vacation by way of Mexico City. He had actually seen it rolled yesterday morning at the Partagas Cigar Factory behind the *Capitolio* in Old Havana. It was as fresh as a Cuban cigar got if you didn't happen to be in Cuba.

I put the cigar on the desk, sat down and looked at the box—large, nondescript, brown cardboard—that had been sent overnight by Pack & Ship in San Francisco and delivered this morning.

My typewriter, usually the focal point of the desk décor, found itself pushed to the side to make room for the package. This particular typewriter was mine by possession but not by right, since its original owner was Raymond Chandler, the mystery writer. I couldn't consider the 1939 Underwood truly mine until I had written at least one story worthy of the master himself. Meg suggested on more than one occasion that I might settle for a paragraph—or even a sentence. I had made several attempts over the years, much to the delight and disgust of the

St. Barnabas choir, on whom I inflicted my efforts. Now, with a fresh Cuban stogie and the sounds of Cab Calloway filling the room, I flipped open a collection of short stories to "Red Wing."

> There was a desert wind blowing that night. It was one of those hot dry Santa Anas that come down through the mountain passes and curl your hair and make your nerves jump and your skin itch. On nights like that every booze party ends in a fight. Meek little wives feel the edge of the carving knife and study their husbands' necks. Anything can happen. You can even get a full glass of beer at a cocktail lounge.

Classic. I put the small book aside, then ran the blade of my pocketknife across the top of the waiting box and opened it. I removed the tissue paper and revealed what I had purchased from a certain Barbara Chandler Forrest. Raymond's grandniece had kept some of her famous uncle's mementos for decades but finally, now having to move into an assisted living facility, she offered them to collectors. And I was one.

I reached in and removed a gray felt hat. A fedora made by the Mallory Hat Company of Danbury, Connecticut. Size 7 3/8. Too small for me, but just large enough to get it sized to my 7 1/2. I tried it on anyway since there wasn't anyone around to laugh. Baxter was looking at me from under a table and if he found the sight to be ludicrous, the only sign he gave was a slight wag of his tail.

I tugged the hat down as low as I dared, not wanting to damage it. My haberdasher in Philadelphia assured me the felt hat could easily be cleaned and professionally stretched one size and I'd told him I would send it up as soon as I received it. But then Meg had taken off for a few days, and I determined to give the hat, the cigar, and the typewriter another try. I looked at a framed photograph that had been included with my purchase. It was a photo of Raymond Chandler, dated 1952, wearing the same hat I now had on my head. I leaned it against the banker's lamp and, with a gentle tug on the chain, illuminated the photo as well as the entire top of the desk.

I lit my cigar, moved the Underwood back to the center of my desk, took a piece of 24 lb. bond and rolled it slowly under the platen. Then I placed my fingers on the glass keys and typed

The Mezzo Wore Mink
Chapter 1

The inspiration was practically palpable.

# Chapter 1

"It's not fair, Hayden," grumbled Pete from behind his copy of the St. Germaine *Tattler*. "She's got no political experience whatsoever."

"Neither did you," I reminded him. "Now, get your head out of the paper and pass me the grits. Even if you lose, what's the big deal? It's not like being mayor is your main source of income. Does it even pay anything?"

"Eight thousand a year, but that's not the point. Being mayor is who I am. It goes with my pony-tail."

"You'll probably win anyway. After twelve years, you're just used to running unopposed."

"And that's the way it should be. I also might point out that as police chief, you should be worried. If I go, I'm not going alone. You, my fine friend, are what we call in the political game a 'crony.' Here, listen to this." Pete snapped the *Tattler* inside out and folded it in half.

"Mayor Peter Moss has done nothing to bring new business to St. Germaine. As a small, quaint, Appalachian town, we should be vying for the same tourist dollars that are going to the nearby communities of Boone, Banner Elk, and Blowing Rock. Yet we have the same tired old stores downtown that we had twelve years ago when he was first elected. Even his own Slab Café hasn't seen a renovation since the '80s."

"So?" I said. "I like the downtown stores. We don't need any new ones. I suggest you point out to Cynthia the recent addition of the Bear and Brew and Noylene's Beautifery. If that isn't progress, I don't know what is. As your crony, I affirm you in this course of non-action."

"What good ol' Cynthia Johnsson doesn't know is that the city council has already passed an incentive package for downtown growth. And I have three new businesses coming into town with a fourth on the hook."

"That should bode well for the probability of your triumphant re-election to public service." I reached across the table and took a biscuit from the red plastic basket sitting next to Pete's elbow. "The article say anything else?"

"Yeah. She says, 'How can any mayor be taken seriously when he doesn't wear any underwear?' How does she know I don't wear underwear?"

"It's common knowledge, Mr. Mayor. You've never tried to hide your strange predilection for being an unfettered nature-boy and you've dated almost every single woman in town. A couple of married ones, too." I waved an empty coffee cup at Noylene. "Didn't you go out with Cynthia a couple of times?"

"Oh, yeah." Pete looked chagrined. "Forgot about that. Hey," he said, looking around for the first time since he picked up the newspaper. "Where is everybody?"

I shrugged. The Slab Café wasn't exactly bustling on this late September morning. In addition to Pete and me, there were only two other customers. Noylene had volunteered to help out on the morning shift until Pete found a permanent waitress to take Collette's place. Noylene's clientele at the Beautifery didn't usually get up and moving before ten. Pete had hired Bootsie Watkins to fill the lunch and dinner slot soon after she'd been let go by New Fellowship Baptist Church. Bootsie discovered, to her dismay, that job security for church secretaries having affairs with head deacons was not especially good.

Noylene brought her coffee pot to the table and filled both cups.

"Thanks, Noylene," Pete said, still grumpy. "Where does Cynthia get off criticizing me for not wearing drawers? She's a belly dancer, for God's sake. Since when can a belly dancer run for mayor?"

"Anyone can run for mayor," I said. "That's what makes our country great. I'd sooner vote for a belly dancer than a lawyer."

"You ain't just whistlin' Dixie," said Noylene. "Hey, wait a minute. You ain't wearin' drawers?"

"No, I'm not," said Pete, "and I'm proud to say it. I gave 'em up in '72."

"What about the time you were in the Navy?" I asked. "Didn't they make you wear them?" I pushed the last bite of the apple-buttered biscuit into my mouth and washed it down with a sip of fresh coffee.

"Army," Pete corrected. "Yes, they did. They forced me. But when I was on leave, I never wore them."

"If I was your campaign manager," said Noylene, "I'd make sure that everybody knew you was wearing your drawers. What if you was in an accident? The voters just cain't trust a man with no drawers."

Pete sniffed. "There's a scientific basis for men not wearing underwear."

"And what would that be?" I asked.

"Well, for one thing, it's been proven that switching from briefs to boxers raises your sperm count. I figure that going commando should be twice as effective."

"And this matters to you because...?"

"Hmm...well, you never know when you might need a high count. Let's say that I needed to get a loan for a new house."

"They look at your sperm count?" said Noylene. "No wonder Wormy can't get a loan."

I shook my head. "Pete, your sperm count isn't like your credit score."

Pete put down the paper. "I know." He lowered his voice and leaned in. Noylene sidled up next to him. "But when I fill out the application," he whispered, "I write my sperm count in the space where they want to know how much I make a year. I just say three to five million. They never actually ask how much *money* I make, so I'm not really lying."

"You can *do* that?" said Noylene. "Dang! Wait till I tell Wormy!" She hurried into the kitchen.

"You've got to stop teasing her," I said.

"I knows it. I jes' cain't hep myself."

The cowbell hanging on the door bounced loudly against the glass and clanged the arrival of another customer. To Pete, it was a sweet sound. The rest of us might prefer the tinkle of a smaller, more delicate chime, but Pete said he always wanted to know when someone came in, even if he was in the kitchen. "It's the sound of cash," he explained. "On the hoof."

Nancy came through the door, attired, as usual, in her uniform, walked over to the table, pulled out a chair and, after adjusting her gun belt, sat down opposite Pete. She ran her fingers through her hair and did her best to fluff her coif back to a semi-normal appearance.

"Helmet hair," she explained. "It's a slight drawback, I'll admit, but being a motorcycle cop is great this time of year. Where's Noylene? I need some coffee."

"She's calling Wormy," said Pete, sipping his own brew. "Needs him to check his sperm count."

Nancy rolled her eyes. "I'm not even going to ask."

"He might have to qualify for a mortgage," I explained.

"I'll need an omelet," said Nancy to no one in particular. "An omelet and some toast."

Noylene came out of the kitchen, spied Nancy and came over to the table with a cup in one hand and the coffee pot in the other.

"Omelet. Toast," mumbled Nancy.

"Will do, hon," said Noylene, deftly filling Nancy's cup. Then she turned to Pete. "It won't work. Wormy says that he's been impudent since he signed up for medical experiments down in Columbia. Course, that's been ten years ago."

"Really?" I said. "Medical experiments can make you impudent?"

"I guess so," shrugged Noylene.

Nancy shook her head and focused her attention on fixing her coffee. Cream and a lot of sugar.

"Y'all going to stay married?" Pete asked. "I mean, if you can't have marital relations, what's the point?"

"I see where y'all are confused," said Noylene with a smile. "Our relations are just fine. Wormy's just impudent. That means he's shootin' blanks."

"Tell me about your master plan for St. Germaine," I said to Pete. "What's your grand scheme?"

Nancy's omelet had arrived at the table and Noylene had brought some sawmill gravy for the remaining biscuits. I helped myself.

"I plan to use strateegery," answered Pete. "Strateegery and paradigms. And tax breaks for new businesses."

"Tax breaks?" said Nancy. "What kind of tax breaks?"

"We're waiving the St. Germaine Privilege Tax for two years."

"You're going to make some folks really mad," I said. "What about Noylene? The Bear and Brew? The Ginger Cat?"

"Sorry," said Pete. "This is the way other towns do it. New businesses only."

"What's this privilege tax?" asked Nancy.

"It's a privilege to have a business in St. Germaine, so we get to tax you."

"That's the dumbest thing I've ever heard."

"It's just a license to do business. The town takes a small percentage," I explained. "Standard procedure."

"What if they close up and re-open under a new name?" Nancy asked. "They'd be a new business and not have to pay the tax. Legally, anyway."

Pete sighed. "I'll talk to the council. Maybe we can waive everybody for two years. It might be worth it in the long run."

"Who's coming in?" I asked.

"There's a bookstore, a high-end day spa, and a music store."

"Really?" said Nancy. "That's great. We need a music store. And a bookstore would be great, too."

"And a coffee house," added Pete. "It's part of the day spa. The owners are very concerned about having a Christian business. They give Christian massages and feed you Christian coffee and Christian cakes. Coffee on the first floor, massage parlor on the second." He paused. "No, that doesn't sound right."

I laughed. "Sounds *delightful*. But you said you had another one on the hook. What's the fourth one?"

"It's a furrier," said Pete. "Fur coats I think, but they won't be downtown. They're too big. They say they'll probably employ six or seven workers at first. It's not a done deal."

"Cynthia will not be pleased. You've just taken away her platform. Now she has to go after your underwear."

"I'm not wearing any," said Pete with a chuckle.

"Me neither," said Nancy.

Pete and I looked at her for a long moment. I could see Pete's eye beginning to twitch.

"Oh, get a grip you guys. I'm just kidding."

Pete relaxed. "Whew...for a moment there I thought I loved you."

Nancy changed the subject. "You batching it for long?"

"Till Friday. Meg will be back on Saturday evening."

"Dave's gone, too," said Nancy. "In case you hadn't noticed."

I hadn't noticed, but it was only Tuesday morning. If Nancy hadn't said anything I might not have noticed until a week from Friday. Dave, with his ubiquitous khakis and light blue button-downs, had an uncanny ability to disappear into the background, even when on duty at the police station.

"Of course I noticed," I said. "Where is he, anyway?"

"He's at banjo camp."

"What?" said Pete.

"He's at banjo camp," repeated Nancy. "He asked for the week off a couple of months ago. Remember?"

"Uh...sure," I said. "Banjo camp. Absolutely."

Nancy smiled and shook her head. "You can't remember anything anymore. Why don't you write this stuff down? Or, better yet, get yourself a PDA or something. How about a BlackBerry?"

"With that silly little stylus? That would just be too embarrassing. Anyway, I don't need one. I keep everything right up here." I tapped on my noggin.

"When's Dave coming back from banjo camp?" asked Pete. "I want to hear him play."

"He's not at banjo camp," said Nancy. "I was kidding. Hayden sent him to Greensboro for a seminar on conflict management and negotiations."

"Huh?" I said. "Oh, yeah. I did."

"Notebook?" asked Nancy.

"I'll try a BlackBerry," I said.

# Chapter 2

Enough money can do many wondrous things, I marveled as I unpacked my resized and newly blocked gray felt hat exactly thirty-eight hours after I had received it from Barbara Chandler Forrest. Expedited FedEx both ways and an extra incentive to my haberdasher to stay up late had hastened the process dramatically. I am not a patient man—especially when the muse is finally knocking on the door. She needed to be let in and welcomed like a rich, elderly maiden aunt.

I placed the hat gently on my head, smiling as the band settled neatly on my brow. A glance into a mirror confirmed my satisfaction, and I added a rakish angle with a self-satisfied grin. It was now or never. I could almost feel the typewriter beckoning me with its "come-hither" keys. I sat at the desk, rolled in a piece of bond, and felt the silent bumps of the carriage return. Then, with a sigh of happiness, I started typing.

A liturgical detective is as welcome in a church as a plumbing inspector in a urologist's office. I pulled my hat down low, lit a stogie, and slumped in my pew as the notes of a Bach fugue beat me about the head like a nun on St. Dorcas Day until I was praying for just one verse of "Softly and Tenderly." I was there to meet a client sent over by the bishop. I work for him. Yeah, I'm a detective.

This was a Baptist church and except for the organist, it was as empty as a Baptist church on Good Friday. I checked my calendar. Good Friday. I pulled the piece of wadded-up paper out of my pocket and looked at the name. AveMaria Gratsyplena. It was a flat cinch this ankle wasn't a Baptist and wasn't looking to convert. I had questions. Questions and queries. Why did the bishop send me over here? How did Noah clean up after those hippos? And, if you have a cold hot-pocket, is it just a pocket?

Suddenly a shot rang out, a knife whizzed by my ear, a hangman's noose dropped ominously from the balcony, and a bottle of cyanide appeared mysteriously in the hymnal rack in front of me next to a little plastic communion cup neatly engraved with a skull and crossbones. I picked up a hymnal and it fell open to hymn number 354--"Where Will You Spend Eternity?"--and I shivered as the cold feet of three baby church mice ran up and down my spine. Something wasn't right. I could feel it. There was a clue here somewhere. Then it came to me. A Bach fugue in a Baptist church? I don't think so.

"Tell me again when Meg is coming home?" Nancy asked. "You're looking distinctly less kempt than usual."

I looked down at my flannel shirt and jeans. "How so? This is what I always wear."

"No. That's what you always wear when Meg is out of town."

I looked out the plate glass window of the police station. The town square wasn't exactly bustling, but there were a few folks out and about.

"Hmm. I don't know what you mean, but Meg will be back tomorrow night."

"Did you open your windows?"

"Windows? Why?"

"Because you've been smoking cigars in the house again, that's why."

"How did you?...Never mind." I changed the subject. "What's the news around town?"

"Dave will be back this afternoon," said Nancy. "And the bookstore is moving in next to Noylene's. I just drove by. Someone's inside painting and there's a sign up."

"Glad to hear it. How about our new music store?"

"Behind the Ginger Cat on North Main. You know...where Beaver Jergenson had his chainsaw repair shop. Beaver says he can't afford the rent, so he's working out of his garage. I looked in the window, but there didn't seem to be any activity. Pete says they'll be in before next week."

"A bookstore and a music store," I mused. "We're really starting to expand. If we could get a donut store here on the square, we wouldn't have to send Dave to the Piggly Wiggly every morning."

"You don't eat the ones we get."

"I'm watching my girlish figure," I said. "Besides, I contend that it's our duty as law enforcement officers to support the donut trade in town."

Nancy harrumphed. "Well, I'm looking forward to the music store. I'm tired of driving into Boone every time I want a new CD."

"You could try the internet," I said.

"Can't get high-speed where I am. I'm still on dial-up. I don't use it except for e-mail."

"Why don't you just use the office internet? That's what Dave does."

"That would be an illegal use of city property. I'm thinking of having

Dave arrested," Nancy laughed. "And besides, I don't have a credit card."

"You'd arrest your own boyfriend?" I chuckled. "Hey, wait a minute. No credit card? Not even one? That's amazing."

"Never needed one, never wanted one," replied Nancy in a very self-satisfied tone. "Mostly I use cash. You'd be amazed at the discounts you can get if you're a cash customer."

"I don't doubt it." I looked back out the window. "How about our new spa? Any news?"

Nancy gestured with a nod. "Down the street from the flower shop. That two-story yellow house on the corner."

"Mrs. McCarty's house?"

"Yep. She's moving down to Gastonia where her daughter lives. Pete's giving them a zoning variance to put in a business. It's only a couple of blocks off the square and the only residence on the block."

I nodded. "What about parking?"

"Customers will have to park behind the house or on the street, but we've been assured there won't be more than three or four cars at a time."

"Three new businesses. Pete will be riding high for a few weeks at least."

"That's his plan." Nancy's eyes narrowed as she looked out the window, across the street and into the park. "Uh oh. Here comes Cynthia. I'll be back by lunch."

"Hey, wait a minute," I said, but Nancy had already disappeared.

"What's going on here?" demanded Cynthia.

"Huh?" I decided that playing innocent was my best defense. "Well, hello, Cynthia."

"Don't you 'Well, hello, Cynthia' me. What's all this about new shops coming into town?"

"Yes," I said. "I believe that there's a bookstore, a music store and a spa joining our downtown community. Also a furrier. But that hasn't been made public yet."

Tears welled up in Cynthia's eyes. "It's not fair. Just when I tell everyone that Pete hasn't done one thing to help grow St. Germaine's tax base, he announces three..."

"Four," I corrected.

"Four new businesses."

I nodded sympathetically. "It certainly is good timing for Pete." I paused before adding apologetically "I'm his crony, you know."

"I know," she said sadly. "I wish I had a crony."

"If it's any consolation, Pete was really scared for a couple of days."

"Now I have to go after his underwear."

"Yeah."

We both stood there silently for a moment; then Cynthia brightened. "Hey," she said, "maybe he'll do something—you know—*unsavory* before the election."

"He's certainly been known to," I said cheerfully. "Pete's a free spirit."

Lunchtime at the Slab was fairly hectic, mostly due to the fact that Noylene was back at her Beautifery by noon and Bootsie didn't quite have the hang of waiting tables even though she'd been at it for a few months. I walked in and spied Georgia and Elaine huddled over a table in the corner by the kitchen. They saw me and waved me over.

"Pull up a chair," Georgia said. "We have terrible news."

"Terrible," echoed Elaine.

"You just found out that Gaylen Weatherall is being considered for bishop of Colorado?" I said.

"You knew?" said Elaine. "You knew and you didn't tell us?"

"Well, I don't tell everything I know. Anyway, she asked me to keep it under my hat. How did you find out?"

"I have a friend in Colorado," Georgia said. "She asked me if I happened to know this particular priest from North Carolina."

"Gaylen," added Elaine glumly. "Just when I thought we were on the right track."

Bootsie came up to our table with a crazed look in her eye. "What do y'all want?"

"Bootsie," I said, "you look a bit harried."

"Cut the chit-chat. What do y'all *want*?" Bootsie repeated. "C'mon. I ain't got all day."

"I shall have the special," Elaine said.

"We got no special," Bootsie answered. "How about a meatloaf sandwich?"

"No, thank you," said Elaine picking up a menu. "Let's see..."

"I'll get you some fries with that," said Bootsie, ignoring her. She slapped her order pad closed. "In fact, meatloaf sandwiches for all of you. And iced tea." She disappeared into the kitchen.

"That was easy," I said. "Sometimes I have a hard time deciding."

"I swear," said Georgia. "I'm going to quit coming in here unless Pete gets some decent help."

"I hate meatloaf," said Elaine. "But back to Gaylen. The election's tomorrow. She's already been out to Colorado twice for the 'meet and greet.'"

"Maybe they won't want her," I suggested, knowing it was a futile hope. Gaylen was one of those rare priests who was intelligent, kind, well published, and not too full of herself. If she weren't elected bishop this time, another diocese would soon snap her up. She was now on the fast track.

"If she gets chosen, when will she leave?" asked Elaine.

"In a couple of weeks, I expect. They tend not to dawdle."

"Then what?"

"I suppose we'll ask the bishop to send us an interim priest."

"How about Tony?" said Georgia, hopefully.

"He's retired," I answered. "No, I take that back. He's now thrice retired. I doubt that he's willing to take the parish again."

We all sat in silence, waiting for our lunches, our hands folded in front of us, listening to the cheery chatter of the other customers, but there was no joy in Mudville. Meatloaf sandwiches and yet another priestly migration were nothing to smile about.

# Chapter 3

A final flood of fugal flatulence drifted out of the organ pipes and off into space like a flock of Easter moths. I got up and was starting toward the baptismal pool, quietly congratulating myself on choosing my new English-Style, double-breasted and fully-lined trench coat, a 60/40 polyester-cotton blend with authentic storm flaps, epaulettes, aged brass hardware and D-rings, like the one in the scene where they say goodbye at the airport, the sound of propellers turning, when I tripped over the corpse.

It was my client, AveMaria Gratsyplena, and she was as stiff as Al Gore on Oscar night. I bent down and lifted her veil. She'd been strangled with a rosary: not a run-of-the-mill rosary like you might get at a Catholic bookstore where Hail Marys are two for a quarter and indulgences are included on the back flap of the May issue of "Nuns and Roses" magazine, but a fancy heirloom rosary with pearls, rubies, and a solid gold cross; a rosary with attitude; the kind of rosary that said, "Get your Jehovah's Witness butt off my front porch."

"I see that you're back in fine form."

I stopped typing, looked back over my shoulder and smiled at Meg. "It's the hat."

"I can tell," she said, lifting the newly acquired prize off my head for a moment, and kissing me on the cheek before dropping it back into position. "It certainly has taken your writing to a new level."

"I can sense your sarcasm, Madam. I'll have you know that the choir has been virtually clamoring for a new story. Virtually *clamoring*, I tell you."

"Virtually?"

"Yep." I took off the hat, placed it on the desk by the typewriter, then stood and greeted her correctly and profoundly, but not exactly according to the Amy Vanderbilt etiquette book. "Welcome home," I growled.

"Mmm, glad to be back."

"Let's rustle up some supper," I suggested. "How was the seminar?"

"Awful." Meg frowned. She was beautiful when she frowned. And she was beautiful when she didn't frown. "Well, actually, the seminar was okay, but we were through every afternoon at three o'clock. There wasn't anything to do."

We walked into the kitchen and I started rummaging around the fridge. "You didn't go lie out on the beach?"

"Sure. From four to six, then back to the hotel room. The rest of the group stayed out partying till two or three a.m."

"May I see your tan lines?"

She giggled. "I haven't decided. Maybe later. What's the news around here?"

I came out of the refrigerator with a couple of old potatoes—old enough to have three inch sprouts shooting from their wrinkled hides. "How about a baked potato?" I asked, handing over one of the spiky spuds.

Meg shuddered and tossed it into the sink. "No thanks."

"Not much news since you've been gone. Cynthia has accused Pete publicly of not wearing underwear. It was in the *Tattler*."

"*That's* news."

"And we have four new businesses coming into town. Two are moving in this week. It's part of Pete's revitalization plan to keep the press out of his pants."

"*That's* news."

"And Gaylen Weatherall is probably being elected Bishop of Colorado tomorrow."

Silence.

"I said..."

"I heard! When did this happen?"

"Well, as I said, the election is tomorrow..."

"Perhaps you didn't hear me correctly," Meg said slowly, carefully enunciating every word.

"Umm," I started. "You see...Gaylen's gone out a couple of times this month to talk to the churches. But I didn't even really know she was seriously in the running until a few days ago."

"And you didn't *tell* me?"

"She asked me not to."

"Let's get one thing straight, Mister. Whenever anyone tells you *not* to tell anyone, that does *not* include me." Sparks flashed from her gray eyes.

I shrugged helplessly.

"Well," Meg admitted, "on second thought, maybe you shouldn't tell me *everything*. But you should have told me about this." She ran her hands through her black hair and leaned against the counter, absently scratching a now-contented Burmese Mountain Dog behind his ears. If Baxter felt his tail smack repeatedly against the table leg, it didn't stop him from enjoying the attention.

"Oh, fine," she huffed. "I guess you're right. You shouldn't have told me if she told you not to."

I walked over and gave her a kiss.

"Don't try to make it up to me," she said, kissing me back. "I'm the one who's right most of the time."

"You *are* right most of the time."

"So, if Gaylen is elected, when would she leave?"

"I don't really know. Maybe a couple of weeks from now?"

Meg sighed. "Oh well. It was too good to last, I suppose. At least she finished putting all the church's money into a trust." She frowned again. "Have you found anything to eat yet? I am rather peckish."

I went back to rummaging. "How about a bologna and strawberry pop-tart sandwich?"

"Nope."

I looked deep into the refrigerator. "I've got a piece of pizza left over from our Fourth of July party. Or you can have one of Archimedes' baby squirrels."

"I refuse to eat owl food, no matter how tempting." She looked thoughtful for a moment, then added, "How would you cook it?"

"Baby squirrel is best served *tartare*," I said. "But wait. Here's something." I pulled out a pot of soup and set it on the stove. "I forgot that I stopped by the Ginger Cat this afternoon and picked up a pot of shrimp bisque."

"Excellent," said Meg. "And?"

"Garlic bread, and a bottle of Shiraz."

"Then I've decided. After supper you may see my tan lines."

# Chapter 4

September turned to October, and with the changing leaves came the tourists. Peak foliage season wouldn't hit St. Germaine for a couple of weeks yet, depending on conditions, but folks were already making their way up into the Appalachians to enjoy the fall weather, the local festivals, art shows and fairs found in almost every small town, and leaf peeping in general. October and early November were the two months that made St. Germaine's economy work. Nancy had to hand out more parking tickets during these two months, as space was at a premium, and out-of-towners insisted that it was their God-given right under the Constitution to leave their cars and SUVs wherever they could find space. This included driving up onto the grass of Sterling Park—our small acre of village green—parking in front of fire hydrants, and even, on occasion, in the spot in front of the police station marked "Reserved for the Chief of Police."

I was drinking a steaming cup of coffee and marveling at my fortuity to be sitting on a bench in Sterling Park on this beautiful October morning. I believe in fate, in chance meetings, and in good fortune. I also believe in the Trinity, salvation by grace, infralapsarianism, non-Darwinian evolution, and possibly unicorns, as they're mentioned nine times in the Old Testament. I wasn't too sure about the unicorns yet. I don't dwell on either fate or theology for too long because it gives me a headache, but on a morning like this, when the crispness in the air snaps you awake and you can almost feel creation in full bloom, I found it impossible not to smile at the wonder of it all. Hayden Konig—Chief of Police of St. Germaine, North Carolina. Hayden Konig—organist and choirmaster of St. Barnabas Episcopal Church. Hayden Konig— wealthy inventor and investor. Fate? Luck? Predestination? Whatever the cosmic answer, I was as happy as the tenth pick on a nine-man jury.

I saw Meg making her way across the park with a coffee cup of her own, attired in a coat and scarf even though the temperature was still in the low fifties and my outerwear consisted of an old cotton sweater.

"Good morning, Miss Farthing," I said with a smile. "Coffee from the new place?" In all, four concerns that Pete had courted had moved in. I suspected that most of them would vanish in January as soon as tourist season waned, but for now, there was a flurry of activity around town and everyone was happy. I looked at Meg's paper cup and knew the answer even as my mouth formed the question, seeing as the logo was emblazoned across both the cup and the protective sleeve. The logo was an ichthys—the Jesus fish—swimming like a shark inside a coffee cup and in bright red letters was the name of the shop, "Holy Grounds."

"Yep. The Ginger Cat doesn't open soon enough to get the early morning coffee drinkers. I'm quite finished drinking coffee by 9:30, thank you."

"Me, too," I said. "It's good coffee. I affirm its Christian goodness."

Meg rolled her eyes. "They can certainly open a Christian coffee shop if they want. You don't have to be so snide about everything."

"I just wonder how drinking this Christian cup of coffee will serve me better in the eternal order of things than drinking a cup of coffee from, let's say, Buddha's Coffee Barn. Hey! Maybe they give part of their profits to convert the unwashed of Appalachia." I took another sip.

Meg harrumphed. "Maybe they do. You don't know one way or the other."

"I've never known a business that *does* do something nice like that not to display the fact prominently in their window."

"You are certainly jaded on this lovely morning."

I nodded. "You're absolutely right. I take it all back. And if this weren't a good cup of coffee, I wouldn't drink it. But if they come out with WWJD cup holders, I'm finished with them."

"What Would Jesus Drink?"

"Exactly."

We sipped our coffee together.

"Their spa opened the day before yesterday," said Meg. "It's on the second floor. Christian massage and holistic healing. That's what Cynthia told me."

"Has Cynthia already been there?" I asked.

"She's working there," said Meg, taking a sip of her coffee and smiling at the corners of her mouth.

"Has she given up belly dancing?"

"Nope. She's been encouraged to incorporate her dancing into the totality of the Christian wellness experience."

"Huh?"

Meg shook her head. "Those are her words, not mine. She can dance, but she's not allowed to give massages. Chad is the only certified Christian massage therapist in this part of the state."

"You don't say."

Meg wasn't looking at me. I suspected she didn't want to give away the punch line too soon, and I knew her too well to believe she wasn't going somewhere with this information.

"That's a shame really. I think Cynthia would make a wonderful Christian masseuse. Especially if she wore the outfit."

"Huh," Meg sniffed. "I don't think *you'll* be going in."

"Not without the Vice Squad."

Meg spun toward me, a big smile finally breaking over her face.

"Okay. I can't stand it any longer," she blurted out. "Do you know the name of the spa?"

Her smile was infectious. "Nope. Do tell." I chuckled and put the cup to my lips.

"The Upper Womb," she laughed. I choked on a sip of coffee and spit it back into my cup.

"Isn't that just *great?* The Upper Womb. Chad took me up there. It's all dark and warm and there was a heartbeat on the sound system."

I shook my head. "All the time? Just a heartbeat?"

"No. He can switch it to anything. Heartbeat, ocean waves, New Age, Contemporary Christian...whatever he wants. He gave me a coupon for a free massage."

"Yes, I'll bet he did."

"Don't worry. I won't use it."

"The heck you won't!" I exclaimed. "I need someone to go up there and scope it out. It's not every day you get a chance for a free Christian massage. Anyway, you'd probably enjoy it."

"Yes," said Meg with a nod of her head. "I probably would. But I don't think I should go. I'll see if Nancy will do it."

"You should go. I'm sure Chad...what's his last name?"

"I have no idea."

"Well, I'm sure Chad Whatshisname will do a good job."

"Yes, I'm sure he would."

"Then what's the problem?" I asked with a shrug.

"You haven't seen Chad."

Meg and I finished up our coffee and wandered over to the Slab for breakfast, an event that was occurring almost daily. Our usual table was empty, although the restaurant was beginning to fill up. It was still early and by eight o'clock, there wouldn't be a table to be had. Noylene was on duty and so was Bootsie, and it was Bootsie who spotted us and made a beeline to the table.

"Coffee?" she asked, already pouring.

"Not this morning," said Meg, causing Bootsie to stop the stream of coffee with a small jerk, spilling some in surprise. Meg gave her a guilty look. "We just had some. Could I get some orange juice instead?"

"I'll have just one more cup," I said quickly. Bootsie relaxed, smiled, and finished pouring the steaming mug. Then she slid it over in front of me.

"I'll get your juice in a sec, Hon," Bootsie said over her shoulder as she disappeared into the kitchen.

"I think you confused her," I whispered. "Don't confuse her. Just take the coffee."

Meg nodded.

Nancy appeared at the table followed closely by Dave. "Expecting anyone?" she asked as she sat down. Dave took the other chair.

"I was just about to ask Meg to raise my illegitimate love-child," I said with as much sarcasm as I could muster, "but please join us, won't you?"

"Yeah, sure. Thanks." Sarcasm wasn't totally lost on Nancy, but she ignored it most of the time. "Hey, I heard you got yourself a BlackBerry."

"I did," I replied, "but I haven't figured it out yet. I can almost make a phone call."

"Almost?" said Dave.

"My fingers are too big for those stupid little buttons."

"You're supposed to use the little stylus," said Meg.

"I lost it. I was using it as a toothpick and I think I left it somewhere. I'm not worried. I don't call anyone anyway."

Meg turned to Nancy. "That's true. I always have to call *him*." Nancy shook her head in disgust.

"I can *answer* the phone," I said, defensively pulling out the BlackBerry from my pants pocket. "I just have to push this button here." I looked at the phone, squinting to see the tiny letters, but not able to make them out. "Or maybe this button."

"How about your notes?" Nancy asked. "Are you taking notes so you don't forget stuff?"

"I lost my stylus..."

"And your calendar," Dave added.

"Calendar?"

"Give me that!" said Meg, taking the BlackBerry out of my hand. She pulled out her own cell phone, deftly popped open the back and pulled out a small card. Then she did the same to the BlackBerry, switched them, closed up both phones and handed me her old flip-phone—the one with the big numbers.

"Use this one," she said.

"But my phone number..."

"Already switched. It's all in the SIM card."

"Great," I said. "Now I don't have to worry where I left that stylus."

"You left it at my house," said Meg. "I have it in my purse."

Nancy laughed and changed the subject. "Has Gaylen Weatherall left yet?"

Meg's shoulders slumped just slightly. "Yes, she's gone. The Reverend has become the Right Reverend Bishop of Colorado."

"Does she need a bodyguard?" asked Nancy. "I think I might like Colorado."

"Probably not," I said, "but I'll be sure and ask."

"What's the priest situation then?" Dave asked. Dave and Nancy had started going back to St. Barnabas as a couple after Dave's break-up with Collette and his subsequent expatriation from the New Life Baptist congregation.

"We're getting an interim rector this week," Meg groused. "Today, in fact. Father Tony won't do it, no matter how many people beg him. I just hope our bishop sends us someone with a little...hmm...how shall I put it...?"

"Ability?" I offered.

"Brains?" added Nancy.

"Intelligence?" said Dave.

Pete had walked up in the middle of this conversation and wasn't shy in chiming in. "Discrimination? Imagination?"

My turn. "Acumen? Prudence? Sagacity?"

Nancy: "Good taste? Resourcefulness? Discernment?"

"Sense," said Meg with finality.

Wednesday meant choir practice. The choir had returned from its summer hiatus in September and was now back in full swing. I was sitting at the organ as the members began to wander up to the choir loft.

"Do we still meet at seven?" asked Rebecca, looking at her watch.

"Yes," I replied. "Seven sharp."

"It's past seven," said Elaine. "Actually, ten past."

"Yes," I said, "I know. We should get started. I think our new rector is coming up to meet you all. It would be good to pretend we're rehearsing."

"Well," said Beverly Greene, "play something."

Beverly was our parish administrator, an appointment made by a previous rector and made semi-permanent by a vote of the vestry. Now she gave a yell worthy of a parish administrator.

"Hey! You people get your butts up here! We've got to get going!"

"Umm. Thanks," I said as the rest of the choir hurried up to the loft.

We rehearsed the anthem for Sunday—a lovely setting of *God Be In My Head* by Mr. Rutter—and were going through the service music when I noticed a collar-clad black shirt standing against the window in the back of the choir loft. We finished the *Gloria*, and I stopped and looked back at the figure. The members of the choir turned and followed my gaze.

"Hello," came the low female voice. "I'm the Reverend Bottoms. Carmel Bottoms."

"That's as scary a voice as I've ever heard," whispered Bev, as she watched the Reverend Bottoms leave the nave by way of the sacristy.

"She'll be fun to have around for Halloween," agreed Fred, from the bass section. "It could be the best Halloween ever."

"Stop looking on the bright side," Elaine said. "She's right out of your first book. Why would the bishop send us someone like that?"

Elaine had a point. If ever there was an alto destined to wear tweed, Carmel Bottoms was the archetype.

"Give her a chance," I said. "She's only an interim priest. You heard her. She just graduated from the seminary. This is her first parish."

"If nothing else," Meg added, "this should be interesting."

"I need a new book," announced Nancy, when I walked in. She threw a tattered paperback into the trash. "I've read this one four times."

I didn't usually come into the station on Saturday morning, but I'd ventured into town to meet Meg and to buy some drill bits. I'd already stopped by the Slab, had a cup of coffee and tried, unsuccessfully, to convince Pete to add a shrimp po-boy to the lunch menu.

Nancy stood up. "I want something saccharine and warmly-fuzzy with a whole bunch of wisteria festooning every page. Have you been in the new bookstore?"

"Nope."

"I thought you were a voracious reader."

"I have about three hundred books I haven't even read yet," I said, "and I'm almost out of room. I promised Meg I wouldn't buy any more until I got rid of a few."

"And you can't bear to part with them?"

I gave a helpless shrug.

"I can take some books off your hands," suggested Nancy. "Just pretend I've borrowed them."

"You know, that's not a bad idea. I don't have any warm-fuzzy books though."

"That's okay. I like chop-em-ups just as well. I'm just in the mood for a warm-fuzzy."

"Well, we might as well hit the new bookstore and introduce ourselves. I have my credit card and I'm not supposed to meet Meg until lunch."

Eden Books was around the square next door to Noylene's Beautifery. We stopped outside and looked in at the window display.

It was pretty typical of small town bookstores: some books placed in a semi-artsy array on a piece of black fabric, a couple of posters, a large stuffed giraffe with a sign around its neck advertising a children's book titled *The Animals Watched,* and some other knick-knacks. I held open the door for Nancy and we went inside, an obnoxious buzzer announcing us to the woman behind the desk.

"Good morning," she said. "Welcome!"

There were four other customers in the shop. Two of them were Meg and her mother, Ruby.

"Well, good morning," said Meg, flipping through a rather large volume of historical fiction. "I just told Hyacinth that you're not allowed to buy anything."

"Good morning, Hayden," called Ruby from the cookbook section.

"Morning, Ruby," I called into the cookbooks, then turned back to Meg. "Methinks you came in here," I accused, "just to thwart my book habit."

"Indeed, sirrah, I did not," said Meg. "I just happened to be in the right place at the right time. I call it Kismet."

"Well...I can't prove anything, but we detectives don't believe in coincidences. Anyway, Nancy says she'll give some of my books a good home."

"I'll believe it when I see it," said Meg. "How about you, Davis? Have you ever voluntarily given away a book?"

Davis Boothe was one shelf over from Meg. He worked at Don's Clothing Store on the next block. I had tried for a while to get him in the church choir because he had quite a nice voice and served on the vestry with Meg, but he didn't seem to be interested. Now his head peeked around the corner of the shelf.

"Nope."

"I didn't think so," said Meg.

I addressed the woman behind the desk. "Pay no attention to the woman in historical fiction," I said. "I am a wealthy bibliophile with plenty of disposable income. However, this morning we just came by to say hello and to introduce ourselves. I'm Hayden Konig, chief of police, and well-compensated public servant. This is Lieutenant Parsky."

"Nancy," corrected Lieutenant Parsky, glaring at me. "Call me Nancy."

"Hello, Nancy. Hayden. I'm Hyacinth Turnipseed, owner of Eden Books."

"Pleased to meet you," said Nancy.

"I wondered when you came in if you'd come for a reading. I couldn't help but notice the uniform." She smiled at Nancy.

Hyacinth Turnipseed was a woman of substance with a grandmotherly comportment who could have played Mrs. Clause in any department store in the country. Her soft white hair was tied in a loose bun framing twinkling blue eyes and dimples that Clement Moore would have envied. She was wearing an apron embroidered with "Eden Books."

"A reading?" said Nancy. I looked over at Meg. She was still thumbing her book, but I could tell her radar was up. Davis', too. Ruby was trying to memorize Martha Stewart's recipe for Lemon Meringue Fluff so she wouldn't have to buy the book, but stopped right in the middle of blending her egg whites and looked up in astonishment. I didn't recognize the other patron, a woman at the counter ready to purchase the latest Mitford book, but she looked startled as well.

Hyacinth smiled a grandmotherly smile and adjusted her round, wire rim spectacles. "I'm very active with several police forces across the country. I help them find missing persons, offer clues to cases...whatever the spirits want them to know."

"Ah, yes," I said. "The spirits."

"Perhaps you've heard of me?" asked Hyacinth.

"Well," I answered, "not you specifically. But I certainly know your type of work."

Hyacinth smiled and nodded. "If you need some help, you know where to come. Of course, I also do private readings."

"And you sell books, too?" asked Nancy, looking at the shelves full of books. "I mean, as well as doing the fortune-telling stuff? You must stay very busy."

"I prefer the term prognostication," Hyacinth said gently. "I'm a clairvoyant. I connect with energies of people who have crossed over."

Nancy and I, apparently both rendered inarticulate at the same moment, nodded in unison like a couple of police bobble-head dolls.

Hyacinth rang up the woman's purchase on an old fashioned cash register and took her money. We listened to the ugly buzz as she opened the door and left the store.

"Can I help you find something?" Hyacinth asked. "I have quite a good Halloween selection."

"I'm sure," said Nancy.

"Any of the Harry Potter books? Stephen King? Ray Bradbury? How about an old classic?"

"Yes," I said. "Maybe a classic."

"No," said Meg. "You have all the classics."

"I have a first edition in the back," Hyacinth cajoled. "Perhaps I could tempt you. It's Washington Irving."

"Washington Irving? It isn't an autographed copy, is it?"

"Why, yes. Yes, it is. I happen to have the first printing by C. S. Van Winkle of New York in 1820. *The Sketchbook of Geoffrey Crayon*. It's an early bind-up of the seven parts, but without the outer wrappers. Near fine condition in contemporary marbled boards, marbled end papers and a modern leather spine. The autograph is on the second of the seven parts."

"You're kidding, of course."

"No," said Hyacinth with a smile. "I'm not."

"What the heck is the *Sketchbook of Geoffrey Crayon*?" asked Meg. "I've never heard of it."

"Washington Irving's collection of essays and short stories," I said. "It was the first published book edition of *The Legend of Sleepy Hollow* and *Rip Van Winkle*. Of course, those are only the two most famous stories. There is a whole set of Christmas essays as well."

"How much is it?" asked Davis, now very curious.

"Are you interested as well, young man?" asked Hyacinth, her blue eyes sparkling. "My, my."

Davis blushed and grinned. "I can't afford it, of course, but I'd love to see it."

"I'll be right back," said Hyacinth, and disappeared into the back of the store.

"I don't even want to know what that book is going to cost," said Ruby. "And here I was worried about spending $35.95 on a Martha Stewart cookbook."

"I'll buy you the cookbook," I said magnanimously. "It's the least I can do to assuage my affluent guilt."

"How about me?" said Davis. "I need a cookbook."

"Nope," I said.

"I love *Rip Van Winkle*," said Meg. She looked over at her mother. "I remember Daddy reading it to me." Ruby nodded.

Hyacinth returned with a book wrapped in tissue paper.

"I prefer *The Legend of Sleepy Hollow*," I said. "It was one of my favorites growing up. I didn't even mind the Disney cartoon. I had a dog named Icky after Ichabod Crane."

Hyacinth laughed and handed the book to Davis. "Where I'm from, the college mascot is the Ichabods," she said.

"How much is it?" asked Davis, opening the book gently and laying it on the counter. He studied the page.

"Four thousand five hundred dollars."

"*What?*" said Ruby. "Really?"

"Really."

"I've really got to go now," said Davis, in a barely audible voice. He closed the book carefully. "It's way too expensive for me anyway. I'd better be getting back to work."

"How about you, Chief Konig?" asked Hyacinth. "Interested?"

"Very. Let me think about it."

Hyacinth smiled and the book disappeared under the counter. "Don't wait too long. Once I put it up for sale on my website, it will go quickly."

"Could you give me a few days?"

"Of course. In fact, I'll hold it for a week. I'd rather you have it than someone I didn't know."

"That's very kind. Thanks."

I bought Ruby the cookbook after eliciting a promise of at least two meals Martha Stewart would be proud of.

"Complete with Lemon Meringue Fluff," I added. "That's the deal."

The ladies said their goodbyes and headed for the door.

"It's been a pleasure meeting you and I'm sure we'll talk soon," I said. "I'm sure you'll sell a lot of books, but I don't know how much... umm...prognosticating you'll be able to do here in St. Germaine. We don't tend to attract the spiritualist community."

"That's just fine, dear," said Hyacinth. "I do mostly internet readings. And St. Germaine needs a good bookstore."

St. Barnabas was a lovely little stone church, rebuilt in 1904 after a fire destroyed the original 1846 building. We could seat three hundred comfortably, and more on Christmas Eve and Easter morning if need be. I looked down from the balcony on this Sunday morning, the twenty-first Sunday after Pentecost, and surveyed the nave, empty except for a couple of altar guild ladies arranging flowers. I'd skipped the hastily called staff meeting on Thursday, and so wasn't quite sure how our new rector would be handling the service. This was the very reason I was early, although a Rite II Eucharist was pretty cut and dried. I just needed to know if she would be intoning the *Sursum Corda* and whether to give her a pitch. Everything else should flow very nicely.

I opened the bulletin and gave it a quick look. Everything seemed to be in order. Maybe I was expecting some new unsingable hymn with appalling lyrics snuck into the service by a newly ordained, middle-aged, female seminary graduate, who decided to enter the priesthood because she had an experience at a Christian retreat weekend and after she'd written a poem about it, knew that God was calling her to a higher purpose because her children had all left home leaving her nothing to do all day but feel guilty about the ozone layer and anyway, she always thought she looked good in black. Or maybe Meg was right and I was getting jaded in my old age. Okay, I decided. Meg was right.

I heard a sound behind me and turned to see the Reverend Carmel Bottoms come into the loft. "Good morning," she said, cheerfully, in a voice so husky it could have won Best of Show at Westminster.

"Morning," I answered.

"Sorry you couldn't make the staff meeting."

"Yeah. Me, too."

"I understand though. I imagine that being the police chief is quite a responsibility. It must take almost all of your time."

I nodded in agreement.

"I didn't change anything in the service," she continued. "I realize I'm just the interim priest, but I may be here for quite a while. Let's just keep everything going until St. Barnabas is settled with its new appointment."

"Huh?" I said. This was not what I expected.

"I'd rather not chant without proper rehearsal, if you don't mind, so I'll just speak the words of institution this morning. Maybe sometime next week we can arrange to go over the chants if that's what you'd prefer. I don't have a great voice, but I don't have a problem staying on pitch. I played the flute in college, so I have a little bit of musicality. Of course, that was a long time ago."

"Huh?" I said again.

"I don't know why Bev said you'd be difficult to work with. You're just delightful." She held out her hand and I shook it almost absently. Then she turned to walk back down the stairs.

"Wait a minute," I said. "What about your poem?"

Carmel Bottoms looked confused for a moment, but smiled almost immediately. "I've written a few, but they aren't very good. I'll just keep them to myself."

"Christian retreat weekend? *Cursillo? Emmaus?*"

"Never been." She shrugged. "I guess I should go to one and see what all the fuss is about. Anyway, it's been great chatting. I need to go have a word with the lay ministers."

"It's about time we got a new story," said Marjorie as she settled into her choir chair and found my newly printed missive in her folder. "*The Mezzo Wore Mink.* Very nice. I have a fondness for mink."

"Me, too," said Georgia, who had just opened her folder and was thumbing through the music. "Although I prefer chinchilla."

"Really?" said Bev.

"Well, I don't know for sure since I don't have either one," admitted Georgia. "But I might."

"I have a mink," said Bev. "I don't wear it very often."

"I was thinking of getting a man-mink," said Mark Wells, one of the basses. "To go with my murse."

"What's a murse?" asked Phil.

"You know. A man-purse."

"You have a man-purse?"

"Nah," answered Mark.

"I have sort of a weasel-stole-thingy that I got from my mother," said Marjorie. "It has a head on one end and a tail on the other and you can clip the tail into the mouth. It's very beautiful. Well, except for the moth-eaten parts." She paused. "And the eyes," she added. "The eyes are creepy."

"Yes," I agreed. "Weasel can be very fetching and creepy. But you all can read the story at your leisure. Let's look at the anthem."

Half an hour and a short run-though later, I began the prelude.

The service started uneventfully as we sang the opening hymn, heard the collect, and began the *Gloria*. The Old Testament readings, the Psalm and the Epistle followed. Another hymn. Then the Gospel and it was time for the sermon. Carmel Bottoms began by introducing herself in her gravelly voice. Then she began her homily on the text "The stone that the builders rejected has become the cornerstone; this was the Lord's doing, and it is amazing in our eyes." She seemed to be doing a pretty good job when the church bell began to ring.

"What's going on?" hissed Meg. "Who's ringing the bell?"

"I'm sure I don't know," Elaine whispered back.

The St. Barnabas church bell was one of the two remaining relics from the old wooden church to survive the fire of 1899, the other being the altar. St. Germaine legend held that when the parishioners arrived on that cold Sunday morning in January to find the ruins of their church still smoldering, the heavy altar, complete with its marble top, had been miraculously carried outside the wooden structure and was sitting on the snow-covered ground with all the communion elements in place. The people of St. Barnabas held the morning service right there in the snow, convinced of God's grace and declaring that the only way the altar could have been removed from the church was by angelic intervention.

The bell, on the other hand, was four hundred pounds of forged bronze and not likely to melt in a wood fire, no matter how intense the inferno. After the church burned, the bell had been used by the city and kept in the clock tower until St. Barnabas was rebuilt, then moved back to the bell tower where it announced services and important civic events. It was still rung to usher in the Fourth of July and Founder's Day, among other less notable occasions such as the mayor's birthday—a tradition started by Pete. Now it was ringing like it was Easter morning.

"What's going on?" said Steve DeMoss, getting up. "Sheesh. And what are the ushers doing? Playing cards again?"

Carmel Bottoms was valiantly trying to continue her sermon, but we could all tell she was distracted beyond measure. Finally, her thought process ground to a halt and she just stood there smiling for a moment before saying, "Could someone see what's going on, please?"

I got up off the organ bench and made my way through the choir and down the stairs. Steve had already headed down, as had Mark Wells, Bev and Meg. As I came down the stairs, I saw quite a crowd standing around the door to the bell tower. In addition to the choir members, the ushers were also in attendance, several of them wringing their hands in distress.

"It's locked!" said Steve. "Whoever's in there won't answer and we don't have a key."

"I'll bet it's that McCollough boy," said Francis Passaglio, the head usher for October. "What's his name? Moosejaw?"

"His name's Moosey," said Meg. "Moosejaw's a city in Canada. Anyway, it's not him."

"I've got a key upstairs in the loft," I said. "At least I think I do."

"The master key doesn't work," said Bev, her voice barely audible over another tremendous clang. "I tried mine."

"I've got some of the old ones," I said. "The choir loft doesn't open with the master either, but we never lock it so it doesn't really matter."

It took me a couple of minutes to run back up the stairs, rummage around the organ trying to find the key ring, and then to hustle back down. There were only three keys on the ring, so it didn't take long to find the right one and give the lock a creaky turn. The door swung open just as the bell clanged again and we all froze at the sight.

Hanging from the bell rope by his neck, swinging like a pendulum, was Davis Boothe.

# Chapter 5

I raced into the room and immediately concluded that Davis must have climbed the old wooden ladder leading to the first landing before tying himself a noose and swinging into space. I looked up. The ceiling was old tongue-in-groove pine, painted dozens of times over the years. In the center of the ceiling, fourteen feet above the floor, was a square hole, roughly two feet across, that had been cut to allow the bell rope to drop to a manageable distance. In fact, when the bell was still, the end of the rope hung about twelve inches above the floor. Now it was tied several times around Davis' neck and looped around his arm. The old wooden ladder was fastened both to the floor and to the cutout in the corner of the ceiling. It was the only way up to the next room that, as far as I knew, was empty and unused except as an access to the pipe chamber by the organ tuner who showed up twice a year.

I pulled my pocketknife out of my pocket and climbed the rickety ladder as fast as I dared, at the same time seeing Mark and Steve come in behind me and grab Davis by the legs. They pushed him towards the ladder and I, reaching the apex, opened the blade and sawed at the heavy braided hemp, silently cursing the slowness with which each strand parted and gave way.

After what seemed an eternity to me, but was probably only thirty seconds, Mark and Steve placed Davis gently on the floor. Bev and Meg bent over him while the two men paused to catch their breath, having held Davis aloft as best they could, given the angle and limited leverage.

"I think he's dead," said Bev. "He's not breathing and his lips are black."

"Can't you do CPR?" Meg asked me, panic on her face.

I skipped the bottom three rungs coming down and landed with a thud. Kneeling, I took Davis' face in my hands and knew immediately there was probably no use. His head swung from side to side like a rag doll. Still, I started the CPR immediately. I could hear Meg behind me calling 911 and, in the distance, the sound of Carmel resuming her sermon. The ushers, I noted, were all standing around slack-jawed and of no help at all.

After three or four minutes, I felt a hand on my shoulder. I looked up at Mark Wells who shook his head sadly.

"His neck's broken," he said. "It's stretched probably two inches or more."

"Yeah, I know."

I fell back off of my knees and sat staring at the corporeal body that had been Davis Boothe. Everyone was deathly quiet. The only sound was the Reverend Carmel Bottoms' concluding sentence, heard as a far-off echo on the church's antiquated sound system. "In the name of the Father, the Son and the Holy Spirit. Amen."

"Amen," muttered everyone in the room.

"Let's leave him for the time being," I said, getting to my feet, "and lock the door until everyone's out." I glared at the crowd of ushers and various choir members peering through the door as I closed it behind me. "Not a word!" I warned, knowing it was a futile threat. "Not until everyone's out of the church." I turned to Meg. "Could you go and whisper to Carmel that we have an emergency and we should cut the service short—maybe after the passing of the peace? Everyone can come back tonight for communion."

She nodded and disappeared.

I could hear the Nicene Creed begin and pointed the ushers toward the front door.

"We believe in one God, the Father, the Almighty, maker of heaven and earth, of all that is, seen and unseen," said the congregation.

"You all can wait outside," I said to the group. Then I turned to Bev. "The choir might as well stay up there until the prayers are over. Could you go up and tell them what's happening after Carmel dismisses the congregation?"

She nodded without a word and disappeared as silently as Meg.

"God from God, light from light, true God from true God, begotten, not made, of one being with the Father," continued the congregation.

I felt exhausted. I sat down on a bench in the narthex, pulled out my cell phone and dialed Nancy's number.

"On my way," came the answer on the first ring. "Meg already called."

I hung up without saying anything.

The entire congregation loitered on the lawn of the church and watched the ambulance pull up and park in front of the double red doors. Nancy had gotten to the church just a few minutes after I'd called her and was in the bell tower room with the two EMTs. Most of the folks had already heard the news as word of the tragedy spread like wildfire among the huddled groups of parishioners. I broke the news to the rector.

"He's *what?!*" exclaimed Carmel Bottoms.

"He's dead," I said. "It was suicide. He hung himself with the bell rope."

34

"Was he a parishioner?"

"Oh, yes," said Meg. "Very active. Well...active for St. Barnabas. He attended services probably once or twice a month."

"Did he have a family?" asked Carmel. "Was he married?"

"I think he may have had a partner—he went out of town a lot—but he wasn't married," said Meg.

"Partner? Was he gay?"

Meg looked at me. "We assumed so," she said. "I don't know for sure."

Carmel's gaze drifted from Meg to me. I lifted my hands and shrugged.

"You know," said the Reverend Bottoms, "Bishop O'Connell said that I shouldn't pay attention to all the rumors going around the diocese."

"What rumors?" asked Meg.

"St. Barnabas is cursed. That's *what rumors!* People are horribly murdered in this church all the time. Horribly!"

"Hey, wait a minute," I said. "They're not *all* murdered. This is a suicide."

"I'm leaving," Carmel said, spinning on her heel. "I haven't even finished unpacking! I'm leaving tomorrow."

"What about the communion service this afternoon?" I asked.

She gave me a withering look over her shoulder and didn't answer.

"Well," said Meg. "That's that. Maybe Tony will fill in."

"He's out of town. We can call Father Tim from...what's the name of that parish?...You know...across the ridge?"

"Lord's Chapel?"

"Yeah, that's it. I have his number in my office."

Nancy and the two EMTs, nice fellows named Mike and Joe, wheeled the gurney out of the front doors and grunted it down the stairs. Our ambulance service came up from Boone—St. Germaine was too small a community to support its own—but considering the distance and the winding roads, Mike and Joe always made good time.

"Another day, another St. Barnabas body," said Mike with a wink as he passed me. I gave him my number two snarl.

"Gives a whole new meaning to 'corpus,'" said Joe. "Corpus! Get it? That's Latin for..."

"I get it," I interrupted. "Take him over to Kent Murphee's, would you? We need to get an autopsy."

"Coroner's closed on Sunday," said Joe. "But we'll drop him at the hospital. Kent can pick him up tomorrow. Just call over there."

They put Davis in the back of the ambulance, closed the doors and drove off without the sirens. Nancy stood at the curb as the crowd of churchgoers began to disperse.

"I really liked Davis," she said.

"Me, too," I said, although I didn't really know him. "He was on the vestry," I added absently.

"We were in a Little Theater production together five or six years ago."

I nodded.

"That man could really dance."

I looked at Nancy, then took out my handkerchief and handed it to her.

"Why'd he do it?" she asked, knowing that none of us had an answer.

# Chapter 6

Nancy and I found ourselves sitting in the station late Monday morning without much to say. We were still waiting for Kent Murphee to give us a call verifying suicide as the cause of death so we could give the go ahead on the funeral arrangements. We had found no next of kin.

Nancy was catching up on reports that had to be filed with the state to fulfill our quota of monthly bureaucracy necessary to receive our all-important government funds. I was in my office staring thoughtfully at a copy of Dave's report on conflict management and negotiations. Seeing as I didn't remember asking him to write it in the first place, I finally gave up and tossed it into an ever-growing pile on my desk.

I sat for a moment listening to the phone not ringing before announcing that I was going out for a while.

"You have your cell?" asked Nancy, not looking up.

"Sure," I said. Then I checked. "Umm. I mean no. Do you see it anywhere around?"

Nancy looked up at me in mock exasperation. Then she flipped open her own phone and hit a number. A couple of seconds later I heard my muffled ring-tone—the theme to the *Muppet Show*. Nancy had put it on my phone as a joke, then somehow locked it, and now I couldn't figure out how to change it. It was no good asking her. "It's distinctive," she said. "You'll always know that it's *your* phone that's ringing."

"How about something by Bach?" I asked. *"That's* distinctive. Or maybe the fugue to the Shostakovich *Second Piano Concerto?"*

"This suits your personality better," said Nancy.

Even listening to the Muppets, it still took me a minute or two to locate my phone, now safely buried on my desk by the scattered pages of Dave's report.

"Got it," I said. "I'm going down to the coroner's office. If Kent calls, tell him I'm on my way."

I found Kent sitting at his desk, clad in the same tweed jacket that had been his uniform, summer and winter, since I met him some twenty years ago. His unlit pipe was clenched between his teeth, and he waved me in as soon as he heard me knock on the jamb of his open door.

"How're you doing, Chief?" he asked.

"Pretty good except for this sad business. We all knew Davis."

Kent nodded and looked professionally sympathetic.

"Can you tell me what you found?"

"Oh, yeah. Sorry." He flipped open a folder on his desk then looked up.

"You want a drink?" he asked. "I just got a wonderful bottle of forty-year-old tawny port."

"Do I need one?"

Kent shrugged.

I looked at my watch. Almost noon. "Okay then. Small one."

Kent pulled a large, amber bottle out of his bottom drawer, then used it to push one of the two coffee cups sitting on his desk across the polished veneer, stopping just short of my lap. Then he opened the bottle and poured me a couple fingers. Kent was right. It was delicious.

"Okay," he said, after he'd taken a sip of his own. "Let's get down to brass tacks. We have here a white male, age thirty-two. That was on his driver's license. He weighed one hundred eighty-two pounds."

I nodded and took a sip of port. "I would have put him younger than that."

"You knew his neck was broken?" asked Kent. I nodded again and he continued. "Between C1 and C2. It's called the hangman's break and usually results in functional decapitation."

"I don't get it."

"His...broken...neck...killed...him," Kent said slowly, seeing the puzzled look on my face.

"Oh, I understand that. But when he came off the ladder, I don't think he dropped far enough to break his neck, and besides, there was plenty of give in the bell rope."

"I thought of that, too," said Kent. "But here's the thing. Nancy sent over the photos. Look here." He laid a photo of the bell tower room on top of the folder and drew a faint line with his pencil. "When he came off the ladder, the bell rope would have given some slack as the bell swung in its first arc. Then, as the bell returned, it would have encountered abrupt resistance from the body moving in the opposite direction. Newton's First Law of Motion."

"And that would have been enough to snap his neck?"

"Like a twig," said Kent.

"If we had gotten there...?"

"Nope," said Kent, before I could finish the question. "He was dead the first time his bell was rung. Hey, that's pretty good!"

"Cute. I guess suicide is the verdict."

Kent nodded. "That's what I'd say. The door was locked from the inside, right?"

"Yep."

"Nancy gave me a heads up that he might be gay. I sent some blood in for an HIV test. The results will be back in a few days. There was one other interesting thing."

"I'm all ears."

"I took an x-ray to see exactly where the break was and found this." He flipped to the back of the file and pulled out a color printout. "Look right here." He spun the picture around and pushed it across the desk.

"What am I looking at?" I asked.

"This." He tapped the picture with a pencil. "Right here in the left parietal lobe. He's got an embolism. Not a small one, either. This sucker would have eventually caused a massive stroke or killed him straight away."

"Elucidize me."

"An embolism is caused when an object migrates, via circulation, from one part of the body and causes a blockage of a blood vessel in another part of the body. It's particularly dangerous if it settles in the lungs, the heart, or the brain. In this case, the occlusion is a blood clot. Just look at the size of this." He tapped a large dark spot on the picture."

"Big?"

"Huge."

"How long before something happened?"

"Can't say, but if a doctor had found it, it would have meant a major operation that I'm not sure the patient would have survived."

"Maybe Davis already knew about it."

"It's a possibility," agreed Kent.

I met Nancy and Dave at the Bear and Brew for lunch. It was Nancy's turn to buy. When I walked in, they were waiting for me, three beers on the table and our pizza already ordered.

"What's the conclusion?" asked Nancy.

"Suicide," I said, sitting down on one end of the bench, across from Dave. "He had a heck of a blood clot though. There was an embolism in his brain. Kent says he was a walking time-bomb."

"Did Davis know?" asked Dave.

I shrugged. "I guess we could ask his doctor, if we knew who his doctor was, if he even had a doctor and if this mythical doctor would tell us if we found him, which I doubt."

"You think there's something else going on?"

I shook my head. "I guess it just caught me by surprise. We all saw Davis on Wednesday at the bookstore. Still, you never know what's going through someone's head."

"Try this," said Nancy, pushing a bottle of Redhook Ale across the table. "Beer and pizza always cheer you up."

"I'll need two," I said, "and most of Dave's slices."

"You can have 'em," said Dave. "I had a late breakfast."

After lunch, Dave headed back to the office to pretend to work. Nancy and I decided that it was time we introduced ourselves to the new business owners in St. Germaine that we hadn't yet met.

"Maybe we can shake them down for a little 'protection' money," said Nancy.

"It's an idea."

Our first stop was the Appalachian Music Shoppe, probably one of about ten stores with the same name within a hundred mile radius of St. Germaine. It wasn't a chain, just a lack of imagination among Appalachian Music Shoppe owners, although Nancy wryly and sarcastically pointed out that the extra "p" and superfluous "e" in 'Shoppe' gave it some class that would have otherwise been sorely lacking. Nancy had surmised, when she first heard about the music store, that it would meet her audiophile needs with bins of CDs— everything from Heavy Metal to Rap to Country to all twelve hundred recordings of Pachelbel's Canon. I figured it for a mountain dulcimer, folk guitar, banjoey type store with some Cherokee flutes on the walls and an expensive handmade hammered dulcimer in the window. We were both wrong.

The Appalachian Music Shoppe was directly across from the Bear and Brew. It was a smallish store. Beaver had moved his chainsaw repair business out of the store and into his garage last winter when the landlord, Russ Stafford, decided to raise his rent. It was a turn-of-the-century storefront; red brick, not complemented much by a plate glass window and a solid oak door painted a greenish brown color that might, at one time, have been a focal point. We swung the door open and walked in to the sound of a trio of shawms playing a Monteverdi canzone on the shop stereo.

"Yikes," said Nancy. "What's that noise?"

"Shawms, I think. Or maybe zinks."

"Sounds like a flock of geese getting their collective necks wrung."

"Yeah, it does."

The store itself was not very big and still smelled faintly of chain oil and gasoline. The old pine floor hadn't been refinished, but the walls had been outfitted with shelves and some fancy display pegboard. Littering the shelves, pegs, and even the floor, were all manner of strange looking musical instruments.

Nancy walked up to the counter and tapped a couple of times on the bell, trying to announce our presence, but the music all but covered up her efforts.

"Hey!" Nancy finally yelled. "Anyone here?"

The music suddenly went down several decibel levels, and a very thin man wearing an oversized sweater walked out of the back room and up to the counter. "Sorry about that," he said. "I was in the back and turned up the music so I could hear it. Can I help you folks with something?"

"Just came in to say hello," I said, reaching across the counter to shake his hand. His grip was weak and his handshake suggested a bag full of turkey bones.

"Glad to meet you," he said. "You must be Chief Konig. You were pointed out to me last week."

"Hayden," I said. "And this is Nancy."

Looking at us from behind the counter, the proprietor of the Music Shoppe conjured up the immediate image of Ichabod Crane: a smallish head, flat on top with large ears and a long snipe nose. He smiled, showing several discolored teeth, and gave Nancy a nod of acknowledgement. Of course, it could be argued that I had Ichabod Crane on my mind. I'd decided yesterday night to purchase *The Sketchbook of Geoffrey Crayon* from Hyacinth Turnipseed. I even got the okay from Meg. So I'd been thinking about Ichabod Crane all morning, and now, here he was, in the flesh.

"That reminds me," I whispered to Nancy. "I've got to go get my Washington Irving book."

"You bought it?"

"Sure," I said.

"My name's Ian Burch," said the unfortunate-looking man in a freakishly high nasal voice. "May I help you?"

"Glad to meet you, Mr. Burch," said Nancy.

"It's Doctor," he corrected. "Dr. Burch. I have a PhD in musicology."

"You don't say," said Nancy, fighting back an evil grin. "Musicology. How interesting." Nancy could size up people in about two minutes and she was rarely mistaken. I already knew what she thought of Dr. Burch.

"Specifically, my work is in late Medieval instrumental music of France and Burgundy," he sniffed. "I've given several papers on the subject."

"Are you an academician?" I asked. "Which faculty?"

"Well," he hesitated, "I *am* a member of several societies and under consideration for a university position." He paused, then continued. "But I haven't heard yet. Until they decide to hire me, I've decided to open a shop. I'm going to sell quality reproductions of Medieval and Renaissance instruments, some instruction books which I have written and perhaps a few select recordings."

"I have a great recording of the Tuntenhausen Bladder-Pipe Ensemble," I said, trying to be nice.

Dr. Burch snorted derisively. "I myself do not care for the bladder instruments. My performing instrument in college was the sopranino rauschpfeife."

"Wow," said Nancy. "I'll bet *that* got you a lot of dates."

Dr. Burch looked at her blankly, then turned to me. "I wonder if you might know if there is a chapter of the American Vegan Society here in town?"

"I don't think so," I said.

"In Boone then?"

I looked over at Nancy. She shrugged.

"Asheville?"

"Oh, sure," said Nancy, nodding. "Asheville for sure!"

"This is fun," said Nancy. "Shall we try the spa next?"

"Let's get my book first."

"Sure."

We stopped by Eden Books and I happily wrote a check for forty-five hundred dollars plus tax, and put the neatly wrapped package under my arm.

"Do come back soon," said Hyacinth, closing the drawer to the old cash register with a solid bang.

"You know where to find me," I answered, "if you find something else of interest."

Nancy didn't say anything about me dropping that kind of money on a book. A couple of years ago, after Nancy had saved my life by shooting a crazed priest's wife, I had thanked her by giving her a motorcycle—a silver Harley-Davidson Dyna Super Glide. She was speechless at the time, and never needled me about spending money again.

We dropped the book off at the station, then continued around the square past St. Barnabas church, stopping on the way to exchange pleasantries with Carol Sterling and Mrs. Kellerman, both taking advantage of the beautiful fall afternoon to take their dogs on a walk. We turned onto Maple Street, walked past the flower shop and up the steps of Mrs. McCarty's old house, now displaying two signs on the front porch. Sign number one had the coffee logo I'd seen a few days ago and advertised "Holy Grounds." Sign number two heralded "The Upper Womb—a place of healing."

We walked into the foyer of the house. Nothing had changed much since Mrs. McCarty had left, save that small tables, some with two chairs, some with four, had replaced the furniture in the two front rooms. I noticed the sounds of Vivaldi softly drifting down from unseen speakers, quite a contrast to the blare of the crumhorns in the Appalachian Music Shoppe. I also noticed that there were no customers.

"Hello," Nancy called. "Anyone here?"

Cynthia appeared in the hallway from what must be the kitchen. She was wiping her hands on a white apron tied around her waist.

"Our city's finest," she said, smiling. "About time you came around. Would you like a cup of coffee?"

"No, thanks," said Nancy. "We're tanked up on Redhook." I gave her a sharp elbow.

"We just came in to meet the proprietor," I said.

"Chad? He's out back. You want me to get him?"

"That's okay," I answered. "We'll find him."

"Right through there." Cynthia pointed down the hall toward a back door, and disappeared back into the kitchen.

Mrs. McCarty's old house was an American Foursquare popular at the turn of the century, two stories tall with a front porch spanning the width off the front and four pillars supporting the porch roof. As was typical with a number of houses built in St. Germaine around this time, this Foursquare had four rooms downstairs, square of course, and four upstairs, each tucked into its own corner of the house. From the entrance, where Nancy and I stood, the hallway ran from the front of the house straight through to the back to take advantage of the mountain breezes. We followed the hall to the back door, exited down a set of stone steps into the backyard, and looked around at a large hedged garden with a gate hanging on one hinge.

"This is where Mrs. McCarty kept her hedgehogs," Nancy muttered under her breath.

In the center was a concrete pad that I reckoned was about twenty feet square. In the middle of the pad was a very well built man in his early thirties, clad in jeans and a white thermal shirt with the sleeves cut off, kneeling and wielding a can of spray paint.

"Chad?" I whispered to Nancy.

"Chad," she whispered back.

Chad stood up when he saw us, smiled, and made his way gingerly across the concrete, obviously avoiding the freshly painted areas. I felt, rather than heard, a sigh escape from Nancy as he approached. Chad was as tall as I—several inches over six feet—but heavier, carrying much more muscle than I ever had, even when young and foolish and convinced of the benefits of excessive weight training. He reached out his hand to me as he approached and I met his grip as best I could, at the same time being slightly envious of forearms wrapped with knotted tendons. His waist was slim, his shoulders broad, his biceps and chest huge, and his curly black hair framed an Adonis' face complete with sparkling blue eyes and a movie star's smile. I disliked him immediately.

"I'm Chad," he said, clasping my hand in a grip of iron. "Chad Parker. You must be the chief."

"Hayden Konig," I said. "You already know Nancy?"

"Nancy's been in a couple of times," Chad said, an overly cute smile playing at the corners of his mouth. I glanced over in her direction and her face was beginning to redden. She sniffed.

"I had this thing going on with my neck. It took a couple of sessions to work it out."

I nodded. "Sounds great. I'm glad we have a masseur in town."

"Christian masseur," corrected Chad. "I'm the only certified Christian masseur in the state. Here at The Womb, we offer holistic and spiritual healing in a Christian atmosphere. Not only massages, but sweats, aroma therapy, drumming classes, acupuncture, yoga, light therapy...the works."

"And a good cup of coffee," I added.

"That too," Chad chuckled.

"What are you working on here?" I asked, walking over to the concrete slab. Chad followed a few steps behind.

"This will be our labyrinth. It used to be the carport, I think, or a picnic shed, but I took down the roof and the posts. Once it's been painted on the slab, it will be perfect for our guided meditations."

I looked down at a paper template, taped at the edges and partially painted. "I recognize the pattern."

"Yes, it's become quite famous over the centuries. Over the past ten years, meditation labyrinths have undergone a dramatic revival as a tool for contemplation, relaxation, and spiritual renewal."

"So, what do you do?" asked Nancy, walking over to inspect Chad's handiwork. "Try to find your way out?"

"Oh no. A labyrinth is an ancient symbol that relates to wholeness. The way in is the way out. There's only one path. It combines the imagery of the circle and the spiral into a meandering but purposeful path. The labyrinth represents a journey to our own center and back again out into the world."

"Oh," I said.

"Your life is a sacred journey," continued Chad. "And it is about change, growth, discovery, transformation, continuously expanding your vision of what is possible. You are on the path, exactly where you are meant to be right now. From here, you can only go forward, shaping your life story into a magnificent tale of triumph, of healing, of courage, of beauty, of wisdom, of dignity, and of love."

"Chad," I said, shaking my head, "that was a memorized speech if I ever heard one."

He laughed. "Well, I *was* a theater major in college. Seriously though, a labyrinth is a metaphor for life's journey with which we can have a direct experience. It is a symbol that creates a sacred space that takes us out of our egos to our inner spirituality. It will be a central part of our spiritual wellness program."

"Certainly something to look forward to," I said. "Is it just you and Cynthia working here?"

"My wife is coming down from New Hampshire next week to join us. She's also a licensed Christian massage therapist. Her name's Lacie. She's been up there packing and selling the house."

"I look forward to meeting her," I said. "I didn't know you were married."

"Sure," said Chad. "By the way, you're going to find out sooner or later..."

My eyebrows went up and Chad shrugged apologetically.

"Lacie and I...we're naturists. Nudists. Do you think that will present a problem?"

"Depends," I said. "Will you be practicing your predilection during business hours?"

"Oh, no. That would be highly unethical."

"Will you be parading around town corrupting our youth and scandalizing our citizens?"

He laughed. "I hardly think so."

"Then I don't have a problem. How about you, Nancy?"

Nancy just stared.

# Chapter 7

Archimedes is a barn owl. He is mostly white, has a wingspan of about two feet, and, by owlish standards, is fairly tame. He's been living with Baxter and me for the past couple of years. Baxter, being a dog of discernment and intelligence, ignores him. I, on the other hand, find him endlessly fascinating. He comes and goes as he pleases, thanks to an electric window in the kitchen, and when he shows up, I feed him deceased mice that I keep in a well-marked coffee can in the refrigerator. Now, seated at my desk, I held one of these treats by its tail and watched Archimedes, standing at attention next to the typewriter, take it gently in his beak, throw his head back, and swallow the snack in two gulps. I held up another, but the owl had had enough. He gave two small hops, spread his wings and, without a sound, took off through the house toward the kitchen, as silent as a ghost.

I watched him disappear through the kitchen door, then picked up my new hat and set it gently on my head, expecting nothing less than literary magic.

I started to head back to the office, then decided to take a short detour into my new favorite bar. Buxtehooters was busy as usual. Piano bars always did pretty well on the south side, but a pipe-organ bar was new to this part of town. I walked in to the sounds of a Jan Pieterszoon Sweelinck sing-along; patrons clanking their beer mugs together while a trio of beer-fraüleins led the tune from the top of the bar clad in their Buxtehooters t-shirts and German dirndls. There was no doubt about it. These girls had talents.

I spotted Pedro LaFleur in the corner nursing a bottle of "Diego's Dog-Oil" and trying to remember the words to the fourth stanza of "Ein Feste Burg." Pedro was a hard guy to miss--about two eighty, cauliflower ear, flat nose, three-inch scar under his eye. He sang counter-tenor for the Presbyterians.

I was walking his way when a hand slithered up from a dimly lit booth like President Nixon coming out of his snake basket, coiling around my waist and wriggling under my trench coat. I looked down at a woman who was half angel, half devil and half mermaid—the good half, not the fish half, her blond hair drifting dreamily in the undercurrents of fruitless pick-up lines and the tidal pools of failed dalliances.

"Sit down, big boy," she burbled. "The name's Ginger. Ginger Snapp."

46

The next morning found the entire police force at the Slab Café, all three of us, doing our best to encourage the Belgian economy in regard to waffles.

"These are great," said Dave, swirling the last bite around the syrup-covered plate like a miniature, bite-sized Dorothy Hamill.

"I concur," I said.

"Ditto," added Nancy.

"We aim to please," said Pete. "I got the mix from the Mennonite bakery. Not bad, eh?"

"Definitely not bad," I said. "By the way, Mr. Mayor, have you checked out any of our new businesses in town? Nancy and I did a walkabout yesterday afternoon."

Pete flushed. "How was I to know? Everybody wanted some new stores in town. 'The town is drying up!' they said. Well, they asked for 'em and now they've got 'em."

"No need to get defensive," said Nancy. "May I have some more waffles?"

"Me, too," said Dave.

Pete waved a vague hand in the direction of Noylene and she came right over.

"Waffles," muttered Pete, "and coffee." Noylene sniffed and headed for the kitchen.

"Don't get depressed," I said. "At least you attracted some interesting folks to our fair community. If I'm not mistaken, that's what Cynthia wanted you to do."

"If you think she won't make a big deal of this, you're mistaken," answered Pete. "A bookstore run by a nutty clairvoyant, a refugee from a Renaissance Fair, and a Christian massage parlor—that's not going to play very well in the *Tattler*."

"Not to mention the fact that the Christians are also nudists," said Nancy.

"*What!?* Oh, that's just *great!*" said Pete in disgust.

"We're off to visit Blueridge Furs this morning," said Nancy. "Have you been out there yet?"

Pete shook his head.

"We're all going," said Dave. "You should come along. After all, you are the mayor."

"They're outside the city limits," Pete exclaimed, throwing up his hands. "I can't be blamed."

"You don't know anything about them," I said. "It may be that you can take credit for bringing them to the area."

"Not the way this month is going," said Pete, as Noylene showed up at the table with a heaping plate of waffles in one hand and a coffee pot in the other. "I'll go with you though. When are you heading over?"

"Soon as we're finished," I said as I looked at the fresh plate of steaming Belgian waffles. "In an hour or so."

"Who's gonna watch the town?"

"Let's leave Noylene in charge," suggested Dave. "These waffles are delicious."

Pete and I got into my '62 Chevy pickup and I turned on the stereo adding the sounds of Zoltan Kodaly's *Psalmus Hungaricus* to the roar of the engine and the squeaks and rattles of the old chassis.

"Nice selection," said Pete. "I can't tell where the music leaves off and the truck begins."

"Spoken like a true jazzer. When was the last time you pulled out your sax?"

"I played with a little combo last month. At the Jazz Parlor down in Lenoir. Nobody was there, of course, and it didn't pay anything, but it helps keep up the chops." He looked down at the seat and picked up the old gray felt hat.

"Is this it? Is this *the* hat?"

"That's the one. I figure that as long as I have it, I might as well wear it."

"May I try it on?"

"Sure."

Pete put the hat on his head, but it was big on him and slid down comically around his ears. He sat thoughtfully for a couple of moments.

"Doesn't do anything for me. I can't think of a single bad sentence. I don't even feel like dangling a participle."

I laughed, took my hat back, and headed out of town on Old Chambers Road, followed by Nancy and Dave in Dave's Ford Escort. Four miles later, I turned right on Highway 53 and soon saw the newly painted sign for Blueridge Furs. We followed a long dirt drive up a meandering hill and came to what looked like an old dairy farm.

"Did you know this was back here?" I asked Pete.

"I had no idea. It looks to me like it hasn't been in operation for a long time."

"It's pretty clean though," I said, getting out of the truck and slamming the door behind me. "I mean, it all looks in pretty good shape. A lot of these old farms are completely falling down."

Nancy and Dave pulled up right behind us and joined Pete and me in our assessment.

"Hey," said Nancy, "you're wearing the hat."

"Yep," I nodded and turned to Dave. "Have you ever been up here?" I asked. "You grew up in St. Germaine, right?"

"Well, practically," said Dave. "This is the old Pierce place—Jed Pierce's grandfather. It hasn't been a working farm since the '80s. Old Man Pierce left it to Jed's father and he sold it to Locust Grove Dairy Farms. They never did open it though. Locust Grove Dairy Farms went belly-up soon after."

"How do you know all this?"

"My mom worked for Old Man Pierce till he sold the place."

Today there wasn't a house on the property but there were three large dairy barns and an office. Most of the fences and chutes had been torn down, but there were a few of the whitewashed posts still standing. In front of the office were two matching, dark green Land Rovers with 'Blueridge Furs' printed on the back doors in white script. We walked up the steps and knocked. After a moment, a very attractive red-haired woman—*very* attractive—opened the door and greeted us.

She was a dish with more curves than a shoebox full of garden snakes, eyes like pimentoed olives, and a face that would make Jimmy Swaggart dress Pat Robertson in petticoats, buy him a beer, and take him dancing.

I immediately whipped off the hat, afraid that, in a moment, I'd have entire chapters racing through my head. "Wow," I said, under my breath. Unfortunately, Nancy heard me and shot me a nasty sideways look, but before I could explain, we were interrupted.

"Hi, y'all!" the redhead said cheerfully. "Won't y'all come in? My name's Muffy."

"Muffy?" said Nancy. "What an *interesting* name. And you know, I've never seen Hayden's hat come off his head quite so fast. Is that spelled with a 'y' or with an 'i'?"

"A 'y'," Muffy said with a small giggle. "Although I spelled it with an 'i-e' when I was in high school. You know how sometimes you can dot the 'i' with a little heart?"

Nancy nodded.

"But then I changed it back." Muffy stepped back from the door. "It was too hard to remember. Come on in."

We entered the spacious office.

"I'm Pete Moss," said Pete. "I'm the mayor of St. Germaine. Running for re-election, by the way. I'd appreciate your vote." He gestured to the rest of us. "And this is Chief Konig, Lieutenant Nancy Parsky and Officer..uh...Dave."

"Dave Vance," said Dave, suddenly remembering that his hat was still on and whisking it away. He was grinning like an idiot. Nancy growled.

49

"Y'all are police? And you're the mayor? Is there a problem?" She looked nervous for a moment. Nervous looked good on her. So did the light blue angora sweater.

"No, no," I answered. "We just came to say hello."

Muffy relaxed. "Whew! That's a relief. My husband's went into Boone with Mr. Bateman to get some more fencing. Roderick Bateman is the owner of Blueridge Furs. My husband's the foreman and I'm the bookkeeper."

"What's your husband's name?" asked Pete. "Maybe I know him."

"Maybe," shrugged Muffy, "but we're from Greensboro. His name is Varmit Lemieux. That's my last name, too. We got married last month." She proudly held her left hand aloft so we could admire her ring.

"Beautiful," said Dave, dodging a withering look from Nancy.

"Breathtaking," said Pete.

"Stunning," I agreed.

"Oh, *brother*," muttered Nancy.

"How many others will be working out here?" Pete asked, hoping for an employment figure that he could tout in the newspaper.

"We have six now, but Mr. Bateman says probably a dozen before long."

Pete smiled happily. "Excellent. A dozen new jobs. That's great!"

"Can I get y'all some coffee and cookies?" asked Muffy.

"Absolutely," I said. "We haven't had anything to eat for a good half hour."

"Hey, wait a minute! Ain't you the choir director over at the Episcopal church?"

"Yes, I am," I answered in surprise. "Have you been over to St. Barnabas?"

"Why, sure! Varmit and I are Episcopalians. Well, Varmit was a back-slid Methodist and I was a Catholic so we sort of ended up in the middle. Anyway, we came over to St. Barnabas last Sunday. We heard the choir sing, but we had to get back here before lunch and I didn't get to talk to anybody." Muffy offered me a homemade chocolate-chip oatmeal cookie from a nicely filled platter. "Hey, can I ask you something?"

"Sure."

"Can me and Varmit join the choir? I have a real good voice and Varmit likes to follow along. It gives him something to do instead of sittin' at home drinking while I'm at choir practice." She lowered her voice. "I've been told," she said, in a confidential tone, "that I sound exactly like Loretta Lynn."

"I'll tell you what," I said. "Choir practice is at seven on Wednesdays." I shot a quick glance at Nancy, but she decided that it was the better part of discretion to suddenly look down at her feet and concentrate on nibbling her cookie. "Why don't you come for a couple of weeks and see how you like it?"

50

"We will!" said Muffy happily. "We'll be there on Wednesday."

We were drinking our coffee and enjoying our snack when we heard a truck drive up outside. I looked out the window and saw another Land Rover, identical to the other two, pull up to the office. A moment later the door opened and two men walked into the office, one of them in jeans and a sweatshirt, the other dressed in khakis with a button down collar jutting out of his v-neck cashmere sweater. Both of them smiled affably when they saw us.

"Pleasure to meet you," said the nattily dressed Roderick Bateman, once we had all introduced ourselves. "I wondered if someone would eventually make a trip out this way to check our operation."

"We're not here to check on anything," I said. "Just to say 'hello.' I expect the Fish and Wildlife Commission has some sort of jurisdiction over fur farms."

"They do," said Roderick, "but we also answer to the Fur Commission of America. They'll be coming in to do our certification."

"Sounds like a fine organization," said Pete. "Muffy here was telling us that you plan to employ about twelve people."

"Maybe more than that," said Roderick, with a sly smile. "We have a completely new product. One that I hope will catch on in the fashion world. If it does, the sky's the limit!"

Pete looked very pleased.

"Would you like the tour?" Roderick asked.

"Of course," Pete and I said in unison. Nancy and Dave both nodded.

Varmit Lemieux didn't have much to say, but he didn't seem to mind following us around, unlocking and opening doors as Roderick showed us the operation. We looked at the manure storage area, a couple of sheds, a cold storage room and the pelting shed.

"One worker," explained Roderick, "can care for five to six hundred breeding females. Then, eventually, we'll need the harvesting personnel as well. In eight months we'll be fully operational."

"How many breeding females will you have?" asked Pete.

"Eventually about four thousand. They'll produce fifteen thousand kits annually for pelting."

"How many do you have now?"

"We have five hundred here at the farm, and a thousand on the way from Louisiana."

"Louisiana?" said Nancy.

"Yep," said Roderick proudly. "That's our secret weapon."

"Can you tell us what it is?" Pete asked.

"As a matter of fact, I can. We just received confirmation from the patent office yesterday and our registered trademark has been approved. Come with me."

Roderick led us to the largest of the three barns and stood aside as Varmit unlocked the twelve-foot-high door and swung it back on giant hinges.

"We have all the stock in these two barns," said Roderick, indicating the structure we were in and the one facing us. "We'll have to build five more over the next couple of years. Not this big, of course—this one was built for cows—but substantial. Very substantial. We'll let the stock outside during the day once we have the pens built, at least during the warmer months. But at night, they'll be kept in here."

"Where are your other employees?" asked Nancy.

"I sent them up to Roanoke. There's a mink farm closing down and we're picking up a trailer full of cages. They'll be back this evening."

He led us into the well-lit barn. The center aisle was wide enough for a large truck to drive from one end to the other, exiting from either end through one of the matching double doors. On both sides of the aisle were pens separated by a four-foot high chain-link fence with a gate on the front. We walked over to the first pen and were startled by a very large animal standing on a hay bale. Upon closer inspection, there were a number of animals in the pen. I counted ten.

"What the heck are those?" asked Dave. "I thought you were raising minks."

"Those are nutrias," said Roderick proudly. "Coypu."

"They're rats!" said Nancy. "Giant rats!"

"Actually, they are," laughed Roderick. "Giant aquatic rats. They're not unlike muskrats and their fur is very desirable."

"I've heard of nutria coats," I said. "But it doesn't have nearly the value of mink or chinchilla." I paused and thought for a moment. "Does it?"

"No, it doesn't," admitted Roderick. "That's where our secret weapon comes in." He smiled. "Varmit, will you be so kind as to get one of our pacaranas?"

Varmit walked to the second pen down, unlatched the gate, disappeared for a moment, then reappeared with a strange creature in his arms. He walked over to us and set the animal on the floor. We surrounded it immediately.

"They're not fast," said Roderick, "and they're very docile."

"What is it again?" asked Nancy, squatting down to get a better look. I joined her.

"It's called a pacarana. Latin name: *dinomys branickii*. They're relatively rare in this part of the world. These little fellows are from the Andes Mountains in Ecuador."

"I'd hardly call him little," I said. The creature was three feet long and weighed about thirty pounds. It looked a bit like a woodchuck, but had a dark brown upper body, two white stripes along its back, and white spots down each side. Its ears were small and curved and I could see a deep cleft on its upper lip. Gray whiskers completed the distinctively strange package.

"The interesting thing about these rodents," said Roderick, "is that they'll mate with a nutria. The offspring are quite extraordinary. First generation offspring of a male pacarana and a female nutria retain all of the desirable fur-bearing characteristics of the nutria, with the distinctive color variations and size of the pacarana. They're one-third bigger than the average nutria. That's one-third more fur."

"What about second generation?" I asked.

"Can't happen," said Roderick. "The offspring are sterile."

"How many male pacaranas do you have?"

"Fourteen," said Roderick. "With more on the way, hopefully. They aren't endangered, but, as I said, they're hard to come by."

"So you're counting on fourteen male pacaranas to impregnate five thousand females. That's..." I tried to do some quick math in my head. "What?...Four hundred females apiece? That's more than King Solomon had."

"Three hundred fifty seven point one four," said Dave. "Roughly."

"A year," said Roderick. " Three hundred fifty seven a *year*. That's only one a day if you give them all the government holidays off. The trick is to give a small dose of hormones to the female nutrias so they don't all come into heat at the same time. We've got it down to an art. Besides, these little guys don't seem to have a problem performing. Like all rats," he laughed, "it's what they do."

"I'll vouch for that," muttered Nancy.

"Sounds like you have it all worked out," said Pete.

"Well, we don't have five thousand female nutrias yet," said Roderick, "and by the time we do, I'm hoping to have a few hundred male pacaranas. We also have two female pacaranas, so we'll be able to breed our own stock."

"You mentioned a patent," I said.

"A patent and a registered trademark. Good for ten years. We're calling the animal 'Minque.' M-I-N-Q-U-E."

"Minque?" I said.

"Minque coats, Minque collars, Minque mittens...you name it. Also," Roderick added, "this isn't public knowledge, but we're hoping for a major celebrity endorsement."

"That will certainly help," said Nancy.

"Minque," said Dave thoughtfully. "With one of those ® signs behind it? I like it. Can we see one of these Minques?"

"Absolutely. They're in the other barn."

# Chapter 8

"I've been waiting for you," Ginger Snapp cooed. "As a shamus, you come highly recommended."

"How 'bout as a good time?" I said smirkily, lighting a stogie.

I'd seen her around, but always hanging off the arm of some up-and-coming bishop. She was an ornament, a decoration, a prize that came with the pointy hat, the dress and the incense pot.

"Hmm. Let me think. As a good time you seem to rate slightly behind Pedro over there." She tossed her head like a hair-covered hand grenade in the direction of Pedro's snoring body, now lying under his table with a drink umbrella sticking out of his mouth.

"I've got information," she said in a voice so low it could have been wearing spike heels and still skittered under Dick Cheney's credibility. "AveMaria was just a warning and I'm afraid that I'm next."

"Beautiful," said Meg. "This is some of the most elegant prose it has ever been my pleasure to dispose of."

"Dispose of?" I said. *"Dispose of?"*

"I meant 'read.' Did I say 'dispose of?' How silly of me." Meg was sitting on the leather couch with a glass of red wine in one hand and my latest literary effort in the other. Her legs were tucked elegantly under her and the flickering light from the fireplace accented her features from continually changing angles. "Now tell me again about this hat thing."

"I was standing at the door of the Blueridge Furs office," I said. "I was wearing the hat. *This* hat. Raymond Chandler's hat."

Meg nodded.

"And this woman opens the door..."

"Muffy Lemieux," said Meg.

"Yes, Muffy Lemieux. And then this sentence just pops into my head."

"Sounds spooky. Just what does this Muffy Lemieux look like?"

"Well, she's...um...sort of...you know...kind of gorgeous. She's got these legs and these other things. You know...accoutrements."

"I know exactly," said Meg. "I would expect someone named Muffy Lemieux to be blonde. Very blonde."

"Nope. Redhead. She says she's going to come and sing in the church choir."

"I'll bet she does."

"Anyway," I said, "it's not like she's single or anything. She's married to a man named Varmit. Apparently she'd like him to join the choir as well. Besides," I added, "she's been told that she has a voice like Loretta Lynn."

"Better and better. But back to the hat, Mr. Hard-Boiled Author. Does this literary phenomenon happen often?"

"So far, whenever I put it on."

"It's on now," she said, with a sly smile. "Anything come to mind?"

She sat reclining on the sofa, her heaving bosom rising and falling like twin boiling Christmas puddings on Boxing Day, and even as her mouth whimpered no, no, no, the rest of her body ached yes, yes, yes, except for her appendix which had been removed the year before and so didn't care very much either way.

I didn't take time to write it down.

Worship Committee meetings at church are to be avoided if at all possible. This is Rule No. 1 in the Hayden Konig Church Musician's Handbook. Rule No. 2 is never, *ever* agree to do anything that Meg asks in her sultry, Lauren Bacall voice while whispering in my ear. Closely following is Rule No. 3: If anyone complains about how loud the organ is, the best possible response is to pull out all the stops. There are a myriad of other rules. For example: Never sing any anthem in which the composer or poet tries to rhyme any word with Jesus. This includes squeeze us, frees us, please us, etcetera. There are exceptions, of course, and one of them was a brilliant Christmas madrigal, penned by myself, in which I managed to rhyme Holy Jesus with Mouldy Cheeses.

Unfortunately, Rule No. 1 had exceptions as well and one of them occurred when a new rector showed up for the first time. That was the canon under which I was currently operating as I sat at the St. Barnabas conference table surrounded by the Worship Committee: Georgia Wester, Carol Sterling, Meg, and Joyce Cooper. Marilyn, the long-suffering church secretary, was there to take notes.

We were busy sharing a pot of coffee and exchanging pleasantries when Beverly Greene walked in wearing her Parish Administrator demeanor, followed by an overweight and extremely muculent man in a priest's collar. His hair was sparse and hung in damp tendrils around his ears. Perched on his nose was a pair of oversized glasses that he was continually pushing back up the slippery slope with his index finger. He was followed into the room by an unsmiling woman of equal girth and humidity, sporting a hairdo reminiscent of Moe Howard, the greatest of the Three Stooges. I shuddered involuntarily.

"This is our new *interim* rector," said Bev, a frozen smile on her face. "The Reverend Dr. Adrian Lemming. Bishop O'Connell called this morning to give me the good news that he's found us a *temporary* priest." She put a lot of stress on the words "interim" and "temporary"—more, in fact, than might have been necessary—but the Reverend Dr. Lemming didn't seem to notice. *Mrs.* Reverend Dr. Lemming *did* notice. Her nostrils flared just a bit and her eyes narrowed oh-so-slightly. Or maybe it was just my imagination.

"Good morning, everyone," said the moist man in an even moister voice. He pulled out a handkerchief and blotted the beads of sweat off his pallid pate—sweat that had formed despite a room temperature in the low seventies. "First of all, I think you should call me Father Lemming. That's really my preference, dontcha know."

I shot a sideways glance at Meg. I knew for a fact that she *hated* it when people said "dontcha know." *Hated it!* She was now displaying the same Arctic smile that spread across Bev's features.

"This is my wife, Fiona Tidball-Lemming, dontcha know," said Father Lemming, gesturing to the woman now seated at the head of the table with a nod.

Scattered "good mornings" and muttered "pleased to meet yous" filtered across the table as Father Lemming took a seat next to his wife.

"Why don't we all introduce ourselves?" suggested Bev. "Father Lemming, perhaps you could start. Tell us a little about yourself."

"The first thing I'd like to say is that Fiona and I are a ministry team, dontcha know."

We nodded as though we *did* know.

"Fiona and I were raised Southern Baptist. In fact, I was a Minister of Music in a Baptist church in Bobo, Alabama, when I started out in church work. Worked there for the better part of twenty years, dontcha know."

I could feel everyone's eyes dart momentarily in my direction.

"Fiona was the church secretary," he continued, smiling over at her, "and Director of Christian Education. After my divorce, she and I were married, and it was God's will that we leave the Southern Baptist denomination. It was clear that He was calling us to the Episcopal Church to continue our ministry, dontcha know."

We nodded again.

"I graduated from the seminary and here I am."

"Your doctorate?" ventured Meg.

"I was granted a Doctor of Ministry degree in 1998 by Liberty University, dontcha know.

"Jerry Falwell's university?" Joyce said.

"Oh yes," said Father Lemming, proudly. "I had my Doctor of

Ministry even before I went to the Episcopal seminary. Did it all from the comfort of my music office at the Baptist church, dontcha know. Liberty has quite a good Doctor of Ministry degree, dontcha know. They count 'life experience' toward your credits for graduation, dontcha know."

The "dontcha knows" were now dropping from his mouth like teeth from Aunt Millie's gums during last year's taffy-pull. I thought Meg might scream.

"We're very pleased to be here," he continued, "and although this is our first position in an Episcopal church, dontcha know, I want you all to be assured that both Fiona and I bring a wealth of ministry experience."

We nodded again and Carol added a "dontcha know" under her breath, but loud enough for me to hear and stifle a snort.

"Now then," said Fiona Tidball-Lemming, offering her first smile of the morning—a smile designed by nature to freeze a predator's prey before pouncing—"you've heard about us. Let's find out about all of you." Her fleshy finger moved around the table and rested on Meg. I could sense a gulp.

"I'm Meg Farthing. I sing in the choir. And I'm on the Worship Committee." She paused. "Vestry, too." It was as succinct a recitation of responsibilities as I'd ever heard from Meg.

Carol was next. "Carol Sterling. Worship Committee. Altar Guild."

"Marilyn Forbis. Secretary," said Marilyn in turn.

We made our way around the table, everyone being as concise as possible. No wasted words with this bunch.

"Georgia Wester. Building and Grounds. Vestry. Worship."

Finally it was my turn. I was the last. "Hayden Konig, organist and choirmaster."

The Lemmings smiled and nodded.

"First things first," said Father Lemming. "It's already mid-October. Do we have our plans for Christmas finalized yet?"

Everyone looked around the table and there seemed to be quite a bit of non-committal shrugging going on.

"Hayden," he said, "tell us about our musical plans."

"Hmm, let's see," I said, pulling out the pad Nancy had given me and flipping it open to the first page. There was nothing written in it, of course, but a little showmanship never hurt. "On the first Sunday of Advent..."

"*Advent?*" snorted Fiona Tidball-Lemming. "We're talking about Christmas."

"Ah," I said, flipping four or five more pages. "Yes, of course. Christmas. On Christmas Eve we'll be having the traditional two services, one at..."

"Not Christmas Eve," said Father Lemming in exasperation. "We mean the Christmas *season*."

"Yes," I said. "The Christmas season. Christmas Eve to January 6th. Actually, as you know, the season of Christmas doesn't really start until Christmas Day, but we always..."

"The *Christmas season*," said Fiona. "December 1st through the 25th. There's no sense in celebrating Christmas after Christmas!"

"Right," I said, flipping back the pages. "So on the first Sunday of Advent—that would be December 2nd—I was planning on doing Bach's Cantata No. 62—*Nun komm, der Heiden Heiland*—in English, of course, maybe with a smallish orchestra. Then on the 9th..."

I'll tell you what," said Father Lemming. "Since we obviously don't have any plans, we've got some really great ideas for Christmas, dontcha know."

"What's the scam, Ginger?" I said. I knew the type. She was beautiful, as sassy as a three-year-old jar of mayonnaise, and so smart she spelled "floozy" with two z's.

"What do you mean?" she jiggled. "Can't a girl buy a gumshoe a drink?"

I sat down and whistled up a beer-fraulein. "I'll have a Mummy Martini," I said. The waitress raised her Arian unibrow in confusion. "So dry I have to blow the dust off the top," I explained, raising an eyebrow of my own at my considerable cleverness as I leaned across the table, Ginger in my sights.

"I'll have a Cement Mixer," said Ginger, leaning in as well. "Hold the pickle."

Our waitress trundled off to get our orders leaving us with nothing more than the space between us, a space that was narrowing as fast as the profit margin at Paris Hilton's "Things Go Better With Coke" discount shoe store.

Ginger's face was close and getting closer. I could smell her breath, a pungent mixture of lilacs, persimmons and furniture wax. Our nose hairs entwined and danced together in the smoke, anorexic ballerinas in a pas de deux of aphrodesia, as our lips reached across the gap, camel-like, and plucked at the thorny twigs of our desire.

"Man," whispered Ginger in a husky whisper, her eyelids dropping to half-mast, "you can really write."

"Baby," I replied. "You ain't heard nothin' yet."

"When we were at Mt. Olivet Baptist Church in Bobo," Mrs. Tidball-Lemming said proudly, "we began a Christmas tradition that still continues even though we left the congregation four years ago. I don't know if you've heard of it up here. It's called *The Singing Christmas Tree*."

Everyone at the table smiled politely.

"We'd like to bring this tradition to St. Barnabas, dontcha know," said Father Lemming, "and make it our gift to the community. In Bobo, we had to keep adding performances to accommodate the crowds, dontcha know." He looked around the table, making contact with each one of us. "People came all the way from Tupelo. Last year, over a thousand people saw the show."

We continued smiling.

"I realize that it's an expensive endeavor in the beginning. After all, the frame has to be bought and configured for the sanctuary, lighting and sound would need to be arranged for. But I think there is just enough time to get everything done if we start immediately. Besides, I understand that St. Barnabas has quite a generous endowment specifically for musical and artistic performances. And," he added, "if we charged ten dollars per ticket—that's what we charged in Bobo—we could easily make back our initial expenses over the course of seven or eight years."

"Well," said Fiona Tidball-Lemming, sitting back triumphantly. "Isn't that a grand idea? What do y'all think?"

Everyone glanced in my direction and waited.

"Well," I said. "I've been wanting to do a *Singing Christmas Tree* for some time, but Cornerstone Baptist over in Boone has been doing one for the past fifteen years."

Father Lemming's face fell, but Fiona was not to be denied. "That's what? Twenty miles from here? There's no reason why we can't do one as well."

"I suppose not," I said. "But the Cornerstone Baptist Tree has quite a following. People might think we're trying to horn in on their Christmas ministry."

"Harrumph," snorted Fiona. "They probably don't even know how to stage a proper *Singing Christmas Tree*. When we did ours, we had solos, children dressed as dancing sheep...the teenagers even rode into the church on four-wheelers singing *Chestnuts Roasting On An Open Fire*. And that wasn't even the grand finale. The people went wild for it!"

"If I might suggest something," I said. "We could consider an alternative that would preempt Cornerstone's *Singing Christmas Tree*."

I felt, rather than heard, a small gasp come from Meg, but undaunted, I rested my elbows on the conference table, templed my fingers and continued.

"Since Cornerstone Baptist is doing a *Singing Christmas Tree*, I suggest something for Thanksgiving. I've been thinking about just such a production."

Meg kicked me under the table. Hard.

"I like it," said Father Lemming with a thoughtful nod. "We could do the show a couple of weeks before Cornerstone's show. What do we call it?"

"We call it *The Living Gobbler*," I said, deftly dodging another kick. "It's like a *Singing Christmas Tree* except with a Thanksgiving theme. We'll have a giant banquet table, Pilgrims, Indians, Thanksgiving carols, the works. I think I can guarantee a huge success."

Father Lemming looked over at his wife who was eyeing me carefully. Then a huge and terrifying smile spread across her pie-like features.

"I think it's a *marvelous* idea!" she chortled. "We could work in some Christmas songs as well. Everyone's used to hearing them in the stores by Thanksgiving anyway."

"It's settled then," said Father Lemming with a clap of his hands.

"I don't think it's quite settled," said Bev, caution evident in her tone. "This really should be approved by the vestry."

"I don't think so," said Fiona. "I've read the by-laws. Actually the vestry at St. Barnabas is charged with the maintenance of the parish finances and its property. The vestry is also responsible for filling various positions of parish leadership. The programs of the church are the responsibility of the rector and the hired staff."

Bev chewed on her lower lip while Father Lemming nodded in agreement before continuing.

"I'd like to appoint Fiona as the Director of Christian Education and Worship." He looked at Bev. "Now, before you say anything, I know that the vestry will have to approve the appointment so we'll have to get it on the agenda of the next meeting, dontcha know." He turned to Marilyn. "When is that?"

Marilyn had stopped taking notes and was sitting motionless, as stunned as the rest of the committee. Suddenly she bustled to life, flipping several pages until she came to the information.

"Not until the end of November," said Marilyn. "We just had one and we're getting ready for the stewardship campaign."

"Fine," said Father Lemming. "Till then, Fiona will be the acting director. We'll get her approved in November."

"We could have a special 'called' vestry meeting," said Bev.

"No need," said Father Lemming, waving a dismissive hand. "Fiona won't be taking a salary, so there should be no problem. By November, the vestry will be able to see the job she's doing, dontcha know. There won't even be any discussion," he said proudly. "Now then, what're the plans for this Sunday?"

# Chapter 9

Lunch at the Slab following a worship committee meeting was more or less required. This particular afternoon, all members were in attendance. Nothing much was said until we were all seated at the large eight top near the kitchen; then, as if on cue, they all turned on me.

"What were you thinking?!" screeched Georgia. "*The Living Gobbler*? Are you crazy?"

"You were just kidding...right?" asked Joyce, her face dropping into her hands.

Bev spun around in her seat and slugged me in the arm.

"Ow!" I yelped.

"This is *not* funny! If we give those people an inch they'll be putting up screens in the nave and using Baywatch videos to explain the mystery of the incarnation!"

"Hang on..." I said. "There's no need..."

Carol slugged me in the other arm.

"Hey. Stop it."

I looked up and saw Pete making his way to the table. Carol slugged me again just for meanness. "First you quit," she growled, "and then you come back and now we're doing *The Living Gobbler*? I oughta hit you again!"

"What's this about *The Living Gobbler*?" asked Pete, sitting down at the table.

"Hayden has decided that St. Barnabas should put on *The Living Gobbler* as a Thanksgiving spectacular," said Meg. "I tried to kick him under the table, but it was no use. He somehow talked the Lemmings into thinking it was a good idea."

"The Lemmings?"

"Our new clergy ministry team. Father Adrian and Fiona, dontcha know."

"Don't I know what?" asked Pete, somewhat confused. Meg didn't elaborate.

"Anyway," continued Pete, "it sounds great. We can advertise it before the election. That'll show everyone we're community minded and might even get a few more folks into town for Thanksgiving weekend shopping."

"I'm glad you can see the advantages," I said. "Of course, the show hasn't actually been written yet."

"How hard can it be?" Meg asked. "Isn't that what you always say? How hard can it be?"

"Yeah," echoed Joyce, sarcasm heavy on her voice. "How hard can it be? A couple of songs...the choir dressed up like tap-dancing broccoli."

"O, Lord," said Georgia. "Tap-dancing broccoli?"

"Sure," I said. "Throw in some Thanksgiving tunes..."

"How about *Just As I Yam*?" said Pete.

"That's a good one," I said. "I was thinking of *Up From The Gravy*."

Bev slugged me again.

"Stop!" I begged.

Pete spread his arms and intoned in his best carnival bark. "St. Barnabas presents *The Living Gobbler*. Come and see the first Thanksgiving as it's never been done before. See the Lemmings as Miles Standish and Squanto, a torrid love story for the ages."

"Torrid indeed," giggled Meg. "Miles Standish and Squanto were both men."

"Although Squanto might be a good character for Mrs. Tidball-Lemming," muttered Georgia. "The name is certainly apropos."

"Come see the choir as they portray the four major food groups," Pete continued unabated. "Watch the alto section do the Sweet Potato Mash. See Carol Sterling as Pocahontas bite the head off a baked chicken. Come take communion from the largest table in North Carolina. See the cast come together for the grand finale in the shape of a *Living Gobbler* and sing that most famous of Thanksgiving hymns *Come Thou Fount of Garlic Dressing*!"

"It's an idea whose time has come," I laughed. "A show so good, it almost writes itself."

"How can it go wrong?" Pete asked.

"How can it go wrong?" asked an incredulous Bev. *"How can it go wrong?!"*

"Excuse me," said a voice. We all turned and saw an older couple standing a few feet away from our table.

"Excuse me," said the woman again. "We couldn't help overhearing. We'll be back in town on Thanksgiving weekend and I wonder if we could get tickets?"

We sat in stunned silence.

"Sure," Pete said finally. "Would you like seating in the Gourmet or Buffet section?"

We had just attacked our cheeseburgers, the Slab Café Wednesday special, when Pete, the only one at the table who had forgone the feast, interrupted our repast.

"Anyone read the paper this morning?" he asked casually.

"Not me," I muttered, managing two words around the side of a mouthful of fries. Everyone else, their mouths being currently occupied with lunch, shook their heads.

"What's the use of getting on the front page if no one reads it?" grumbled Pete. "There's a big article about all the increased economic activity in St. Germaine."

I shrugged and swallowed. "So?"

"So?" said Pete. "*So?* I'm in the political fight of my life here, people!"

"Pete," said Meg, "you're running for mayor of St. Germaine, a town of barely three thousand residents, against a woman whose only qualifications are that she's belly danced for Bill Clinton."

"Really?" asked Joyce. "She belly danced for Bill Clinton?"

"Oh, sure," said Carol. "Back when Clinton was president. His first term, I think. Before Monica. It was in the *Tattler*."

"Well, that sheds a whole new light on everything," I said. "I didn't know that Cynthia belly danced for the president. Maybe she *is* qualified to be mayor." I motioned for Pete to pass the ketchup. "I hope for your sake that she doesn't advertise her political expertise, or you're in big trouble."

"I'm sure it'll come up in the debate," said Pete.

"Debate?" said Georgia.

"Yep," said Pete with a grimace. "There's going to be a debate. A week from today. I hear that Cynthia has hired a publicist from Boone to help her prepare."

"That sounds like great fun," I said. "What time and where?"

"Eight o'clock at the courthouse."

"No problem. We'll cut choir practice a little short."

"What about *Living Gobbler* practice?" asked Georgia.

"That doesn't start until Thursday."

"Hey," said Joyce. "Where's Noylene? Isn't anyone waiting on tables in here? I'd like another iced tea."

Pete rolled his eyes. "Noylene only works in the morning. Then Bootsie takes over around eleven. Hey!" he yelled. "Anyone seen Bootsie?"

Bear Niederman, enjoying his Wednesday special at a table by the front plate glass window, hollered back, "She's outside having a cigarette."

"That's *it!*" said Pete, standing up and throwing his paper napkin to the floor in a huff, an angry gesture that lost its dramatic flourish when the napkin fluttered to the ground like a wounded butterfly. He stomped it in disgust. "I've had enough!"

He sighed heavily, walked behind the counter, got a pitcher of tea out of the cooler and commenced to visit the tables, seeing what the Slab clientele required in the way of additional victuals. But he was not happy.

Our lunch and pressing Gobbler business finished—or at least, on hold—Joyce excused herself, followed shortly by Carol, Bev and Georgia, leaving Meg and me to enjoy a cup of coffee before strolling back to work. I really enjoyed the pace of autumn and this early October afternoon was a perfect example. The crowds hadn't yet descended on the town for peak leaf season (although there was plenty of color dotting the mountains), the weather was brisk and sunny, and we weren't close enough to the holidays to feel the pressure inherent in any musician's life during Advent and Christmas.

"You're not *really* putting on *The Living Gobbler*, are you?" asked Meg, lifting the steaming cup to her lips and blowing gently across the top.

"I sincerely doubt it," I replied. "The Lemmings will need costumes, a children's choir director—not to mention a children's choir, stage hands, set builders, five octaves of handbells, bagpipers, twelve live turkeys...you know...a cast of thousands. That's what the show demands, of course. A cast of thousands. And an orchestra," I added. "Don't forget the orchestra."

"So it was a ruse."

"Yep."

"You have no intention of writing it?"

"Oh, I'll be happy to write it," I said. "It's a show that practically gobbles to be written. I just don't think it will be performed."

"I hope you're right."

"Have I ever been wrong before?"

"Oh, my dear, let me count the ways."

We were still sipping our coffee and contemplating the last piece of rhubarb pie in the pie case when the door of the Slab banged open, causing Pete's cowbell to dance noisily against the glass. Nancy strode in, Dave in her wake, and both of them moved hastily over to our table.

"Better come quick," said Nancy, bending down and whispering in my ear. "Right now."

I recognized the tone and knew better than to ask questions in a crowded restaurant. Meg and I followed Nancy and Dave onto the sidewalk outside without a word.

"We might as well walk," said Nancy as we crossed the road into the park. "It's just a couple of blocks. That new spa just called. There's a dead woman behind the house."

We were there in three minutes—straight across the park, a quick detour beside St. Barnabas and two doors over on Maple Street. Cynthia was waiting on the porch of the coffee shop with another woman. Both their faces were paler than their natural pallor might indicate. Cynthia's hands were entwined inside her apron, the lower half of which was now a knot of material at her waist. The other woman—tall and very attractive—had her arm around Cynthia's shoulder.

"Lacie?" I asked, as we climbed the steps up to the covered porch.

"That's right," said the woman. "Lacie Ravencroft."

"You're married to Chad?"

"Yes."

"I'm Chief Konig. This is Lieutenant Parsky, Officer Vance, and Meg Farthing." I looked over at Cynthia. "Cynthia, would you like to sit down?"

She shook her head.

"Can you tell us what's happened?"

"I'll *show* you," said Lacie. "Come on with me. Chad's in the back."

We followed Lacie into the front door, straight through the house and out the back. There, in the hedged garden, lying face down on Chad's newly painted labyrinth, was a woman. All five of us walked up to the edge of the concrete slab. Chad was sitting about four feet from the body, cross-legged, and staring at it as though in a trance. He didn't seem to hear us approach, or, if he did, he didn't acknowledge our presence until Lacie called out to him.

"Chad? Honey?"

Chad looked over at us a moment later, then shrugged himself out of his seated position and stood. Nancy and I stepped onto the slab and walked over to the body.

"You didn't touch anything, did you?" asked Nancy, snapping on a pair of Latex gloves.

"No."

I bent over the lifeless form as Nancy took her shoulder and rolled her over.

"She's stiff," said Nancy, "but not in full rigor. I'd say maybe last night sometime. The EMTs are on the way. Kent can probably give us a time of death if they hustle her down there."

"Who is it?" asked Meg. "Someone we know?"

"Thelma Wingler," I said. Thelma was one of those many women of a certain age whose actual chronology was made almost impossible to approximate by black hair dye, face powder, rouge, lipstick and a couple of face lifts. She might have been born anytime from the beginning of Theodore Roosevelt's term to the end of Harry Truman's. I knew her as a long-time parishioner of St. Barnabas and the owner of Watauga County's only crematorium.

"Oh, my Lord," said Meg. "Thelma? Mother just had lunch with her on Saturday."

Thelma was wearing a housedress, a light blue floral print, with a cardigan sweater on top. She had on her sensible no-nonsense support hose and a pair of black Nurse Ratchet shoes. Her eyes were closed but there was no peaceful expression on her face. Hers was a countenance of considerable fear; lips drawn back, brow furrowed and hands clenched, claw-like, with fists full of sweater.

I stood up and turned to Chad. "You found her?"

"Yes," he answered softly.

"Is she a client?"

"Yes."

"Want to give us a little more information?" growled Nancy, standing up beside me.

Chad sighed. "We've been gone since Sunday evening, but on Sunday afternoon, we had a guided meditation in the labyrinth for a few folks. There were five of us including myself and Lacie."

"We'll need their names," said Nancy.

Chad nodded and continued. "We were here for about an hour. It was a great session. Everyone really got in touch with their spiritual path."

"Thelma was one of them?" I asked. "Just to be clear?"

"She was."

I nodded and watched Nancy jotting notes, suddenly trying to remember where I'd left my pad and pen. Chad continued.

"We finished around four o'clock. This woman," Chad gestured toward Thelma's body, "and the two other ladies asked if they could come back and try the labyrinth themselves. I didn't see the harm, so I gave them a key to the back gate."

I looked around the garden. It was as secluded a spot as you could find and still be in town. The privet hedge was at least eight feet tall and probably planted when the house was built. It had been well cared for over the years and there were no gaping holes in the dark mossy wall. At the back of the garden was an iron gate—the same one I had seen hanging by one hinge. Now it was fixed, closed securely, and offering a view of the back of St. Barnabas' garden.

"We left on Sunday night," said Chad. "And we didn't get back into town until about eleven this morning. I didn't even look in the garden until right before we called."

"You have people who can verify your whereabouts since Sunday?" asked Nancy, still writing.

"Of course we do!" said Lacie. "What are you implying?"

"We're not implying anything," I said. "Just asking."

"We were at our naturist meeting," said Chad. "In Galax. There were plenty of witnesses."

66

I nodded to him and headed toward the back gate, leaving Nancy to get the names of the witnesses and the other two women on the labyrinth walk. It was a walk of about twenty feet from the back edge of the concrete slab to the gate. The shape of the garden was square, like the house, and I judged one side of the hedge to be close to sixty feet in length. Sixty by sixty with a twenty-foot square slab smack dab in the middle. Those Victorians liked their symmetry.

The gate had been recently painted and looked to be original to the house. It was wrought iron and heavy. It was also closed and latched with a new padlock on the clasp. The lock was hanging open.

"Check and see if Thelma has a key on her," I called back to Nancy.

I lifted the latch and the gate swung in easily. I knelt down and saw evidence of recent painting and what was probably some spilled oil used on the hinges.

"No key, boss," Nancy called back. "She doesn't even have any pockets."

"Look for her purse then."

I walked around the east side of the hedge toward the house, not knowing what I was looking for. It was a good hedge and would probably be fine for keeping a flock of sheep out of Old Mrs. McCarty's back yard, but it would hardly have stopped anyone who wanted to come in, lock or no lock.

"We don't see a purse," said Meg.

"Dave," I said, "why don't you put on some gloves and look in the bushes? See if her purse was tossed in there somehow. She wouldn't have gone out without her purse. Not without a pocket to put her own keys in, not to mention the one that Chad gave her."

Dave gave me a mock salute and began his search while the rest of us went back inside to wait for the ambulance.

There are some beautiful women in St. Germaine. Meg, for one. Reisa Walker for another. But in the past two days, the company of beautiful women had risen (in my mind at least) by one hundred percent. Muffy Lemieux was a vision of dark red hair, emerald eyes, a voluptuous figure and a baby doll face that projected innocence and sensuality in equal measure; a dangerous combination to be sure. Lacie Ravencroft, in contrast, was dark—dark complexion, thick dark hair, brown, almond eyes, more well-toned than voluptuous, startlingly tall with a lean but curvaceous body, and a smile that would make Pete give away free pie if she asked him to. So I admit that I wasn't totally put out when I found myself interrogating her in the kitchen of the Holy Grounds Coffee Shop.

Nancy had given me a spare pad and I pulled it from my shirt pocket along with a pen, also courtesy of my well-prepared lieutenant.

"Name?" I asked. "Just for the record."

"Lacie Ravencroft," she said, trying out her low wattage smile for my reaction.

"No. I mean your *real* name."

"Pardon?"

"Your real name." I gave her my own low wattage smile. "What's your real name? C'mon," I cajoled, "*Lacie Ravencroft?*"

Her smile increased to forty watts. I could feel it from four feet away. "It's really Lacie," she said. "Well, Lacie Peckelsham. Ravencroft is my professional name." She turned her smile up to fifty.

I smiled back at her, matching her tooth for tooth. It was nice for a couple of moments—just two people smiling at each other like a couple of game show hosts, but my face was beginning to tire and I wasn't as young as I used to be. "Occupation?" I finally asked, feeling my smile slip down my chest. "Just for the record."

"Licensed Christian massage therapist."

"You left St. Germaine on Sunday afternoon?"

"Late afternoon. We were out at the labyrinth until about four. Then the guests left and we headed for Galax about an hour later. We've been there since Sunday night."

"Galax, Virginia?"

"Yes."

"A little chilly for nudists, isn't it?" I asked.

"No, our group is used to it. We actually prefer a bit of a chill in the air. Until it gets down around forty-five degrees we're pretty comfortable. And if there's a bonfire going, we're just fine. It's amazing how quickly you can warm up next to a fire when you have no clothes on."

I nodded thoughtfully and pretended to write down this important warming-up information on my pad, at the same time doing my best not to conjure up any mental images.

"You got back this morning?"

"About eleven. Cynthia was working in the coffee bar. We didn't go into the garden until about one. Actually, it was Chad who found her. It's such a tragedy. When will we find out what happened?"

"I don't know," I said. "We'll wait for the coroner to tell us." I snapped the pad closed and put it back into my pocket. "Do you think I might have a cup of coffee?"

"Oh, absolutely!" Lacie walked around the kitchen table to the three thermoses of coffee sitting on the counter by the sink. "What kind would you like? We have *Jamaican Me Crazy, Vietnamese Robusta* and *Sumatran Decaf*. If you don't like one of those I can brew you another."

"The Jamaican one sounds fine," I answered as I followed her to the counter. "And maybe a muffin, unless you have a piece of pie. I'll be glad to pay for it. I don't want you to think the police force comes in for free coffee and snacks."

Lacie laughed and filled a mug from the nearest thermos. "It's on the house, but we don't serve pie I'm afraid. What kind of muffin would you like? Blueberry, banana-nut, raspberry..."

"How about rhubarb?"

She looked at me quizzically and handed me the mug of coffee. "No. Sorry."

"Ah," I said. "I was hoping for a rhubarb fix."

Lacie looked confused.

"I was just about to order the last piece of rhubarb pie when we were called over," I explained. "It's that time of year—pumpkin and rhubarb. I thought you might have made some rhubarb muffins."

Lacie still looked confused.

"Since you have some rhubarb sitting in the sink," I said with a laugh, pointing to the cleaned stalks resting under the faucet.

"Oh, sure," she said, comprehension spreading across her face. "We have a new recipe, but we haven't made them yet. We'll make some up next week."

"How about pumpkin?"

"Pumpkin we have," Lacie said, going over to a glass case and removing a large, dark orange muffin the size of a grapefruit. "Would you like me to heat that up?"

"No, thanks," I said, pulling out a chair and sitting down at the table. Lacie put the muffin on a plate and set it in front of me along with a paper napkin and a fork. I ignored the fork, broke off a piece of the muffin and followed the bite by a sip of coffee.

"Delicious. The coffee, too."

Lacie sat down across from me. "Thanks. Glad you like it."

I broke off another bite, this time smaller, and took the time to savor the coffee that followed it into my mouth. I wiped the corners of my mouth with the paper napkin and asked, "How many people are in your Naked Club?"

She managed an offended look, but the upturned corners of her mouth gave her away. Then she giggled. "We prefer the term 'Naturists,' although 'Nudists' isn't considered incorrect. 'Naked Club' is definitely out."

I gave a chuckle. "Pardon me. I shall rephrase the question. How many nudists are in your hangout?"

"Oh, puhleease," she groaned. "Hangout? *Really!* Save me from any more nudist jokes. Anyway, there're about fifty. Ours is a Christian group. We're the Galax Chapter of the Daystar Naturists for God and Love. You should come out and try it. You're a Christian, aren't you?"

"Absolutely. But I'm pretty sure my particular religious affiliation forbids nudism."

"Which one is that?" she asked, dazzling me with another dental display.

"Whichever one forbids it," I answered.

Mike and Joe, our two EMTs, had loaded Thelma into the ambulance and were pulling away when Dave joined us on the front porch.

"I didn't find a purse," he said, "but I did find this. It was hanging in the hedge by the strap."

He produced a carved, J-shaped wooden object about sixteen inches long with a leather thong attached to one end.

"What the heck is it?" Dave asked.

"Hey!" said Nancy. "That's one of those...uh..thingys."

"It certainly is," I said, pulling out my handkerchief and using it to take the object from Dave's gloved hand. "If I'm not mistaken, it's a krummhorn."

"What's a krummhorn?" asked Chad.

"You mean it's not yours?"

"Never seen it before."

I looked over at Lacie. "Nope," she said, no longer smiling.

"Cynthia?"

She just shook her head.

# Chapter 10

Cynthia had taken the rest of the day off and Holy Grounds closed early. The four of us went back to the station after Nancy and I had one more look around the back yard. We didn't find anything.

"Okay," said Meg. "What's a krummhorn?"

"A Renaissance reed instrument," I said.

"Just like that fellow sells over at the Appalachian Music Shoppe," said Nancy, flipping her pad open. "Ian Burch, PhD."

"Just like it," I said.

"What was it doing in the bushes?" asked Meg.

"That's what we'd all like to know," I said. "Check it for fingerprints, will you?"

"You think she was killed?" asked Dave. "She was pretty old. Maybe she just...you know...expired."

"Maybe," I said. "But why was the krummhorn in the bushes? First Davis and now Thelma?"

"It could be a coincidence," Meg offered. "We know that Davis committed suicide. Maybe Thelma had a heart attack or something."

"I'm sure that's it," I said. "Kent will tell us soon enough." I turned to Nancy. "When's Davis going to be cremated?"

Nancy picked up a clipboard and flipped through some papers. "Kent was sending the body over this afternoon. The HIV test was negative, by the way. They'll probably do the cremation tonight."

"Call Kent and put it on hold, will you? Let's leave Davis in the morgue. He can stay on ice for a little longer."

"What are you thinking?"

"Don't know yet. Did you ever find his doctor?"

"I never really looked," said Nancy. "I thought we were going with suicide."

"We were. But now let's look."

"Did you hear?" said Marjorie. "Thelma Wingler died!"

I was seated at the organ and choir rehearsal was minutes away; that is, if we'd manage to start on time, a thin hope at best.

"I heard," I answered.

"I heard she was murdered at the spa," said Mark Wells. "By a talking gorilla."

"You shouldn't make jokes," said Elaine. "She's dead, for heaven's sake."

"Well," said Mark, running a hand through his sparse beard, "I

71

didn't much care for Thelma. She was a nasty piece of work. Double charged me to cremate my grandfather."

"Double charged you?" said Elaine.

"Yeah. She told me that anyone over three hundred pounds cost double due to fuel consumption. And grandpa was a big ol' boy."

"That seems reasonable."

"You'd think," said Mark. "I found out later that fat folks actually only use *half* the fuel. They get them cookin' and then shut the burners down. Their own juices take care of the rest."

"Ewww!" said the entire soprano section.

"That's more information than any of us needed," said Elaine.

"How old was the old bat?" asked Mark.

"She was at least eighty," said Steve DeMoss. "Or ninety."

"I didn't care for her either," said Elaine, "but we don't speak ill of the departed. She is, after all, now safe in the arms of Jesus."

"I sincerely doubt that," said Mark. "I'd say she's down there giving the devil his due."

"We don't have to sing for the funeral, do we?" asked Rebecca.

"I don't think so," I said. "I'm not sure that Father Lemming knows we do that sort of thing."

"Well, don't tell him," said Mark. "I'm busy anyway."

"You don't even know when it is," said Georgia, who'd just sat down.

"Doesn't matter."

"We'll worry about it when it happens," I said. "We don't need to rehearse anything new." It was true. We had three or four nice funeral anthems under our belt, and could sing them without much notice.

"What about the schedule next week?" asked Meg. "Don't forget to announce the debate."

"Right," I said. "Next Wednesday we'll start at 6:30 instead of seven. There's a mayoral debate at eight o'clock over at the courthouse. We need to go over and support Pete."

"Or Cynthia," said Marjorie, with a sniff.

"Or Cynthia," I agreed.

"Hi y'all!" called a voice from the back of the choir loft. Everyone turned at once and saw a lively redhead bounce down the steps followed doggedly by a man wearing jeans, a sweater with "Blueridge Furs" etched across the left breast and an expression that said "Choir practice? Just kill me now."

"I'm Muffy Lemieux," she said, giddier than a cheerleader in a pom-pom store. "This here is my husband, Varmit. We've come to join the choir!"

The choir was momentarily stunned, but recovered quickly.

"Well, come on in," said Marjorie. "Are y'all a soprano?"

"I sure am," gushed Muffy. "I've been a soprano since I was old enough to squeal!"

"How about you, Varmit?" asked Marjorie. "You're not a soprano, are you?"

"Nope."

Marjorie was the only woman in the St. Barnabas choir who was over seventy. She started out as a soprano when she joined the choir in 1952. Sometime in the '80s she moved to the alto section and started keeping a small flask in her hymnal rack. No one asked what was in it. By the time I came along in the '90s, she was singing tenor and I didn't mind a bit. She certainly had the notes. Being safely in her seventies, Marjorie could afford to be friendly. The rest of the women were eyeing Muffy carefully in the way that both altos and sopranos can just *look* at a gorgeous redhead wearing a tight angora sweater—this one a light green—and know immediately if she's choir material. The men were speechless.

"Welcome," I said. "It's good to have you. Are you a bass, Varmit?"

"I guess I am."

"Great. Why don't you sit next to Phil. Elaine? Would you get these two some music?"

"Kin I sit on the front row?" giggled Muffy.

"Yes, dear, of course you may," said Bev, with a forced smile. "Come sit next to Meg."

Tell me your story, Ginger," I said. Ginger Snapp was a doll with more twist than a Moravian pretzel.

"AveMaria and I were doing a gig for the Bishops' Council on Church Reform. One of their underwear parties. Nothing smutty—just lingerie."

"Isn't that a bit chilly this time of year?"

"Oh," said Ginger in surprise, making her mouth into one of those O's—like a smoke ring or maybe a lipstick-covered donut. "Not for us. It's the bishops that wear the lingerie. We just serve drinks."

"Don't those bishops get a little grabby?"

"Sometimes that one from New Hampshire," Ginger admitted. "But only when Raoul's there. Anyway, it's harmless fun."

"Go on."

"So we're working the room and one of these bishops is talking to another one."

"How'd you know they were bishops," I asked, "and not just their toadies?"

"Even in their underwear, they still wear their pointy hats," said Ginger, "and their big ol' crosses."

"I see," I said, seeing.

"And they're talking about a mink farm in Russia and how they're going to corner the market on Liturgical Hairpieces."

"Liturgical Hairpieces?"

"You know, the big swoopy kind like they wear on TV."

"Ah," I said. "You mean the Evangelical Wiglet...the Glory Fringe...the Clerical Coiffure."

"Yeah. That's it."

"Did AveMaria know about this?"

"Sure. She's the one that told me! She said that the bishops are going to corner the market. They'll make a killing."

"Sweetheart, it looks like they already did."

"That's some real good writin'," said Meg, reading over my shoulder. She took the hat off my head and put it on the desk next to the typewriter. "Enough for now. Put on some music and come have a sandwich."

I put a new CD by Judie Cochill on the stereo, then followed Meg into the kitchen as the sounds of *Let's Do It* filled the house. There was a pimento cheese sandwich waiting for me at the table, along with a cold bottle of Hummingbird Ale.

"Great music!" said Meg. "I love Cole Porter."

"They don't write 'em like they used to," I agreed. "Can I ask you something? Was your mother a friend of Thelma's?"

"I suppose you could say that. I asked her about Thelma once and Mother said she really just felt sorry for her. They had lunch about once a week. Dutch treat, of course. Why do you ask?"

"I can't find anyone that liked her."

"That's sad, isn't it," said Meg. "But I don't think Mother liked her, either.

"By the way, how did Muffy do in the choir?"

"I never heard her utter a note. I think she was a bit flummoxed."

"Flummoxed, you say?"

"I think so. When we were singing the Saint-Saëns *Ave Verum*, she was just sort of frowning and following the Latin words with her finger.

"But we were singing it in English."

"Yes. I know." Meg sat down across from me and tasted her sandwich. "Hey, this is good. Mother made the pimento cheese á la Martha Stewart."

I nodded and gave an affirmative grunt, having been taught from an early age not to talk with my mouth full. Grunting was okay.

"Don't fill up too fast. There's Lemon Meringue Fluff for dessert."

"Excellent!"

"You know," said Meg, "I don't think Muffy actually reads music."

"She'll get better. I should call her up and encourage her."

"She might get better if she sticks with it," agreed Meg, all too sweetly. "Have you ever called anyone *else* up to encourage *them*?"

"Hmm...Not that I recall."

I watched one of Meg's eyebrows go up.

"She probably doesn't need any encouragement," I decided, taking another bite of my sandwich.

# Chapter 11

"What's the verdict, Kent?" I asked, balancing the phone between my shoulder and my ear as I rooted across the top of the desk for a pen and a piece of paper. Nancy, usually the first one to the station, was in Boone doing some investigating and Dave wasn't due in until eleven.

"Looks like coronary arrest," Kent answered. "I just finished the autopsy, but I did a prelim when they brought her in. I would say she died sometime on Tuesday evening. Maybe between seven and ten o'clock."

"Maybe?"

"Give or take a few hours. It's tough to tell when the body's been outside all night. It was cold on Tuesday. Thirty-four degrees according to the weather service."

"But Tuesday night for sure."

"Tuesday night," agreed Kent. "Nancy was in here a little while ago and brought in the courthouse records. Thelma Wingler was eighty-eight years old, so a heart attack isn't anything out of the ordinary. There wasn't any prior indication of a heart episode though. Other than being dead, as far as her heart was concerned, she was healthy as a horse. She had a red throat and some swelling of her vocal cords. Nothing out of the ordinary. Probably the onset of a cold. Nancy said she was on the way to talk to Thelma's doctor."

"Yeah. The whole thing's fishy. She didn't have her purse or her keys. There was nothing else in the garden except a krummhorn hanging in the bushes."

"Ah, yes," said Kent, his smile evident, even over the phone lines. "Isn't that what you detectives call 'a clue?' It sounds to me like the old 'krummhorn in the bushes' caper."

"Mock me if you will. I shall solve this conundrum."

Kent laughed. "I have no doubt. Anyway, I can tell you that she wasn't killed by a krummhorn."

"Aren't you going to ask me what a krummhorn is?" I said.

"No, I'm not," said Kent. "I know what a krummhorn is. I was forced to be part of a *Collegium Musicum* in college. It's probably the reason I hate music to this day. If *I* had a krummhorn, I'd throw it in the bushes as well."

"You played the krummhorn?"

"Yes," he sighed. "And the cornamuse. I was drafted because I also played the oboe in the orchestra. The Medieval history professor thought it should be part of my scholarship. They even made me dress up in tights and wear one of those stupid hats with a feather in it. I think I still have the hat somewhere. I will go on record as stating that the krummhorn has all the musical range and beauty of a piglet caught in a vacuum cleaner."

I laughed. "Then how do you know the krummhorn wasn't responsible for her heart attack?"

"Easy," replied Kent, with a chuckle. "Because her ears weren't bleeding."

"Will you look at this?" said Pete, thrusting a newspaper across the table. The Slab was void of customers except for myself. I'd missed the lunch rush by at least an hour.

I picked up *The Tattler*—Pete had thoughtfully folded it open to the editorial page—and skimmed quickly down the "Letters to the Editor" until I saw Pete's name.

"Wow," I said, reading Cynthia's letter, "Cynthia's not letting up on this underwear thing, is she?"

"No, she isn't," said Pete. "I can't believe it's become an issue. I thought she was going to let it go, but now that she's hired this yahoo from Boone, that's all they're going to talk about."

"Do you know them?"

"Nope. It's a new public relations firm."

"I guess it's a pretty good strategy. She doesn't actually have a political platform now that you've brought all that business to town."

"It doesn't matter. I have a new plan. I need you to do something for me."

"Is it illegal?"

"Nope. I need you to write a rebuttal to Cynthia's letter. Quote some scripture or something. There's got to be some biblical precedent for not wearing underwear. I mean, it's not like I'm one of those nudists or anything."

"I'll see what I can do."

"Thanks. Now how about some lunch?"

"Sounds great. Reuben sandwich?"

"Coming right up," said Pete with a grin. "Hey, Collette!" he hollered.

"Collette? Collette's back?"

"She called me last night and asked for her old job back."

"Nancy isn't going to be happy about this. Now that she and Dave are a couple..." I let the thought trail off, then continued. "As you may recall, Collette's and Dave's breakup wasn't exactly amicable."

"Oh, I recall all right," said Pete. "And I appreciate you chipping in to pay for the damage. Collette tore this place up. But here's the thing. I've got to have a waitress during the day. Noylene can't do it—she's got to be at the Beautifery at eleven. Bootsie is a disaster, and I can't find anyone else. I've had a 'Help Wanted' sign in the window, an ad in the paper…I even put up flyers at the university."

Collette came through the kitchen door and put a Reuben sandwich with a side of coleslaw down in front of me.

"How'd you fix this so fast?" I asked.

"I saw you come in and figured you'd want one," said Collette with a smile. "Was I right?"

"You were right," I said. I took a bite and chewed slowly, savoring the sauerkraut and corned beef for a long moment before swallowing. I closed my eyes in culinary rapture.

"Ah. Delicious," I proclaimed, settling back in my chair. "Now tell me, Collette, why'd you decide to come back?"

"The Holy Spirit has told me that Dave and I are meant to be married," stated Collette, as matter-of-factly as you please. "I've come back to fight for him. I plan to witness to him until he sees that this is the Lord's will for us." She gave us a peaceful smile, turned primly and proceeded to walk back into the kitchen.

"Well, that should work," mumbled Pete under his breath.

"Mmm," I agreed, another bite of my sandwich disappearing.

"I didn't know about that thing with Dave and the Holy Spirit," said Pete, shaking his head. "She just asked me if she could have her old job back. I swear…"

Pete's swear didn't quite make it out of his mouth before it was interrupted by Collette's blood-curdling scream. He and I were both out of our seats and through the kitchen door in a matter of seconds.

"*Help!* Oh, help, help, *help!*" she screeched.

"What?" hollered Pete, looking around for an imminent disaster. "Why are you screaming?"

"In the walk-in! In the walk-in!" screamed Collette, dancing from one foot to the other and pointing with one hand toward the walk-in refrigerator while the other hand clutched at her apron. "Down by the lettuce!"

"*What?*" yelled Pete. "I don't see anything. The stupid light bulb's out again!"

"It ran behind the onions! Oh, Lord!" shrieked Collette. "Oh, Lord! *It's a rat from the pit of hell!*"

"We do *not* have rats!" hissed Pete, looking around for any customers that might have come into the Slab during our brief absence, and wandered into the kitchen to see what all the fuss was about. He needn't have worried. "Keep your voice down!" he said.

I spotted a furry face looking out from behind a bag of potatoes. "There it is," I said quietly, pointing it out in the semi-dark walk-in.

"Sweet Jesus," whispered Pete, "it *is* a rat! Look at the size of that head! Give me your gun, will you?"

Collette screamed one last time, fainted against the dishwasher and slid to the floor.

"I don't carry it with me," I said. "It's in the organ bench. Anyway, I don't think rats eat salad. Get me the flashlight, will you?"

Pete kept a big flashlight sitting on top of the fire extinguisher and in a moment it was in my hand. The beam swept the floor of the walk-in and settled on a dark brown shape sitting up behind a fifty-pound sack of Idaho spuds, a head of cabbage securely in its paws. We both recognized it at the same time. A Minque.

"Aw, geeze," said Pete. "How did that thing get all the way over here from Blueridge Furs?"

"I don't know," I admitted. "But if there's one loose there's bound to be more."

I left Pete to call the Minque farm and headed over to St. Barnabas to practice my prelude for Sunday. I had very cleverly entered through the transept door, making my way up to the choir loft unnoticed. I wouldn't be unnoticed, of course, as soon as I started playing, but at that point, most folks were loathe to interrupt the artistic process.

Most folks didn't include Father Lemming.

"Glad I caught you!" he barked from the nave, finally hearing a slight cessation of music. Unfortunately for him, the pause was only long enough for me to pull the stop for the trompette en chamade. I grabbed a handful of notes and pretended I hadn't heard him. That much was easy. He was harder to ignore when he came up into the loft, leaned against the console, and began drumming his fingers on top of the organ. I stopped playing.

"May I help you with something?" I asked, not bothering to keep the irritation out of my voice.

"Yes. I need to see you in my office immediately."

"I'll come down as soon as I'm finished practicing."

"Well, hurry up. There's someone waiting," he said and disappeared down the stairs.

I didn't bother to rush, but eventually I'd done all the improving I was going to do and made my way downstairs to the suite of offices. Marilyn was typing away at her computer and, when she saw me, rolled her eyes and nodded in the direction of Father Lemming's office.

"Go right in," she said. "They're waiting for you."

"They?"

Marilyn just smiled.

"Have a seat, Hayden," said Father Lemming. "You remember Carmel Bottoms?"

"Yes, I do," I said shaking her hand. "It's nice to see you again, Carmel." I turned to Father Lemming who was perched behind his desk like a Poobah. "I really can't stay and chat," I said. "I have another appointment. Is there something you need?"

"I've called Carmel in as a spiritual consultant, dontcha know." Father Lemming pushed his glasses up his nose. "We were in seminary together. I discerned very early on in our Spiritual Gifts seminar during our first year together that Carmel had a tremendous affinity for identifying unwanted spirits."

"Really?" I said.

"With these two latest deaths, it has become clear that St. Barnabas has an unhealthy influence residing within its walls, dontcha know."

"Unhealthy influence?"

"I suspect demons," said Carmel Bottoms. "More than one. I felt them as soon as I came in this morning."

"You didn't feel them the first time you were here?" I asked. "Last month?"

"They're able to shield their presence from me," she explained. "For a while."

"Well, you know," I said, "Thelma Wingler wasn't killed in St. Barnabas. In fact, she wasn't killed at all. As far as we know, she had a heart attack. Davis' suicide was terrible, but I don't think that it was due to demons. At least not demons living in the church."

"I knew you'd say that." She pulled out a piece of paper. "What about Willie Boyd? Darlene Puckett? Kris Toth? Peppermint the Clown?" She looked down at a page of notes and read off a list of names. "Lester Gifford, Randall Stamps, Agnes Day, Kenny Frazier, Little Bubba Haggarty, Jimmy Kilroy and Junior Jameson. All associated with St. Barnabas."

"Well, not exactly," I said. "Okay. Willie Boyd, sure. And Agnes. You might count Randall Stamps, although he was killed in his house and not in the church. But Lester Gifford was killed over sixty years ago..."

"Demons don't measure time in the same way we do," said Carmel. "Sixty years could be yesterday for all they care."

"And," I continued, "Kenny Frazier isn't dead. He was shot, but he's fine now. Darlene was a traffic accident. Little Bubba Haggarty was killed by his wife in his trailer and wasn't a member of St. Barnabas. Neither was Ruthie. In fact, I think they were Catholic."

"Doesn't she go to church here?" asked Father Lemming. "I thought I saw her on the list."

"She does now," I admitted, "but when she killed Little Bubba she was attending the Catholic church. Anyway, she was acquitted."

80

Carmel Bottoms gave me the look that said, "she's still a murderer," but I let it go.

"Jimmy Kilroy was the pastor at New Fellowship Baptist. I doubt that he'd even been inside an Episcopal church. And Kris Toth was killed in England, for heaven's sake."

"Yet, all the killings are intertwined with the fabric of St. Barnabas," sniffed Carmel, with a sardonic smile. "What are the chances?"

"In this town, and with me being the police chief, I'd say about one hundred percent." I looked at her pointedly. "Do you also think it's fascinating that almost all the cases involve the clergy in one way or another?"

Carmel ignored me, but I could see her stiffen.

I continued. "Junior Jameson wasn't even from St. Germaine. He was killed in a racing accident in South Carolina. Peppermint the Clown was not a well man. His death was an unfortunate series of unrelated events."

"I doubt that either of them would have been killed if it weren't for their involvement with the church," said Carmel.

"Maybe not," I admitted. "But that's like saying that if Thelma hadn't come to services on Sunday, she wouldn't be dead now."

Carmel shrugged and was about to speak when she was interrupted by Father Lemming.

"It does us no good to argue, dontcha know," he said. "It's obvious that there're spiritual forces at work here—forces that Carmel is uniquely equipped to deal with."

"Fine with me," I said. "I'm not arguing. I'm always in favor of prayer."

"Oh, it's more than prayer," said Carmel. "We're going to need a full blown exorcism."

I shrugged and raised both hands affably. "Well, whatever you think. Let me know how it goes. I certainly am in favor of nobody else getting killed—especially someone connected with St. Barnabas."

"I'm glad you see it that way," said Father Lemming. "I've authorized Bev to write the Rev. Bottoms a check for fifteen thousand dollars."

"Excuse me?" I said incredulously. "Fifteen thousand dollars? That's the fee?"

"It's not like the church is hurting for money," said Father Lemming. "We have millions of dollars at our disposal, dontcha know."

"I'll be bringing in my associates," said Carmel. "We met in seminary and formed a ministry that is uniquely equipped to deal with demonic influence. We're based in Asheville, but our associates are in place across the country."

"Your associates are priests?"

"Of course. Five total. One of us has a parish, but the rest are now working exclusively in the demonic area."

"*Ordained* priests?" I asked.

"Ordained by God," came the self-satisfied answer. "We are the Exorkizein.

"So let me get this straight," I said. "You..." I pointed at Father Lemming, "are paying five priests fifteen thousand dollars to get rid of some demons that Carmel says are lurking in the walls of St. Barnabas."

"No," insisted Father Lemming. "You misunderstand. I don't think the vestry would ever go for that. Quite frankly, I don't think they can see the danger, dontcha know. What I'm going to do is to have Carmel's group come in and exorcise the demons. I will then make a donation to their non-profit ministry from my discretionary fund."

"You have that much in your discretionary fund?"

"Sure," replied Father Lemming. "Gaylen Weatherall had all kinds of money in there."

"Oh, yeah," I said, remembering my conversation with Gaylen. "I talked to her about it in August. She was going to send a large donation to the women's shelter in Boone, start a soup kitchen here when the weather turned cold, fund some scholarships to a summer camp...I can't remember what else."

"Yes, well...whatever." Father Lemming waved his hand dismissively. "I'm sure we can make some donations to her causes as well, dontcha know."

"I don't think the vestry will approve this expense," I said.

"They don't have to," he answered. "It's *discretionary*."

"So why tell me?"

"You, above all, know the danger and we may need your help," said Carmel Bottoms. She folded her hands in a prayerful position in front of her and suddenly I knew.

"This isn't a scam is it?" I said. "You're serious."

"This is a matter of life and death," said Carmel gravely. "It is a battle in the spiritual realm for the very existence of St. Barnabas."

Father Lemming nodded.

Nancy was in the station when I came through the door. I meandered to the counter to see if perchance there was a rogue donut that had survived the morning foraging. The box was empty.

"Need a donut?" she asked.

"Or a stiff drink."

"I have some news about Thelma," said Nancy. "I talked to her doctor and her psychiatrist."

"Psychiatrist?" I said, flopping down in one of the two office chairs. "Okay. Go."

"Dr. Weber says Thelma called in Friday with a sore throat but otherwise, as far as he knew, was physically fine. Just had a check-up last month. Then he sent me over to the psychiatrist. It seems that Thelma had OCD—a severe case apparently—and it was worse every time Doctor Sawyer saw her."

"Dr. Sawyer is the psychiatrist?"

"Yep. Helen Sawyer."

"Hmm. Obsessive compulsive disorder," I said. "I didn't ever see any signs. Of course, I wasn't around her very much."

"It had very specific manifestations."

"Which were?"

"According to Dr. Sawyer, she wouldn't—or couldn't—step on a line."

"Step on a crack, break your mother's back," I said, repeating the children's rhyme.

Nancy pulled out her pad to check her notes. "Like that. Apparently her OCD didn't apply to small lines that were part of a pattern, like wood grain or small tiles. But larger lines, big cracks in the pavement, painted street markers, large tiles of contrasting colors—all these could set her off. It really sort of depended on the situation. Dr. Sawyer said that she could give us a rough idea, but she never knew exactly how Thelma would react to any one thing."

"And how did Thelma deal with it?"

"Dr. Sawyer said that, basically, as long as Thelma stayed on her meds she was fine. Even if she was off them and found herself outside, she could walk around whatever lines she saw until she could return home. They'd put wall-to-wall carpet throughout Thelma's house so she was fine once she got back."

"What happened if she got stranded?"

"It only happened once, according to Dr. Sawyer," said Nancy. "She was in the Piggly Wiggly and dropped a gallon of grape drink. It broke open and splattered purple lines all over the floor. Thelma couldn't move until they mopped it all up. They tried to help her over to a chair, but she wouldn't go—just stood there shaking, unable to talk. Roger called the paramedics. He thought she was having heart failure. The hospital called it a panic attack and released her the next day."

"Have you checked her meds? Was she on them?"

"I got a list from both doctors and Kent ran a scan. She was supposed to be taking Zoloft for the OCD, but her blood work came up negative for that. She was also taking something for osteoporosis and a cholesterol medication. Those drugs were both present. Her medical doctor had called in something to the pharmacy on Monday morning for a sore throat, but Thelma never picked it up."

"So what's your conclusion?" I asked.

83

"I think she got stuck inside that labyrinth," said Nancy. "She walked into the middle, had a panic attack and couldn't get out. She might have been there for two days for all we know. Finally she had a heart attack and died."

"I agree," I said. "There are a couple of questions remaining."

Nancy nodded. "Where's her purse?"

"Right. And why was there a krummhorn in the bushes? Have you looked in her house?"

"Dave's over there now."

"Make sure he looks for her meds. Purse, too. Any prints on the krummhorn?"

"Just hers and some smudges."

"How about Davis Boothe's doctor?"

"What am I, three people?" said Nancy. "I'm still looking. There are one hundred ninety-two doctors or clinics in Boone. That doesn't even include the rest of Watauga County."

"Sorry," I said with a grin. "I'm going to get a donut and head over to talk with the two ladies who accompanied Thelma Wingler to the labyrinth on Sunday."

Nancy flipped a few pages in her pad looking for the names she'd gotten from Chad Parker. "Wynette Winslow and Mattie Lou Entriken."

"I know just where to find them. I'll stop by the Appalachian Music Shoppe, as well."

"Have a good time," said Nancy. "I'll keep calling doctors' offices."

"By the way," I said, "did you hear that Collette was back in town? She's working at the Slab."

I heard Nancy's growl as the door of the office closed behind me.

# Chapter 12

Wynette Winslow and Mattie Lou Entriken were in the church kitchen. I'd seen them earlier on my way out. They were fixing chicken salad sandwiches for the Salvation Army kitchen in Boone, something they did every Thursday afternoon.

"Afternoon, ladies," I said. "I was sorry to hear about Thelma."

Mattie Lou looked up and smiled a greeting. "Yes," she said. "It was a shock."

"It certainly was," added Wynette. "We just saw her on Sunday."

"That's what I wanted to talk to you about."

"Really, dear?" said Mattie Lou. "Whatever for?"

"I heard that you two and Thelma had an appointment at the new spa."

"Yes, dear, we certainly did," said Mattie Lou.

"Can you tell me about it?"

"I'll be happy to tell you about it," said Wynette. "I thought the whole thing was ridiculous."

"Really?"

"Absolutely." Wynette put down her knife and wiped her hands on her apron. Wynette and Mattie Lou were a pair of apple-cheeked grandmothers, both in their seventies, that had been best friends since childhood. Now their hair was snowy and their figures a good deal rounder than the pictures I'd seen of them in ancient church directories—always together, always laughing. They were two of the matriarchs of St. Barnabas.

"As you may know," Wynette began, "I didn't care much for Thelma Wingler. She was a mean woman. Petty and vindictive."

"Malicious," added Mattie Lou.

"Spiteful," said Wynette. She looked over at Mattie Lou for help.

"Unforgiving."

"Exactly. Unforgiving and cruel."

"Positively malignant," finished Mattie Lou. "Not that we wish to speak ill of the dead."

"Of course not," I said. "Could you tell me about Sunday?"

"Certainly," said Wynette. "Would you care for a sandwich, dear?"

"No, thanks."

"Are you sure?" asked Mattie Lou. "We have plenty."

"No, I'm fine. Thanks though. About Sunday...?"

"Thelma called us up on Sunday afternoon, didn't she?" said Wynette.

"She did," said Mattie Lou. "She hadn't even been to church. In fact, I hadn't seen her in church for several weeks." She looked at me and laid a finger beside her nose. "The reason will soon become evident."

"She'd been having appointments at the spa every Sunday morning. 'The Upper Womb' she called it," said Wynette.

"That's the name of the spa," I said.

"Huh," snorted Wynette. "Anyway, Thelma had been going to her 'appointments' for several weeks." Wynette used finger quotes around the word "appointments."

"That floozy," said Mattie Lou, under her breath. "Appointments indeed..."

"Could you elaborate?" I asked.

"Well, we don't like to speak ill of the dead," said Wynette sweetly.

"Oh, hell," said Mattie Lou. "I don't mind. Thelma had been going over there for massages every day since she saw that man in the Piggly Wiggly."

"Chad Parker?"

"That's him," said Wynette. "Big, good-looking boy."

"Very good-looking," added Mattie Lou. "If I was forty years younger..."

"Yes, but you're not. And neither was Thelma. That didn't stop her though. And she didn't mind telling us about the affair in graphic detail."

"She was having an affair with Chad Parker?" I asked. "Thelma?"

"Well," said Wynette, "*she* called it an 'affaire de coeur.' I'm not at all sure Mr. Parker was reciprocal in his involvement. At least not unless he was paid."

"Let me understand," I said. "Thelma said that she was having a tryst with Chad Parker."

"Not exactly," said Mattie Lou. "Oh, I'm sure she was smitten. She always fancied herself quite the siren, even in her later years. And she *always* lied about her age."

Wynette nodded in agreement. "She was much older than us, of course. She married right before the war, but her husband was in the infantry and killed in Italy. Anzio, I think. She had one daughter who was behind us a few years in school."

"Did Thelma marry again?" I asked.

"No, she didn't," said Mattie Lou. "And she's been a harridan ever since. I can't tell you the number of marriages she's broken up."

"Is the daughter still around?"

"Dead," said Mattie Lou.

"Dead," agreed Wynette.

"Any other family? Next of kin?"

"Not that we know of," answered Wynette.

"The coroner says she was eighty-eight."

"That's about right," said Mattie Lou. "Eighty-eight years old and getting massages—buck naked—from a thirty year old! Scandalous!"

"Well, I think that's the way they do it," I said. "Massages, I mean."

"Oh, I know, dear. I'm not a *complete* moron. Still, at *her* age!"

I laughed. "Back to Sunday?"

Wynette continued the narrative. "On Sunday afternoon, Thelma called me up after church and asked if we would go with her to the Upper Womb. I said no, of course."

"Of course," agreed Mattie Lou.

Wynette went on. "Ask Ruby, I said."

"Sure, ask Ruby. She's your best friend," added Mattie Lou.

"So Thelma started crying. 'Ruby's out with Meg,' she says. Then she tells me she's been doing therapy with Chad Parker. Massages every day, herbal teas, some kind of aroma nonsense, the works. Now he wants her to do this labyrinth thing."

"You see," explained Mattie Lou, "they've painted this labyrinth on the concrete behind the house. In the garden."

"I've seen it," I said.

Wynette picked up a butter knife and a piece of bread. "You don't mind if we keep spreading chicken salad while we talk, do you, dear?"

"No, of course not."

"So," Wynette said, "Thelma wanted us to go with her. She was scared to death of this labyrinth but told me that Chad insisted that she do it. She said that *he* said that it would help her overcome her fears and find spiritual renewal."

"You know about Thelma's...umm...disorder?" asked Mattie Lou.

"Yes. OCD."

"Right," said Wynette. "Can't step on a line. So she tells me 'you can just imagine how scared I am.' 'What about your medication?' I ask. 'Chad is teaching me how to live without it," she says. 'Please come with me. I'm still scared.' I think she was lying. She just wanted to show off. She certainly wouldn't have asked us otherwise. When we got there, she was hanging all over Chad Parker like a cheap suit."

"It was disgusting," Mattie Lou agreed.

"But we said we'd do it," said Wynette.

Mattie Lou shrugged. "Actually, I was a little curious."

"Me, too. Not that I'd get one of those naked massages or anything. Anyway," continued Wynette, "we walked into the house and Chad and his wife..." She paused and pursed her lips, trying to remember a name.

"Lacie Ravencroft," I said.

"Yes, Lacie. They gave us a tour of the house and then invited us into the kitchen for a cup of tea while they explained the labyrinth."

"Then they took us into the garden," said Mattie Lou, "and did what they called a Guided Meditation. There was this Celtic sounding harp music playing and we walked around the maze."

"It took an hour!" exclaimed Wynette in disgust. "Lacie kept making us stop and 'center our spirit selves,' whatever *that* means! I could have been in and out of that thing in about two minutes! I mean, it wasn't hard."

"Well," I said, "I don't think it's a puzzle."

"Whatever it is," Wynette sniffed, "I wasn't impressed. The tea was good though."

"Then you left?"

"Yes," said Mattie Lou. "But Chad gave Thelma a key to the back gate. He told her that she should do the labyrinth every day now that she knew how. He said we were welcome to come along."

"Did Thelma have any problem with the labyrinth? I mean, as far as her OCD was concerned?"

Both ladies shook their head.

"She was fine," said Mattie Lou. "And on the way home, she was happy to describe her private sessions with Chad. Did you know they use scented oils?"

I nodded.

"She was getting a cold," said Wynette. "Said her throat was hurting. Probably from lying naked on that massage table."

"I doubt it," said Mattie Lou, shaking her head. "That upstairs was very warm. Anyway, now that the weather'll be warming up a bit, we'll probably all get colds."

Wynette nodded her agreement. "Hot, cold, hot, cold. It'll play havoc with your sinuses."

"It's going to warm up?" I said.

"Just for a bit," said Mattie Lou. "Don't you watch the Weather Channel?"

"Nope," I admitted.

"Well, you should."

Ian Burch was in front of the Appalachian Music Shoppe, locking the front door, when I walked up.

"Dr. Burch," I said, "I wonder if I might ask you a few questions before you lock up?"

Ian Burch, PhD, gave a huff and a shrug of resignation and unlocked the door to the shop. "Come in, if you must," he said. "But I really must leave in about half an hour."

"That's not a problem. I just need a couple of minutes."

"All right then." Ian folded his arms, chewed on his lower lip and stood in expectation of the third degree.

I had stopped by the police station and picked up the krummhorn on the way to the Music Shoppe. Now I opened the plastic bag and took it out, making a production of holding it carefully in a handkerchief.

"Do you recognize this?" I asked.

"It's a krummhorn."

"Yes," I said, "I know. Is it from your shop?"

"Umm. It could be, I suppose."

"Let me help you out, Dr. Burch. Did you sell a krummhorn to an eighty-eight year old woman on Monday morning?"

"I'd have to check my records."

"You're not in any trouble and you only have a half hour," I said. "So, let's start again. How many instruments have you sold since you've been open?"

Ian Burch's shoulders slumped. "Umm...that would be one."

"Was it a krummhorn?"

"Yes."

"Did you sell it on Monday?"

"Yes."

"To Thelma Wingler?"

"Yes."

"Is this it?"

"I suppose so. I mean, how many krummhorns are floating around? But it was in a box. Brand new."

"Can you tell me why it doesn't work?"

"Doesn't work?"

"We tried to play it down at the police station. No luck."

"Let me see." Ian took the krummhorn with the handkerchief. "Can I touch it?"

"Sure."

Ian handed me back the handkerchief, put the krummhorn to his lips and blew. As I expected, there was a burst of air but no sound.

"Huh," said Ian. He pulled the mouthpiece off the instrument and looked down the barrel. "Well, here's the problem. There's no reed."

"No reed?"

"I showed the woman how to play it. Well, how to make a sound anyway. But we used the one here." He took an identical krummhorn off the wall and pulled off the mouthpiece.

"See?" He pulled a reed loose and handed it to me.

"So what happened to the one in Thelma's krummhorn?"

"I have no idea. Maybe she didn't put it in."

"Excuse me?"

"The reed comes separately. It's in the box in a small plastic case. You have to put it in the instrument."

"Did you tell Thelma this?"

"Well, no," he admitted. "But it's all right there in the instructions."

89

"What time did she come in?"

"It was about ten o'clock Monday morning."

"Okay. Thanks."

"They came and got the Minque," said Pete. "Took 'em long enough. I had to leave it in the walk-in till they got there. The stupid thing ate about a case of lettuce."

"Well, I'm glad it's back at the farm," I said.

"Oh, sure," said Pete. "*That* one. Unfortunately, it wasn't the only one to escape."

"No?"

"No."

"How many?" I asked, dreading the answer.

"One hundred eighty-seven."

"Holy Moses! How did this happen?"

"Roderick Bateman said that one of the employees left the gate unlocked after feeding. It didn't take them long to scatter."

# Chapter 13

Liturgical hairpieces. It was the best idea for televangelists since Oral Roberts got his makeup tattooed on. Making them out of mink was a stroke of genius. Mink had a sheen that showed up under television lights like six pounds of pomade without the stink. The only problem was the cost. Televangelists usually went through four or five wigs a week and I didn't see them dishing out the big money when regular squirrel wigs could be had for seven bucks apiece.

"That pig won't hunt," I said to Ginger, thinking about a pig I used to have that wouldn't hunt, mainly because he was just a pig and not some sort of weird Chinese hunting pig. "There are only a handful of televangelists that could afford mink wigs. It's a specialized market."

"That's the beauty of their plan," whispered Ginger, her eyes darting around Buxtehooters like a couple of humming-birds doing Tequila shooters. "They've found a way to make them affordable. Every televangelist in the country could buy them."

I took a sip of my martini and considered the consequences. Right now, there were probably only a handful of televangelists that could afford the mink wigs, but once they became available to every rapscallion hawking his wares on cable TV, the whole balance of economic power would shift. Who could resist the glistening coif glowing under the bright lights of the studio? The money would pour in like they were Democrats and Hillary wasn't on the ticket.

"Okay," I said to Ginger. "I've got the picture. Now spell it out."

"I've decided to become a 'hat man,'" I announced. "I'm going to single handedly bring back the fedora as a fashion statement."

"I affirm you in that decision," said Meg. "I think you look great in a hat. What brought this on?"

"Well, I have this hat..."

"I know. It looks very fetching, but I thought you were only going to use it for writing. It's too dangerous to wear around town. Before long, you'll be spouting prose as bad as Jackie Collins'."

"Bite your tongue. It doesn't always happen. Just sometimes."

"Okay," said Meg. "Then go for it."

"Found him," said Nancy as soon as I walked into the station. Dave was sitting behind the desk reading the morning edition of *The Tattler*.

"Found who?" I asked.

"Try to keep up, boss. I found Davis Boothe's doctor. Nice hat, by the way."

"Thanks. Did you talk to him?"

"Them, actually. It's a clinic. I have to take a death certificate over there and they'll give me Davis' records. The nurse said that Davis didn't indicate any next-of-kin on his information sheet."

"Can you do that this morning?"

"Sure," said Nancy. "I can head over to Boone right now."

"Hey!" said Dave, thwapping the newspaper with a flicked finger. "Here's your letter to the editor."

"Yeah," I said. "I sent it in yesterday. But before you delve into St. Germaine's political intrigue, tell me about what you found in Thelma's house."

"Oh, sorry. I forgot." Dave put the paper down and picked up a shoebox that had been resting on the counter.

"I brought all of Thelma's medications that I could find. There are quite a few."

"Zoloft?"

Dave opened the box and reached in. "Yep. That's here. Also Zocor, Boniva, Resperate, Allegra..." He rummaged around the bottles of pills. "...Orencia, Crestor, Lipitor, Ambien, Frontline...hey, here's a bottle of Viagra!"

"Frontline is for fleas," said Nancy. "Thelma had fleas?"

"It sounds to me like Thelma was watching too many TV commercials," I said. "At least three of those are cholesterol medications, if I remember correctly.

"It does sound like that," admitted Dave. "Maybe her doctor can shed some light."

"Who's the prescribing physician?"

"Dr. Sam Weber. Except for the Zoloft. That was Helen Sawyer."

"Sam Weber's her principal doctor, right?" I asked. Nancy nodded. "What's he doing prescribing Viagra, for heaven's sake?"

"I heard that some of these patients come in and demand this stuff once they've seen it on television," said Nancy. "Maybe that's what Thelma was doing."

"That would explain the Frontline and the Viagra. But that didn't mean that Weber had to prescribe them."

"Probably not against the law," said Dave. "Is it?"

"I don't know," I admitted. "Some combination of these drugs might have killed her though. What did Kent find in her blood? He told me, but I can't remember."

Nancy opened her pad and skimmed through the pages. "No Zoloft. She had simvastatin in her system. That's the Zocor, a cholesteral drug. Also present was..." Nancy stumbled over the next word "...ibandronate sodium. That's the Boniva for osteoporosis."

"None of this other stuff?"

"Nope. I guess she wasn't taking it."

"I think she was," said Dave, shaking one of the plastic pill bottles. "Every bottle is about half empty."

"I'll have a talk with Dr. Weber," I said. "Did you find her purse?"

"Nope. No purse."

"Anything else of interest?"

"There was a rhubarb pie on the kitchen table. I guess she put it there to cool. I put it in the refrigerator, but it had been sitting out since Tuesday, I guess. She bought the rhubarb on Tuesday morning. There was a receipt for it in the grocery bag in the trash."

"So, we know she was alive on Tuesday, anyway," I said. "Nice work."

"Here you go," said Nancy, handing me a piece of paper. "Dr. Samuel Weber's address and phone number."

"Thanks."

The door of the police station opened and Pete Moss walked in carrying a copy of *The Tattler*.

"I just saw your letter to the editor," he said with a grin. "I hope it keeps Cynthia at bay long enough to get through the debate next week."

"Here, let me see," said Nancy. She took Dave's newspaper, flipped to the second page and started reading.

Dear Editor,

It has come to my attention that Cynthia Johnsson, one of our mayoral candidates, has been casting aspersions on her worthy opponent, Peter Moss, for declining to wear underpants. This is an unfair obloquy of a public official whose moral guidelines, at least as applied to the donning of unmentionables, come directly from the Holy Scriptures. In fact, most of Mayor Moss' convictions concerning his wearing of underpants are based on Biblical precedents.

When looking for a spiritual guidance on this matter, we need go no further than Genesis 24. Abraham said to the chief servant in his household, "Put your hand under my loins. I want you to swear by the Lord, the God of heaven and the God of earth."

It's fairly obvious that, unlike most politicians today, when someone made a promise in Genesis, that promise was taken seriously. I'm not saying that Mr. Moss is in the habit of swearing "loin oaths," but I *am* saying that if he did, the level of intimacy that this oath entails would not be possible if our mayor wasn't unencumbered.

Isaiah says it best in Chapter 33. "Your rigging hangs loose: The mast is not held secure, the sail is not spread." Can this scripture be taken blatantly out of context to make a point? Of course it can! As can many others!

We should strive to judge our public officials on their merit and talent—whether it be belly dancing or playing saxophone in a jazz club—rather than dangling their shortcomings in public.

Signed,
Hayden Konig, voter

"Excellent work," laughed Nancy. "And Mr. Mayor, I would ask that you not dangle your shortcomings in public."

"Don't you worry," said Pete.

"Dr. Weber?" I asked.

"Speaking."

"This is Chief Konig."

"Yes, Chief. My nurse said you'd be calling." On the phone, Dr. Weber sounded as if he was as old as Thelma Wingler. Maybe older.

"Did she tell you why I was calling?" I asked.

"Yes," said Dr. Weber. I could hear some pages being ruffled. "Thelma Wingler, right?"

"I'm afraid so. She was found dead on Wednesday morning."

"I heard. I'm very sorry. Thelma's been a patient of mine for fifty-some-odd years."

"Listen, Doctor, the reason I'm calling is because we found several... no, change that...we found *many* bottles of medication in Thelma's house."

Dr. Weber sighed over the phone. "Yes, I know."

"Could you explain? It'd help us out."

"I guess there's no reason not to. Thelma didn't have any next-of-kin. Her only daughter died many years ago."

I waited.

"Thelma was one of those patients who..." He paused. "Let's just say that, although she was a hypochondriac in the strictest sense of the word, she was easily swayed by television advertising."

"That's sort of what we thought."

"She was in here every month or so telling me she needed Ambien or Minoxidil or Viagra or some such thing. Finally, we did what we do for several of our patients."

"What was that?" I asked.

"Sugar pills. We put a label on a bottle of sugar pills. If you look closely, you'll see that the labels simply have the name of the drug. The instructions say to take one a day. There's no dosage, there's no RX number."

"Is that legal, Doctor?"

"Well, it's not *illegal*. You see, with these type of older patients, if we don't placate their hypochondria, it's been our experience that they'll go to several different doctors to get what they think they need. This can result in patients taking medications that cause adverse effects when taken together. They don't often confide in each of the doctors."

"Makes sense. Can you tell me what she was actually supposed to be taking?"

I heard the papers rustling again. "I had her on a very low dosage of Boniva. That's for osteoporosis—just a preventative measure in her case. Of course, she'd seen Sally Field touting the benefits on television. The only other thing that I prescribed was taking a drug for cholesterol. Zocor. She wouldn't take the generic equivalent. Had to be Zocor."

"What about the Frontline?"

"I remember that day," laughed Dr. Weber. "I just shook my head and had the nurse give her a bottle of 'Frontline.' I have a note here from her psychiatrist..."

"Helen Sawyer?"

"Yes. Dr. Sawyer had her on Zoloft. That was for her anxiety disorder. Have you spoken with her?"

"We've talked to her."

"Then you know about her OCD?"

"Yes."

"Anything else?"

"No. Thanks, Doctor."

"Okay, I talked to Davis Boothe's doctor," said Nancy when she finally found me. I was in Sterling Park having an afternoon cup of coffee. "Well, actually his clinic. He didn't actually have one doctor. He was going to a walk-in clinic in Banner Elk. There were several doctors who saw him."

"A walk-in clinic?" I said, tipping my hat and motioning to the spot beside me on the bench. "Have a seat. It's a lovely day."

Nancy was a female cop that every egg who thought he was tough had on his Ten Most Wanted list until he was left hammered and spent like a punch-drunk boxer on the ring ropes of love.

"Yep. He didn't have any health insurance."

"Huh?" I said.

"Health insurance. He didn't have any health insurance."

"Oh. Sorry. I was thinking of something else." I took off the hat, smoothed my hair with my free hand, then replaced it at what I hoped was a rakish angle. "So what did the clinic say?"

"I talked to the nurse. She said that Davis knew about the embolism, but was waiting to see if it went away with the medication he was on. Blood thinners."

"Wasn't that dangerous?"

"Very. But he didn't have the money for the operation."

"Still, hardly a reason to commit suicide. Especially since he was on the blood thinners. He hadn't given up on the treatment."

"That's what I think," said Nancy, getting back to her feet. "I guess I'll head back to the station."

"Why don't you take the rest of the day off?" I suggested magnanimously.

"It's already 4:30," she said. "I was off half an hour ago."

Billy and Elaine Hixon were coming out of St. Barnabas when they spotted me and walked over. Billy was the senior warden, but more important to most of the members, had a lawn service that was responsible for the upkeep of the grounds.

"Hayden," called Billy. "How you doin'?"

"Pretty well. What are you two up to?"

"I had a meeting with the new priest," Billy said, making a face. "What a...."

"Billy," interrupted Elaine. "You're the senior warden." She waggled a finger at him. "Be nice."

"It's okay," I said. "I've met him. I know what you mean. Did he tell you about *The Living Gobbler*?"

"I should have known that was *your* idea," said Elaine.

I shrugged modestly.

"I'll bet you haven't heard *this*," said Elaine with a smirk.

"I don't know," I said. "I hear a lot of stuff."

"Really? Did you know that the Christian nudists have a contract to buy the old summer camp in Grinder's Mill?"

"Camp Possumtickle? I thought the camp was still open. Who told you?"

"Well, Noylene spilled the beans, but she didn't have any particulars. Anyway, Camp Possumtickle closed up in June. The nudists have a retreat scheduled for the fourth week of November. Thanksgiving weekend."

Camp Possumtickle had been struggling financially for several years. It had started out in the 1950s as a summer camp for privileged city kids, but, as fancier camps had sprung up in the mountains of North Carolina—camps with indoor plumbing—Camp Possumtickle had failed to keep up. I remembered a run-down lodge, about ten individual cabins, a bath-house and a small dining room. The camp was located on Possumtickle Lake, about three miles from town.

"Could be cold out there," said Billy. "I mean, if you're nekkid."

"They'll be here for a week in November," said Elaine, "but after the first of the year, it'll be a full-time Christian nudist retreat. They're planning improvements."

"How do you find out this stuff?"

"Well, after Noylene filled me in on what she knew, which wasn't much, I went over to the Upper Womb and asked Chad Parker. He told me that the Daystar Naturists for God and Love are purchasing the property. They'll be having Bible studies, bonfires, singing, playing games, hiking, and there will be revival services at night in the lodge. The public is invited to the services."

"Will the services be clothing optional?" I asked.

Elaine smiled and said in her sweetest voice, "What do you think?"

# Chapter 14

The Slab Café on an autumn Saturday morning was generally packed to the rafters and this morning was no exception. Pete had saved a table so Meg and I didn't have the half hour wait that most of the patrons endured. The smell of coffee hung in the air mixed with various other wafting scents that I had no trouble identifying: country ham, cheese grits, bacon, waffles, pancakes and scrambled eggs. Noylene, Collette and Pauli Girl McCollough were working the floor and had everything under control. The six booths were full, as were all the tables and the four red-vinyl upholstered stools at the counter. We walked across the big black and white tiles, greeting folks we knew, nodding cordially to those we didn't, and made our way to Pete's table. I gave him the bad news.

"The Daystar Naturists for God and Love?" Pete was despondent. "They bought the camp? Maybe they'll change their minds. Maybe we'll have a monsoon or an earthquake or something."

"Maybe," said Meg, looking toward the door as the cowbell jangled against the glass. "Do you mind if Mother joins us? I texted her that we would save her a seat."

"Fine with me," said Pete.

"You *texted* her?" I added. "Is that even a *word?*"

"I texted her on your BlackBerry. She texted me back that she had news."

"She texted you *back?*"

"Sure." Meg gave me a demure smile. "After all, this is the 21st century."

"Well, I hope it's good news," I said. "We could use some good news."

"Ask her yourself."

I looked up and saw Ruby approaching. Then I stood and pulled out a chair, still practicing to be the good son-in-law.

"Thank you, Hayden," said Ruby with a delightful smile. Ruby was an older version of Meg. Her hair was still black, although now, as she neared seventy, it was streaked with silver. She was a striking woman, slightly taller than Meg, statuesque and elegant. "I have news."

"We heard," I said. "Do tell."

"Well," started Ruby, "you know that Thelma Wingler died on Wednesday."

"Tuesday, actually," I said. "But we found her on Wednesday."

"Of course, you're right," said Ruby. "Now don't interrupt, dear."

"Sorry," I said.

"Well, apparently Thelma had no family."

Meg, Pete and I nodded.

"Also, I suppose she had no friends."

We nodded.

"I used to have lunch with her once a week. I didn't much care for her, but I thought it was my Christian responsibility."

We nodded again.

"Anyway, it seems that when she made out her last will, she left everything to me. She didn't have any family. Did I mention that?"

Ruby looked at us. We nodded.

"Oh, for heaven's sake, say something."

"That's great!" said Meg. "The house? Everything?"

"No. Not the house. She left the house to the church."

"All her money?" said Pete. "She was loaded! Man, what a windfall!"

"No, not the money," said Ruby, scrunching up her nose in that wonderful way that reminded me of Meg. "The money goes to the Humane Society. Well, most of it anyway. Five thousand dollars goes to Upper Womb Ministries."

"Really? The Upper Womb?" said Pete. "Now there's a surprise."

"Definitely worth looking into," I said. "Let's see then. Not the house. Not the money. That leaves..."

"The crematorium," said Ruby. "She left me the crematorium."

"*What?*" said Meg. "The crematorium?"

"I understand it does quite a bit of business," said Ruby, "and that if I don't want to keep it, I could certainly sell it."

"Not to mention the advantages if one of us dies unexpectedly," said Pete. "I would hope I'd get a special deal. After all, I did save you a place at my table."

"You may all have special deals," said Ruby. "I always like to remember the little people."

The McColloughs lived up in the hills in a mobile home that hadn't been mobile in thirty years. Ardine had been married to a nasty piece of work named PeeDee McCollough, an abusive man who managed a moonshine still and a couple of welfare scams to make ends meet. The ends didn't meet often and when they did, PeeDee soon drank up the excess. He had dropped off the face of the earth seven or eight years ago and although Ardine had never been officially questioned about his disappearance, it was the general consensus that PeeDee probably got what was coming to him and wouldn't be missed. His family certainly didn't miss him. Ardine worked part time at a Christmas tree farm and made quilts that she sold in gift shops. She made ends meet quite well and, although they didn't have a lot, her children were growing up healthy and happy.

The McColloughs had three children. The only contribution that PeeDee made to his children's lives was to name them and this he did with great deliberation; this deliberation consisting of walking over to the refrigerator. Hence, his children were all named after beers. Ardine had been too tired to argue.

Bud was the eldest. He had a unique talent that made him, even at the tender age of sixteen, well respected and in high demand in St. Germaine. He was a genuine wine connoisseur. Well, not a connoisseur in the strict sense—he didn't actually drink the wine—but did, however, have the knowledge and the wine-speak to compete with any sommelier on the East coast, and that included Boston and New York. If asked about a certain Sauvignon Blanc on sale at the Ginger Cat, he might tell you that it was "ripe and well-balanced with fresh citrus and passion fruit characteristics. A good value at eleven dollars a bottle." If your interest went a bit further, he'd tell you that this particular Sauvignon Blanc was from the Marlborough region of New Zealand and that the Kiwi winemakers consider it essential that, in addition to the fruitiness, their wines have the "true Marlborough" hints of armpit and cat pee. "Cat pee?" you'd ask incredulously. "A slightly musky, pungently perfumed mix of herbs, asparagus, green bean and bell pepper," he'd answer. And he'd be right.

Bud was a voracious reader and single handedly kept the St. Germaine public library in business, or so it seemed. Rebecca Watts, the librarian, told me that he frequently checked out thirty books at a time.

"Isn't there a limit?" I asked.

"Sure," was the reply, "but not for Bud."

Bud had just gotten his driver's license, so now he was relegated to driving his brother and sister around town when Ardine couldn't do it. Although he'd been driving his father's old pick-up truck since he was twelve, she hadn't let him drive the other kids until he was "legal." Ardine was a good mother.

Pauli Girl was fifteen going on twenty-seven. She looked a lot like Daisy Mae in *Little Abner* and was, by a long shot, the prettiest girl in town. It wasn't uncommon to see her walking down the street with a gaggle of adolescent boys trailing in her wake like sharks following a tuna boat. Now that school had started, she worked on the weekends in various food establishments in town, depending on which one called her first. I'd seen her lately at the Bear and Brew, the Ginger Cat and now, on this particularly lovely autumn morning, waiting tables at the Slab.

Moose-Head was the youngest of the McCollough brood. He was now eight, but still small for his age. Known to everyone in town as "Moosey," he could be easily identified by his tattered, old-fashioned, high top Keds running down the street, the mop of uncombed straw that passed for hair, and the half eaten candy bar in his hand. Moosey had the metabolism and attention span of a garden shrew.

It was Moosey who banged into the Slab just as Noylene had poured us our second cup of coffee. He hit the door so hard that the cowbell flew off the rope, skidded across the linoleum floor, and clanked against the counter.

"Careful!" called Pete. "That cowbell cost a dollar and a quarter!"

"Hey, Chief!" Moosey yelled, standing in the doorway and holding the door open. He'd taken to calling me 'Chief' during the summer after his mother had lectured him on the proper way to address his elders. "Chief, come quick! There's some giant rats in the library!"

To say the patrons of Pete's establishment were startled by the announcement would be an understatement.

"Gotta go," I said, rising to my feet.

"We're coming, too," said Meg. Ruby nodded.

"You guys go ahead," said Pete. "I've already seen the giant rats." He looked around the Slab and noticed the other customers fidgeting, as if trying to decide whether giant rats were a viable tourist attraction worthy of leaving their tables to the line of hungry patrons waiting next to Moosey by the door.

"If y'all leave now, you still have to pay," announced Pete in a loud voice. That seemed to settle the question and the diners went back to enjoying their breakfasts.

We arrived at the library behind Moosey, a one-block walk from the Slab, just in time to see Rebecca Watts chase two of the Minques out of the front door and down the steps with a broom.

"There's still one inside," she called when she saw us. "Bring your gun." She disappeared back inside with Moosey at her heels. The Minques seemed to be quite nonplused about the whole episode. They calmly walked over to the flowerbeds on either side of the front steps and started munching happily on the chrysanthemums.

"Do you have your gun?" asked Ruby.

"Nope."

"It's in the organ bench," said Meg with the sideways look that always followed the mention of my 9mm Glock stashed in the church.

"Very handy for rats in the choir loft," I said. "And tenors."

"Well, *those* aren't rats," said Ruby, looking at the creatures now gobbling the flowers like a couple of fur-covered weed-eaters.

"They're Minques," said Meg. "M-I-N-Q-U-E. Don't get too close. They're a cross between a nutria and a...a something else from South America. They're pretty aggressive."

101

"A pacarana," I said. "The pacaranas are pretty docile, but the Minques are not. It's one of the breed characteristics."

"Well, isn't that special," said Ruby sweetly. "Aggressive Minques that eat flowers. And just in time for mum season."

Another Minque came scurrying out of the library with Rebecca in hot pursuit. "Get out!" she yelled. "You stupid rat!"

"They're not rats," I called to her from the sidewalk. "They're..."

"I *know* what they are. I already talked to the fur farm. They're sending over a crew. The stupid things got hold of an entire bottom shelf of biographies. Benjamin Franklin to John Stuart Mill."

"John *who?*" asked Meg.

"John Stuart Mill. Nineteenth century British philosopher," said Rebecca. "Chewed right through him and kept on going."

"Well, the flowers should keep them busy until the fur farmers get here," I said.

Rebecca looked down at the decimated flowerbeds and let out a wail. "Oh, man! Give me your pistol, Hayden. I'll kill them myself!"

"This," I whispered to Ruby, "is why I keep the gun in the organ bench."

"Hey," yelled Moosey from somewhere inside. "I found another one!"

"C'mon, boy," I called and gave a whistle. I didn't need to whistle. Baxter was out of the door and headed up the driveway before the sound died away in the kitchen. He was used to these morning runs, and although he could run to his heart's content up here in the mountains, he dutifully hung around the house until invited to partake in an outing.

An October morning is a wonderful thing in the Appalachians. The "smoke" that the Smoky Mountains was known for hung in clumps on the side of the mountains, a heavy fog that would finally give way mid-morning, dispersing slowly, gradually exposing the patches of orange and yellow that now dotted the hills. By the time I'd run out to the main road and turned north to begin my two-mile loop, Baxter had chased up a couple of deer and was worrying something that had taken shelter in a nearby tree—a squirrel, or maybe a raccoon. I couldn't see it. He barked at it happily until I jogged past, then took off ahead of me again to see what other interesting things he might find.

There was no traffic early on Sunday mornings. There was barely traffic during what the residents of Green Holler Road jokingly called "rush hour." The church service was still hours away, and my shoes kicked up dust on the unpaved road as I headed up the slope.

Running and thinking went together like possum and sweet

taters. I was investigating two deaths within three days of each other. Coincidence? Maybe. Davis Boothe was thirty-two but looked younger. He had no family and that in itself was odd. If he was older, maybe, but at thirty-two, it seemed strange that he had no surviving parents, no brothers or sisters, no grandparents and no record of anyone who might be related to him. What else did we know about him? He hadn't been to college, but showed up in the area about twelve years ago. He got a job waiting tables in Boone and then selling suits at Don's Clothing Store. He was a member of the vestry at St. Barnabas and active in the local Little Theater. He had been diagnosed with a blood clot in his brain, and was taking blood thinners. Surgery—medically, a better option for Davis—wasn't really an option because he had no health insurance. Other than the blood clot, he seemed to be in good health, productive and happy. We had all assumed he was gay, but we may have been way off base. He was single, attractive and available, but had never been linked with anyone of either sex that I knew of. Still, if he was gay, we had no evidence of it.

Davis had hanged himself on a Sunday morning. I had seen him the day before at the bookstore when I first saw the book I had purchased a few days later, *The Sketchbook of Geoffrey Crayon*. Davis had been looking at it with me when he had suddenly left the bookstore. I thought back on the scene. He'd closed the book, said he had to leave and disappeared. The next morning, he killed himself. Did he see something in the book, and if so, what? This particular book was one hundred eighty-five years old.

I rounded a bend and the road now followed a rushing creek that drowned out the sounds of the surrounding woods. I caught a glimpse of Baxter as he tore up a hill and disappeared into a thicket of mountain laurel. Without breaking stride, I kicked absently at a large hickory nut lying on the side of the road and watched it bounce off a rock and splash into the swirling water.

Thelma Wingler had died two days later of coronary arrest. Her heart had stopped, but I wasn't buying "died of natural causes." Thelma had quit taking her OCD meds and had become trapped in the Upper Womb's labyrinth under circumstances that any normal person would have found ludicrous. "Just walk away," they might have laughed. But Thelma couldn't "just walk away." She was a prisoner of her obsessive compulsive disorder as surely as if she were walled into Minos' own maze.

Chad Parker and Lacie Ravencroft had painted the labyrinth for their spa patrons to use as a tool to help guide their meditative experience. Or so it seemed. I had seen labyrinths before and, although I didn't necessarily feel the fascination, I'd concede its viability as a spiritual guide. Had Thelma been instructed by Chad to discard her medication, use his techniques to deal with her OCD like Wynette had said, then become lost in the labyrinth and, unable to extricate herself, finally died there? Whatever the reasons behind her demise, I didn't think she died alone. The lock was left open, hanging from the latch, and Thelma had no key on her person. More than that, she didn't even have any pockets. If she'd had her purse with her—something I considered probable—it was missing. Someone was in the garden with her. There was a krummhorn hanging in the bushes, a very loud instrument that she had purchased earlier that morning, but she hadn't known that she needed to put a reed into the horn to make it work. She'd had some swelling of her vocal cords and had been complaining of a cold coming on. She'd even had a prescription, called in by Dr. Weber, that she never picked up.

I skipped around a box turtle that I hadn't noticed until the last moment. Baxter was nowhere to be seen.

What about Lacie? Where did she figure in all this? True, both Chad and Lacie were in Virginia during the time in question, but could they have masterminded the entire episode? If so, what was their motive? Money? The five thousand dollars that the Upper Womb received from Thelma's estate would hardly be worth a murder, although I'd seen it done for a lot less.

I had more questions than answers as I jogged around the final turn and headed back to the house. When I arrived, Baxter was already on the porch, soaking wet from chasing frogs into the creek, deliriously content, and ready for breakfast.

Most of the members of St. Barnabas had heard about the Lemmings long before Sunday, so it was no surprise that the church was full for their first service. The Rev. Dr. Adrian Lemming, being an ex-Baptist minister of music and well-versed in the hymns of the faith, had chosen *Onward Christian Soldiers* as the opening hymn. *Rock of Ages* and *Just As I Am* rounded out the selections. I figured he was going with the old favorites, but suspected he'd be in trouble in a couple of weeks when those old favorites ran out. The Episcopal hymnal hadn't been kind to the old favorites and for every *Stand Up, Stand Up for Jesus,* there were ten *Lo, He Comes With Clouds Descending,* great tunes and texts unknown to most of the folks who had grown up on Fanny Crosby and the Sunday School hymns of the early 20th century. I certainly didn't fault them. People like to sing what they know and most of our parishioners were not of the Frozen Chosen—that is to say, cradle Episcopalians—but had moved their memberships over to St. Barnabas from other denominations. In addition to the handful of chestnuts and popular standards that crossed all denominations, our hymnal included quite a number of *Earth and All Stars*—tricky tunes with texts that made people want to become Amish just to get away from them. Every denominational hymnal had its share of dogs to be sure, and this one could bark with the best of them, but I figured there were plenty of hymns in it for everyone's taste. Added to that, it was the only hymnal we had and, for now at least, it was the one we used. Choosing hymns was a balancing act, of old favorites and new finds, but every congregation had their own repertoire and I knew ours pretty well. I was sure that the Lemmings did not.

Fiona Tidball-Lemming came down to give the children's sermon, but the children, not knowing they would be required, had left during the second hymn and gone on to Children's Church as was their custom. Father Lemming, singing the hymn with gusto, didn't see them depart and, when the hymn was over, invited the now-absent children to come forward while Mrs. Tidball-Lemming waited on the chancel steps. She was dressed in a white alb like her husband, complete with a matching ministerial stole and looked more than a little put out when there were no children to attend to her ministrations. Knowing the children of St. Barnabas as I did, she got away easy, but she huffed her way back to her position as lay Eucharistic minister with her children's sermon still in her pocket. Father Lemming gave *his* sermon a few moments later. It wasn't a particularly memorable message, but it wasn't awful. It did, however, contain more than a few "dontcha know"s.

Our new priest seemed quite happy—almost giddy, in fact—when, during his welcome and announcements, he invited all interested parties to come in and audition for *The Living Gobbler*. He and Fiona would be personally holding the auditions on Tuesday and Wednesday afternoon with rehearsals to begin the following week.

"Hey, great news, dontcha know," said Meg to the rest of the soprano section as they were passing the peace. "If we don't audition, we don't have to be in it."

"Au contraire," I said, overhearing their nefarious plan. "The whole choir is in it. I've already ordered your rutabaga and pilgrim costumes."

"I'd like to be Pocahontas," said Marjorie as demurely as she could manage in her whisky tenor.

"You're pushing eighty, Marjorie," said Phil. "And pushing it pretty hard. Pocahontas was an Indian maiden."

"Bite your tongue, you little whippersnapper," said Marjorie.

"You'll have to audition for the Lemmings," I said. "I'm afraid I hold no sway in the casting process. Pocahontas has a lot of lines though. And there's the big love scene with Squanto."

"John Smith," corrected Meg.

"Whoever."

"I don't mind," said Marjorie. "I could use a little lovin'."

"Meg said that you haven't even started writing it," said Bev. "How do you know how many lines Pocahontas has?"

"It's all right up here," I answered, tapping my noggin. "Almost finished."

"It's a good thing *Whispering Hope* isn't in the hymnal," said Elaine. "It'd be the grand finale."

Suddenly several screams emanated from the nave below. Those of us on the front row leaned over the edge of the balcony to see what had precipitated such a Pentecostal outburst. Those choir members seated further back stood up and craned forward to get a look. Running down the aisle and heading for the open doors was a Minque.

# Chapter 15

"Okay," I said to Ginger. "I've got the picture. Now spell it out."

Ginger leaned in and spilled her guts like a sorority pledge after the Homecoming dance.

"Here's the grift, goombah. The bishops are opening a Mexican mink farm to supply the Liturgical Hairpiece industry. They're going to smuggle mink skins up to the border in a Taco Bell truck."

I nodded. The old mink skin disguised as a burrito trick.

"No, not the old mink skin disguised as a burrito trick," said Ginger, reading my thought bubble. "They're going to load the skins into a giant cannon and shoot them across the border. They'll be picked up on the other side. You see?"

"Yeah," I said, thoughtfully running one hand across Ginger's grizzled chin. "The Taco Bell cannon indeed. But how can they make the scam pay off?"

"That's the best part," said Ginger. "Here's the way it works. They're going to start with one million minks."

I nodded. A million minks. Sure.

"Each mink averages twelve minklets a year. The skins can be sold for 33¢ a piece. This will give them twelve million skins at three for a dollar. You with me so far?"

I nodded again and started counting on my fingers.

"That's a gross revenue of almost four million per year."

"Four million," I said. "Got it." One thing was for sure. I was going to need more fingers.

"That's about $10,000 per day," said Ginger, "not including Sundays and holidays. A good Mexican worker can skin about 50 minks per day and will work all day for $3. It will take 566 workers to operate the mink farm. That's $1700 for the workers. So the profit will be $8300 per day."

I'd run out of fingers and had taken off my shoes.

"Now," continued Ginger, "the minks will be fed exclusively on rats. The bishops are going to start a rat farm right next to the mink farm. They're going to import one million rats from New York."

"Sounds about right."

"Rats multiply four times as fast as the minks so there will be four rats per mink every day."

"Good eatin'," I agreed.

"Then the rats will be fed on the carcasses of the minks that they skin. That will give each rat a quarter of a mink."

I was beginning to see the beauty of the operation. "Of course!" I said. "The minks eat the rats, the rats eat the minks and the bishops get the skins!"

"Exactly!"

"It's brilliant," I said.

"There's more!" said Ginger. "Eventually, the bishops are going to cross the minks with snakes. Sninks. This will launch them into the Liturgical Cowboy Boot market as well as get the minks to skin themselves twice a year."

"Not only that," I said, "but they could get two skins for one mink."

"If word gets out, they'll never get those cheap skins across the border. That's why..."

Ginger never finished her sentence. Her eyes grew wide and her head suddenly hit the table and bounced twice exactly the way a bowling ball wouldn't.

She was dead.

"Is Davis' body still down at the morgue?" I asked. I had the phone pressed to the side of my head and my shoulder was doing the best it could to keep it there. My two hands were busy—a plate of nachos in one and the TV remote in the other as I tried to keep track of three football games at once.

"Yes," said Nancy's voice. "I had Kent keep him on ice. There's no next of kin, so it wasn't a problem."

"Do me a favor...hang on a minute." I flipped through the channels. "I think the Colts just scored."

"They did. A fifty-five yard field goal. "

"You watching the Colts and the Broncos?"

"Yep. Dave and me."

"Listen, tomorrow morning would you go down to the morgue and take Davis' fingerprints? Then run them through the FBI data base."

"You think he's wanted somewhere?"

"It's a possibility," I said. "Young, single guy just shows up in town seven years ago. No family, no connections to the area. It's worth a look."

I could hear Nancy thinking on the other end. "Makes sense," she finally said. "I'll do it first thing. It'll be a few days before we hear anything though. Those FBI searches take forever."

"Dagnabbit! Tampa Bay just scored on the Panthers."

"What channel?" she asked.

"Thirty-five." Nancy and I both had satellite TV and could get thirteen pro football games on any given Sunday. She was a Denver fan but, like me, flipped between games as soon as a commercial came on or the outcome was no longer in doubt.

"Like I was saying," said Nancy, "first thing tomorrow. Oh, crap... now Jay Cutler's down."

"See you then."

Noylene's Beautifery was bustling. Many hair salons were closed on Mondays but Noylene only took one day off, preferring to take her free time in the mornings. The Beautifery didn't open until eleven. Along with hair styling, Noylene's also offered manicures, pedicures, and, in the back room, did quite a brisk business with an invention she had cooked up called the Dip 'n Tan. Her son D'Artagnan, and his friend Skeeter Donalson had built the contraption, an absolute marvel of engineering that consisted of a winch, a trapeze bar, and a five-hundred gallon vat of spray-on tanning fluid. A brave customer could hold onto this bar and be lowered into the vat for an all-over tan. Early on, many folks could be seen around St. Germaine sporting the pallor of giant carrots, but as Noylene refined the formula and the timing, her customers looked, more or less, like people who were native to the Brazilian rain forests. Still, as Noylene so delicately put it, "brown fat looks better than white fat," and the Dip 'n Tan had its devotees.

Noylene Fabergé and Woodrow "Wormy" DuPont had gotten married by Judge Adams early in August. They'd been planning a double ceremony with Collette and Dave, but after Brother Kilroy, the pastor of New Fellowship Baptist Church, was murdered and Dave broke his engagement with Collette, Noylene had decided on a private ceremony. She and Wormy were first cousins on the Fabergé side, but that wasn't an obstacle to marriage in North Carolina and Judge Adams was happy to oblige. Noylene had decided to hyphenate for professional reasons and was now officially and legally Noylene Fabergé-DuPont. D'Artagnan, age twenty-four, for reasons known only to himself, had decided to adopt the hyphenated moniker as well.

I stopped in at the Beautifery on Monday afternoon to talk to Ruby. Meg's mother had a standing appointment at the Beautifery every Monday at 2:15 pm. The three cubicles were all in use. Noylene was in the one farthest from the door and gave me a wave as I walked in. The other two licensed beauticians, Darla and Debbie, were snipping, coloring, and razoring like the professionals they were, all the while keeping up a continuous and simultaneous chatter with the three customers. Ruby wasn't one of them.

"Afternoon, ladies, " I said, tipping my gray felt hat. The chairs were occupied by Hannah, Grace, and Amelia, the three checkout girls from the Piggly Wiggly. "Checkout girls" was really a misnomer. All three ladies were in their early sixties and, since the robbery last spring, were all known for packing heat.

"I love a man in a hat," said Hannah from the chair nearest the door. "It's lucky I'm sitting down or I'd swoon straight away."

"Thank you," I said. "I'm trying to bring the fedora back into style."

"You and Brad Pitt," said Grace. Grace had a head full of aluminum foil. I didn't ask.

"Who's minding the Pig?" I asked.

"Roger's working the register," said Amelia. "He's not very good at it, but Mondays are slow."

"I thought Ruby would be here."

"She called this morning and cancelled," said Noylene. "Said she was going out to the crematorium."

"Isn't that something?" said Darla. "Ruby inheriting the crematorium."

"I would have been nicer to that old bat," said Debbie, "if I'd known she was rich. She was as tight as a tick and as mean as a boiled owl. Never tipped me. Not once."

"Me, neither," said Darla.

"I almost shot her once," said Grace. "She deserved it, too. Called me white trash because I wouldn't give her double coupons on a Tuesday. A Tuesday! Can you believe it?"

"Pshaw!" said Amelia. "You *should* have shot her. Everyone knows double coupons is on Wednesday."

Nancy was sitting at my desk studying intently. Dave was looking over her shoulder and both of them had looks of concentration on their faces. They both looked up when they heard me come in.

"Found anything yet?" I asked.

"Nothing," said Nancy. "We're not reading the whole thing. Just looking for something that would have jumped out at Davis."

"Yeah," I said. I'd told the force, i.e. Nancy and Dave, about Davis' sudden departure from Eden Books after viewing *The Sketchbook of Geoffrey Crayon* and they'd been scouring it for any kind of clue.

"Be careful of those pages," I admonished. "It's an antique. One of a kind. A signed first edition."

Nancy held up her hands. She was wearing her cotton dress gloves.

"Ah," I said. "Very well. Carry on."

I was cutting across the park, heading for the Upper Womb with a few questions for Chad Parker. Suddenly a voice rang out.

"Hayden!"

I turned and saw Muffy Lemieux waving and hurrying toward me.

I waved back at her. She saw me stop and slowed her pace from a skip to a languid sway. I tipped my hat back and admired her perambulation.

"Hi, Hayden," she said, smiling as she walked up.

"Good afternoon," I said, returning the smile and touching the brim of my hat.

"Hey, can I ask you a big favor?"

"Doesn't hurt to ask," I said.

"Me and Varmit are going to audition for *The Living Gobbler* and we need a song. I was hoping you'd have a suggestion."

"Hmm. I would suggest some sort of duet. Do you know any musicals?"

"I do, but Varmit doesn't."

"Well, what does he know?"

"Country songs, mostly," shrugged Muffy.

"Any duets?"

She brightened. "I'm pretty sure he knows *Get Your Biscuits In The Oven And Your Buns In The Bed*. It's 'our' song."

"Do that one, then," I suggested. "I'm sure you'll be a hit."

"Why, *thank you*," she said in an accent just a little too Southern to be real. "You're the best!"

I nodded to her and doffed my hat again. Then I turned and headed toward the spa. I could get used to this hat thing. It saved a lot of talking.

"Hey," Muffy said again, suddenly appearing in step beside me. "Are you going over to the Upper Womb? I'm headed that way, myself."

"Yep. I was hoping to talk to Chad."

"You'll probably have to make an appointment."

"Really?"

"Oh, yes. I had a massage scheduled for two weeks from Thursday, but he had an unexpected cancellation so I'm getting in early." Muffy lowered her voice. "Someone died."

I nodded. "So, he's pretty busy?"

"Well, duh," Muffy said. "Have you seen him? Every woman in town's been scheduling massages." Muffy was nothing if not delicate.

"It's just a massage though. Right? Nothing else."

Muffy's mouth dropped open and she looked quite offended. "Of *course*, it's just a massage." Then she giggled. "And a little fantasizing."

111

We walked up on the front porch of the spa-coffee shop and I held the door for her as she walked in.

"You know," she said in a conspiratorial whisper, "Lacie Ravencroft is doing massages, too. Varmit came in last Friday. You might want to give it a try."

Muffy was a few minutes early for her appointment, but disappeared up the long staircase and into a waiting room on the second floor. Cynthia was in the coffee bar, bussing a table. Sitting at another table were Annette Passaglio and Wendy Bolling.

"Afternoon, ladies," I said.

"Hey there," said Cynthia, putting the last of the dirty dishes onto a tray. Annette and Wendy smiled pleasantly and nodded, but I noticed the conversation had stopped.

"Here for a massage?" I asked them.

"Not today," Wendy answered. Annette gave her a kick under the table, but never stopped smiling.

"We just stopped in for a cup of coffee," said Annette pleasantly. "Do they give massages here, too?"

"Why, you know," said Wendy, "I believe they do. I think that I heard that somewhere."

"Perhaps we should try it sometime," said Annette. Wendy nodded.

"That sounds like a good idea," I said. "I hear it's very relaxing. Y'all have a nice day."

Annette smiled. Wendy looked nervous. I followed Cynthia into the kitchen. She set the tray on the counter and started unloading it into the dishwasher.

"Annette's been here four times in the last five days," Cynthia whispered. "And that's only because we're closed on Sundays. Chad's doing a brisk business."

I nodded. "How about Lacie?"

"She does okay. Men aren't as apt to come in for massages—at least not in this town. She does have some female clients though. Most of her business consists of consultations. Holistic and wellness programs."

"Hey! You ready for the big debate?"

"Sure, I'm ready. But, to tell you the truth, I'm scared to death. This is all my new publicist's idea."

"You'll do fine," I said. "Is Lacie here?"

"I think so. I didn't see her leave. I could check the appointment book."

"Would you?" I asked.

"Sure."

Cynthia, drying her hands on a dishtowel, headed for a door in the kitchen marked "office."

"Could you also look and see if Davis Boothe came in for an appointment? Maybe two weeks ago?"

Cynthia looked at me and pursed her lips but didn't answer.

"Look, I won't say anything to Chad or Lacie—at least not directly. It would help."

Cynthia gave a faint nod, opened the door to the office and disappeared.

I leaned against the counter, tugged the brim of my hat into what might be a rakish angle, then folded my arms in front of me and felt, for all the world, just like a detective. Cynthia appeared a moment later.

"It's the hat," she said. "Who can resist the hat?"

"Of all the coffee joints in all the towns in all the world, I walked into yours," I snarled, in my best Bogeyese. "Here's lookin' at you, kid."

Cynthia laughed. "As far as I know, Lacie's upstairs with a client for another..." she looked at her watch, "five minutes or so. As for Davis Boothe, he had a 1:00 appointment with Chad on September 29th. That was a Saturday."

"The day before he died."

Cynthia shrugged. "I guess so."

"Do you think that you could go up and tell Chad and Lacie I need to speak with them for a few moments?"

"Sure. They usually take a five minute break between clients in the afternoon."

"Thanks, Sweetheart," I Bogeyed. "You're the best. By the way, do you have any of those rhubarb muffins?"

"What rhubarb muffins?"

"Lacie said you were going to put rhubarb muffins on the menu."

"Nope." Cynthia shook her head. "We have pumpkin-spice, blueberry, banana-nut, raspberry, and cranberry. No rhubarb."

"Pity," I said. "I love rhubarb."

I waited in the hallway while Cynthia went upstairs to get Chad Parker and Lacie Ravencroft.

The plastered hallway of Old Mrs. McCarty's house was still mostly covered in 1940's vintage flowered wallpaper. Where someone had begun to remove it, probably Mrs. McCarty's daughter during one of her visits home, some lathe peeked out from underneath the plaster. The old house was in good shape, but definitely needed some updating. The light switches were still the old pushbutton type and I could glimpse the old knob and tube wiring through a gap in the boards.

I looked up when I heard footfalls on the stairs and saw Lacie coming down followed by Cynthia and Chad. I smiled as I greeted them. Mr. Congeniality.

"Good afternoon, Chief," said Lacie.

"Afternoon," I said. "Could I have a couple of minutes?"

"Sure," said Chad. "How can we help?"

"Can we go out on the porch?"

"Great idea," said Lacie. "Can I get us some tea?"

"No, thanks. I won't be here that long."

Cynthia excused herself back to the coffee bar while Chad, Lacie, and I repaired to the front porch.

"I just have a couple of questions," I said. "You know about Thelma Wingler's will?"

"Yes," said Chad. "We found out on Friday. It was a very generous gift to our ministry."

"It certainly was," I said. "Especially since she'd known you less than a month before she died."

"Well, I won't tell you I was surprised by her death," said Chad. "I was saddened, certainly, but Thelma had many problems of which I'm sure you are now aware."

I nodded. "This gift to your ministry. Was this her idea or yours?"

"Just what are you implying?" bristled Lacie.

"I'm implying that perhaps you suggested that your ministry be included in her will. I'm implying that she might not have included the Upper Womb in her will if you hadn't mentioned it to her." I smiled amiably. "Nothing wrong with that; nothing illegal and there's no one to contest it."

"All right, then," said Chad, "I might have said something to her. The Upper Womb is a legitimate non-profit organization. She told me the week before she died that she'd changed her will to include Upper Womb ministries."

I heard a sharp intake of breath from Lacie Ravencroft.

"Did you know how much she left you?" I asked. "I mean before the will was read."

"Of course not," said Chad petulantly.

"Yes, we did, honey," said Lacie. "Remember? She told us that she was leaving us five thousand dollars."

Lacie was obviously the brains of this operation and I mentally kicked myself for not seeing it sooner.

"Five thousand dollars is hardly enough money to kill someone over," said Lacie. "We do five thousand dollars a week."

Chad was still looking confused. "Kill who?" he asked. "Thelma?"

"Yes, honey," said Lacie, sweetly. "Chief Konig is trying to discover if we had a motive to kill Thelma."

"Of course we didn't!" said Chad.

"I guess not," I said. "By the way, you didn't happen to see Davis Boothe the week or so before he committed suicide, did you?"

Lacie huffed. "I wasn't here. I was still in New York." She looked over at Chad. I did, too.

"Sure," he said. "I saw him on that Saturday afternoon. I remember because after our session, he cancelled his next appointment."

"Did he happen to say anything?"

"He was very agitated when he came in, but he calmed down considerably during his massage. He didn't say why, but he was very tense."

"He didn't happen to leave the Upper Womb anything in his will, did he?"

"No!" said Lacie.

"Maybe a life insurance policy?"

Lacie turned on her heel and left the porch with a stomp and a bang of the door.

"How did you know about the life insurance?" asked Chad.

# Chapter 16

I was in my office, studying the computer screen, when Meg and Ruby walked in. Nancy had taken off at about five o'clock. I hadn't seen Dave since earlier in the afternoon.

"How about some supper?" Ruby called from the counter. "My treat. I'm a very wealthy crematorium owner."

"Sounds great," I said. "You two c'mere a minute."

Meg and Ruby made their way around the counter and wandered carefully through the stacks of papers Dave had piled neatly on the floor. Dave was in charge of filing reports with the state and however he wanted to do them was fine with Nancy and me.

"Did you know," I said, "that during World War I, the British government advised people to eat rhubarb leaves? Like they were collard greens or something."

"The internet is a wonderful thing," said Meg. "So?"

"So," I continued. "The thing is, they're poisonous. Quite a number of people were poisoned until the British government reversed their recommendation."

"Really? They'll kill you?" Ruby asked.

"No. They won't kill you. At least they're listed here as 'generally not toxic.' The leaves contain oxalic acid in the form of oxalate crystals. They cause swelling of the mouth and throat and paralyze the vocal cords."

"Sort of like Thelma?" asked Meg.

"Uh-huh."

"So where did you see rhubarb leaves?"

"In the kitchen at the spa. The day we found Thelma. It was in the sink."

"A lot of people have rhubarb this time of year," said Ruby. "I have some myself. Maybe they were cooking something up."

"Maybe they were."

The Ginger Cat was doing a brisk business. Just inside the door of the restaurant, was a small gift shop that catered to out-of-towners. It carried local foodstuffs—jams, jellies and relishes—cookbooks, a couple of Ardine's quilts, some pottery, knick-knacks and a few paintings by area artists. It was a nice browse while waiting for your table. Cynthia Johnsson greeted us and put us on the table list.

"Didn't I just see you over at the coffee bar?" I kidded.

"They close at four and a girl's got to make a living," she said with a smile. "I'm on at the Ginger Cat Monday and Thursday nights. Pauli

Girl's here, too. She'll be over at the Bear and Brew tomorrow. I'm off until Thursday unless someone calls me in, which they probably will. October's busy."

"I don't know how you two keep up," said Ruby.

"I only have the two jobs, plus belly dancing," said Cynthia. "When I'm the mayor, I'll have to cut back."

"Speaking of politics," I said, "did you *really* belly dance for Bill Clinton?"

"I really did," Cynthia said proudly. "He even tipped me a twenty. Tucked it right here." She pointed to her chest. "I was going to keep it and frame it, but I needed cab fare."

"I'm going to need a belly dancer for *The Living Gobbler*," I said. "Do you think you could work it into your schedule?"

"Oh, absolutely!"

"Actually, come to think of it, I'm going to need a *couple* of belly dancers. Maybe you could give Meg a few lessons?"

"Why, sure!" said Cynthia. "I'd love to."

Meg was smiling, but only on the outside.

"I was just kidding. I only need one belly dancer."

We'd been seated at our table and our drinks were on the way.

"You don't need *any* belly dancers," said Meg. "I'm fairly certain that belly dancing isn't part nor parcel of any Thanksgiving celebration either here or abroad."

"Au contraire," I said. "It's an old English tradition dating back to the sixth century, started by Abercrombie the Thankful after his victory at the battle of Pumpkin Hill. His Celtic belly dancers so hypnotized the Viking invaders that they threw down their Horns of Plenty and headed for America."

"Abraham Lincoln started Thanksgiving in 1863," said Meg.

"Well," I said, "if you're going to muck up this conversation by quoting actual facts, the original Thanksgiving feast was in 1621. In fact, there were a number of states that celebrated Thanksgiving even before Honest Abe declared it a National Holiday. I looked it up."

"What has that got to do with belly dancing?" asked Ruby.

"Probably about as much as having twelve kids dressed up like elves and riding in on a four-wheeler singing *Grandma Got Run Over By A Reindeer* has to do with Christmas."

"You have a point," conceded Ruby, "but that doesn't make it right. How's your *Gobbler* show coming along? Is it finished?"

"Luckily, the Lemmings have taken the reins on this one. It seems that Fiona Tidball-Lemming is a bit of a poetess and playwright, and of course, Adrian is an ex-Baptist minister of music. She's acquiesced to provide the script and he's helping as needed. I just need to drop in a few tunes. No problem."

"And Fiona included a belly dancer?" said Meg.

"Well, that's my own touch. A bit of local flavor, if you will. Cynthia will be belly-dancing to *Over the River and Through the Woods.*"

Meg lay her head down on the table.

"Cheer up," I said. "At least you don't have to be one of the singing Brussels sprouts. I put you down as a beautiful Indian squaw."

Meg said something, but, with her face still resting on her arms, all I could hear was a whimper.

"If you'd like a speaking role or a solo, the try-outs are tomorrow and Wednesday," I said. "I'm pretty sure that Muffy and Varmit are auditioning."

"Hey," said Ruby, "I think the nudists will be in town. Maybe you can work them into the show somehow."

"They'll be confined to Camp Possumtickle, I believe."

"You mean 'Camp Daystar,'" corrected Ruby. "Chad Parker told me they've renamed it 'Camp Daystar.'"

"When did you talk to Chad?" asked Meg.

"Why, when I went over for my massage, dear."

"You went over for a massage?" Meg was incredulous.

"Sure. All the ladies in our prayer group are going. He's a licensed Christian Massage Therapist."

"Did you?...You know?..." Meg mimed unbuttoning her blouse.

"Of course. You can't get a massage with your clothes on." Ruby gave Meg a matter-of-fact look. "Oh, don't look so shocked, dear. It's nothing really. You have a sheet covering you. Well...partially. It's all very discreet and very relaxing. Chad has very strong hands."

"*Mother!*" said Meg. "Well, I *never...*"

"Oh, I'll bet you did," laughed Ruby. "Anyway, what were we talking about? Oh, yes. Camp Daystar. They're going to have a retreat on Thanksgiving weekend."

"Is this a national organization?" asked Meg. "Or local?"

"National, I think," I answered. "The Daystar Naturists of God and Love. A Christian nudist association."

"You're not going to join, are you?" Meg asked her mother.

"Of course not," Ruby replied. "I have no intention of becoming a member of DANGL."

Ruby, good as her word, happily paid for our supper, then bid us good night and headed for home. She and Meg lived just a few blocks from the downtown square and it was still early evening. Standing in front of the Ginger Cat, and looking east down Oak Street, we could just make out the fourth street light, the one that marked their house, now glowing yellow in the dusk. Up and down the street children were playing tag, a few dogs were running loose, some families were out walking, others just sitting on their front porch. We saw a couple of bike riders and watched a game of catch start up. Ruby walked briskly in their direction, stopping here and there to chat with her neighbors.

We held hands and watched for what seemed to be a long time, neither of us saying anything. Then we crossed Main Street and wandered into Sterling Park, joining a growing number of people who were intent on enjoying the autumn evening. The breeze picked up and carried with it the scent of pine and fir along with the smell of the wood smoke emanating from chimneys all over town. Meg put her arm in mine and snuggled up against the chill.

"I should have worn a coat."

"That sweater looks pretty warm."

"Not warm enough. And I don't have a hat."

"Would you like to borrow mine?"

"Nope. It'll muss my hair. Anyway, it looks good on you. Very dashing."

She was a dame with a lot of vim. A real looker with brains, moxy, and gams till Tuesday.

"Hey, Toots," I said. "I like your style. I know I've asked you before, but how 'bout you and me gettin' hitched?"

"Absolutely," she answered quietly. Then she kissed me. "I'll be happy to marry you. I was just waiting for you to ask me again."

"Huh?"

"I wanted to make sure you really wanted to marry me. You were under duress the first time you proposed."

"So we could have gotten married a while ago?"

"Oh, yes. But you never asked me again."

"Ah," I said. "I'm sorry. I didn't know the rules. It all makes perfect sense."

"No, it doesn't," she laughed. "But you're sweet to say so. Anyway, I never could resist a man in a hat."

# Chapter 17

"DANGL?" said Pete. "DANGL?"

"Yep," I said. "The Daystar Naturists of God and Love. They'll be here Thanksgiving weekend."

"That's our biggest weekend of the year. The town will be packed. Can we keep them out at the camp?"

I laughed. "I don't think they'll come into town naked. That's why they have a camp. They're not militant nudists. They're Christian nudists."

"Are they still having revival services?"

"That's what the flyer says."

Pete shook his head.

"Are you ready for the debate tonight?" I asked.

"I suppose so. I have a surprise for Cynthia if she goes for my drawers."

"Really? Like what?"

"Like, I'm wearing some!"

I was shocked. "Huh?"

"Boxers. Just till after the election."

I waved my empty coffee cup at Collette who was busy chatting up some out-of-town customers. Pete got up, went to the counter and brought a pot of coffee over to the table.

"Might as well do it myself," he grumped. "Noylene said she'd be in late and Collette keeps passing out salvation tracts to the customers. I'll have to fire her, I guess."

Collette finally walked over to our table. "Need some coffee?"

"No," said Pete sullenly. "We have some. It walked over to our table and poured itself into our cups. Thanks, anyway."

The sarcasm was lost on Collette, who remained disturbingly cheerful. "Have you seen Dave this morning? I need to tell him something."

"I haven't been over to the station," I said. I glanced at my watch. "It's seven in the morning, Collette. Dave probably won't be in until eight or so."

"Would you give my Snookie-Pie a message for me?"

"Sure," I said.

"Would you tell him that God forgives him for his sins?"

"I'll tell him, but I'm sure he knows that." I smiled at Collette but there was fire in her eyes.

"No. I mean specifically for his sins against *me*."

"Oh. *Those* sins."

"Tell him that I forgive him, too. And that I have received a Word of Knowledge that since I've forgiven him, he is to forsake the Great Harlot and come back to the fold."

I looked at Pete. He sipped his coffee and rolled his eyes.

"The Great Harlot?"

"The Jezebel. The Whore of Babylon."

I glanced at Pete again. "Nancy," he said with a shrug.

I let out a slow breath. "I don't believe I'd say that too loudly, Collette," I suggested. "Nancy doesn't take kindly to name calling."

"The Lord is my strength," said Collette with a smile. "Ask and it shall be given—Matthew 7:7. If you abide in me and my words abide in you, ask whatever you wish, and it shall be done for you—John 15:7. Whatever things you ask when you pray, believe that you receive them, and you will have them—Mark 11:24." Collette narrowed her eyes. "I've prayed that Dave will be my husband and I believe it. Whatever I bind in heaven shall be bound on earth—Matthew 16:19. We'll be married before Christmas." She handed me a tract entitled *Name it, Claim it! Fourteen "Can't Miss" Promises Straight From God.*

"You certainly know your scriptures," I said, as Collette walked smugly away.

"Blessed are the insane," said Pete.

"Great news," said Noylene. She'd come in the back door, through the kitchen, and now appeared behind the counter donning a clean white apron. She didn't waste a moment clearing the dirty dishes off the counter and running a rag across the red Formica top.

"Wormy got his loan!" she said, grinning at us and swiping at some toast crumbs.

"I didn't know he was applying for one," I said. "Are you guys buying a house?"

Noylene shook her head. "We have a nice new double-wide."

"New truck?" said Pete.

"Nope. Wormy's buying a Ferris wheel."

I looked at Pete. He sighed.

"We didn't think he would get it," said Noylene, "but then he did what you told him. He put his sperm count down as income."

"I thought you said he was impudent," I said.

"He was, but the little fellers came back," said Noylene. "He went down and got checked. His count was still pretty low, but high enough to get a loan, I guess."

"You know..." I started, but then thought better of it. I shook my head. "Never mind. Tell us about this Ferris wheel."

"He's going to keep it out at the cemetery. For rides and such."

Wormy had bought Kenny Frazier's family farm and turned it into a graveyard. Officially, the name was Woodrow DuPont's Bellefontaine

Cemetery, but it was known locally as Wormy Acres. It featured all the latest in perpetual trappings including "Eternizak," music piped into your coffin for as long as the bill was paid. So far, about twelve folks had availed themselves of the new digs including Junior Jameson, the NASCAR driver, whose wife, Kimmy Jo, had chosen to bury him in his racecar. St. Germaine's other memorial garden, Mountainview Cemetery, was full. That is, plots were no longer being sold. Most families had purchased their final resting places long ago. Any Johnny-Come-Latelys would have to settle for Wormy Acres if they wanted to stay in St. Germaine.

"So," I asked, "why a Ferris wheel?"

"It's for the kids. I mean, most kids don't want to hang around the grave during a funeral. They'll want to have a little fun. So, while the adults do the burying, Wormy's going to run the ride for the kids."

"And why not?" asked Pete, throwing up his hands in dismay. "Why not?" He put his head down on the table.

"What's wrong with him?" asked Noylene.

"It's the stress," I said. "You know he has a debate tonight."

I was walking out the door of the Slab Café when my cell phone rang. It was Nancy.

"Come on over to Patricia Nakamura's house when you get finished with your breakfast."

"Why? What's up?"

"One of those Minques ate her toy poodle."

"Ate it?" I asked.

"Well, didn't actually eat it. Killed it though. The dog..."

"Mr. Cuddles," I heard a voice sob in the background. "His name was Mr. Cuddles."

"Mr. Cuddles," continued Nancy, "was tied up in the backyard. Patricia heard him barking, then heard him not barking."

"She saw it? The Minque?"

"She saw it, but it's long gone. It tore that dog's throat and took off."

"Patricia's sure it wasn't a coyote?"

"She's sure."

"Poor Mr. Cuddles."

"Yeah," said Nancy.

Nancy and I borrowed Patricia's shovel and buried Mr. Cuddles in the back yard. It was all part of the job.

122

"I called Varmit Lemieux over at Blueridge Furs on my way over," I said. "They've caught fifty-seven of the missing Minques. That means there's one hundred thirty still loose. They've got live traps out all over town, but they only have twenty of them and those are the ones they borrowed from Fish and Game."

"If those Minques are mean enough to kill a dog, they're mean enough to hurt a child," said Nancy. "I think the time has come to get rid of the Minques."

"I agree. Let me talk to Varmit again. I'll bet we can get the Fur Farm to offer a bounty. That way they can reclaim some of their losses by getting the pelts back."

St. Barnabas was bustling at four o'clock. The Lemmings were just finishing up *The Living Gobbler* auditions when I walked into the choir room. Moosey met me at the door.

"Hi, Chief! I'm 'ditioning for the *Gobbler*."

"That's great, Moosey. Did you sing?"

"Shore did. I sang *Lead On, O Kinky Turtle*. Father Lemming says I might get to be an Indian."

There were five or six people sitting in the room other than the Lemmings. I looked over at Adrian. He was beaming. "We had some great auditions. Lots of kids, too."

"Everyone likes a Thanksgiving show," I said. "Did you get the script finished?"

"Just now," said Fiona, with a flourish of her red pencil. "Mossy was so good, we just had to add a song for him."

"Moosey," I corrected.

"Whatever," said Fiona. "We'll start rehearsals tomorrow evening. Did you get the belly dancer?"

"Absolutely. Cynthia says she'll be happy to do it."

"Can I wear my Indian suit for Halloween?" Moosey asked. "It's next week and I don't have a costume yet."

"If you get to be an Indian, we'll get you a costume," I promised. "I guess you'll know by tomorrow." I looked over at Adrian for confirmation.

"We'll go over the auditions this evening and post the cast list tomorrow at the first rehearsal. Everyone who auditioned will get a part, that I can promise you. Thank you all for coming."

A few minutes later I was in the choir loft fencing with a Johann Kuhnau organ fugue. A well-constructed Baroque fugue is like a complex work of architecture, and as I wandered my way through the subject and countersubject, the series of expositions and finally deep into the development, I became lost in the music and didn't hear Meg and Ruby come up the steps. I don't know how long they'd been standing there when I reached the final chord, but they both applauded as I lifted my hands off the console.

"Brilliant," said Ruby.

"Not bad," said Meg.

"Not bad?"

"I don't want you to get a big head."

"No chance of that," I laughed. "Too many notes."

"I understand congratulations are in order," said Ruby. "And may I say that it's about time."

"Thank you very much," I said.

""I'm very happy for you both," said Ruby. "Have you two decided on a date?"

I looked over at Meg. She shrugged and smiled.

"Not yet," I said.

"I have a thought," said Meg. "What if we got married during *The Living Gobbler*?"

"Excuse *me*?" said Ruby.

"Well, it certainly would be apropos," said Meg. "Don't you think? But only if we could get Father Tony to perform the actual ceremony. I don't want to have the Lemmings do it."

"Hmm," I said. "We'd have to wear costumes. Maybe dress up as pilgrims."

"As long as we don't have to dress up like giblets," said Meg. "I've already had the thirty-thousand dollar wedding. A pilgrim wedding might be just the right touch. All our friends would already be there."

"This is exactly why I'm marrying you, you know."

"Yes, I know."

Ruby wasn't smiling.

I cut our choir practice short, just taking enough time to put the finishing touches on Sunday's anthem. *How Lovely Is Thy Dwelling Place* from Brahms' *Requiem* was an anthem we'd sung before and an old favorite with the choir. Better than that, if the priest stuck with the lectionary, we'd be right in step.

We headed over to the courthouse for the first mayoral debate in St. Germaine's history. The festivities would be held in the rotunda on the ground floor. Offices and the old, unused courtroom were up the stairs and off the balcony that surrounded and looked down on the rotunda. There was plenty of room for the hundred or so chairs that the St. Germaine chapter of the Daughters of the American Revolution, headed by Wynette Winslow, had set up in front of the dais, beautifully draped with red, white, and blue political bunting. Two podiums stood on the platform from which, according to the format that Pete had shown me earlier, the candidates would answer questions from the floor and from each other. Billy Hixon was the moderator, since he was also the St. Germaine Election Commissioner, but his real job, according to Pete, was to call for questions and break up fistfights.

We were about fifteen minutes early. In addition to most of the choir members, there were maybe twenty other folks milling about exchanging pleasantries. I noticed Calvin Denton, the editor of *The Tattler,* sitting in the front row with pad in hand. Marjorie had a placard on a yardstick proclaiming her allegiance to Cynthia's candidacy. Marjorie and Pete had a long running feud stemming from her insistence on raising chickens in her backyard on Poplar Avenue, a scant two blocks from downtown. She'd already spoken to Cynthia and gotten her okay on the chicken question. Her poster had Cynthia's name in handwritten letters and was decorated with ribbons, crepe paper streamers and a couple of homemade bumper-stickers.

Meg and I were scouting out seats when we were approached by a very large and very exuberant African-American woman.

"Hi, y'all!" she said. "So glad you could make it!" She pressed a brochure into my hand and turned to Meg. "May I assume that your husband will not be influencing your decision on whom to vote for?"

"You may so assume," said Meg, "but he's not my husband. And that was a very slick question. Separating our votes like that."

The woman beamed. "It's what I do." She stuck out a hand the size of a canned ham. "My name's Crayonella. Crayonella Washington. I work with Cynthia Johnsson." She looked in my direction and glowered. "I think I know who *you* are."

"Hayden Konig at your service. I'm very pleased to meet you," I said. "I'd heard that Cynthia had hired a publicist."

"A political advisor."

"Exactly," I said, looking down at the color brochure. Cynthia, decked out in her belly-dancing regalia, adorned the front. She was pictured in full swerve with both hands poised artistically above her head. You could almost hear the "ching" of the finger-cymbals and the rattle of the bells on her hips. It was a good photo. Really good. I opened the brochure. There was Cynthia again, this time in a dark blue business suit, her blonde hair pulled back and a no-nonsense look on her face. Another good photo. Underneath was a caption "Cynthia Johnsson for Mayor—A New Face, A New Step, A New Direction." A brief bio followed with a few bullet points highlighting some general political positions.

"Everyone knows she's a belly dancer," said Crayonella. "No sense in hiding the fact. May as well make the most of it."

"I have to agree," I said. "In fact, I'm going to hang this brochure on the bulletin board at work."

Crayonella sniffed. "But will you vote for her?"

"No. I don't live within the city limits. But I'm very impressed."

"How about you?" she asked Meg. "I hope we can count on your vote. It's high time that St. Germaine had a new mayor."

"I'll certainly consider it," said Meg.

"Will Cynthia be belly-dancing this evening?" I asked.

"Good question," said Crayonella. "Here's another. Will Mr. Moss be wearing underwear, and if so, is he prepared to prove it?"

At eight o'clock, Billy got up and walked to one of the podium mikes. Cynthia and Pete followed him onto the dais and each took a seat in one of the two chairs. Cynthia was in her two-piece, tailored blue suit, looking very accomplished and capable. Her hair was tied loosely behind her head and she had discarded her contacts in favor of a pair of fashionable glasses that any Fifth Avenue exec would have been comfortable wearing. Pete was wearing his Hawaiian shirt, khaki expando-pants and sandals. His gray hair was tied back in a ponytail. I did notice that he put on his good earring and a nice gold chain obviously left over from the '80s.

"Settle down, you people," Billy said, tapping on the microphone. "Is this thing on?" It wasn't, of course. It wasn't even hooked up. The rotunda didn't have a sound system and the ladies of the D.A.R. hadn't thought to bring one in.

"Pay attention!" Billy hollered. We did.

"Welcome to the St. Germaine mayoral debate. I'm in charge, so don't go yelling at each other or I'll throw your butts out of here."

I looked around the room. The crowd had swelled to fifty and was sprinkled across the hundred chairs giving the impression of a larger audience. It looked like a sedate group, all except for Marjorie, who was waving her sign and obviously chomping at the bit, waiting to be called on.

"We'll start with opening statements," said Billy. "Cynthia will go first."

Cynthia got up and walked to her podium. She adjusted her glasses and smoothed her skirt with both hands.

"Good evening," she said. "I would like to say, right off the bat, that no matter what any of the voters might say, I don't want to make this campaign about whether Mayor Moss wears any underwear or not. I refuse to discuss it."

I looked over at Crayonella Washington, her moon face smiling and nodding.

"Hey, just one second," interrupted Pete.

"Quiet, Pete," said Billy. "You'll get your turn."

"But..."

"Hush up!" said Billy, waggling a threatening finger.

Cynthia continued. "No, I won't have Mr. Moss' unsanitary personal habits become an issue when we should be concentrating on what's really important for the future of St. Germaine. I ask you..." She gestured toward the audience. "...what do *you* think are the pressing issues?"

"Education," came a call from the back.

"Property taxes," came another.

"Gas prices," said a third.

"Chickens," hollered Marjorie, waving her sign.

"And new businesses," added Crayonella, in her loud voice.

"Exactly," said Cynthia. "We're tired of this lackadaisical effort by our city officials to address these problems."

"*What* problems?" asked Pete, genuinely confused. "These aren't problems."

"Quiet," warned Billy again.

"Our childrens' test scores are down, property taxes and gas prices are going up, we *still* have no cable TV, and the new businesses that Pete invited into town won't be paying any taxes for two years."

"And our chickens aren't safe!" added Marjorie.

"Wait!" said Pete. "That's just not..."

"I'm not going to tell you again," said Billy. "Next time, you forfeit your opening remarks. Them's the rules."

Pete slumped back in his chair and folded his arms across his chest in disgust.

Cynthia went on for another minute decrying the woeful state of our little township, finally finishing with "We don't want any more excuses. No matter what you may think of Mayor Moss' failure to wear underwear, his failure to provide this town with badly needed services is the real crime."

Marjorie stood and gave her a standing ovation, waving her poster wildly. Cynthia nodded and took her seat.

"Okay, Pete," said Billy. "Your turn."

"I hardly know where to begin," said Pete. "Listen. Sure, the kids' test scores are down, but that's not our fault. We don't even have a school! I suggest you blame the Watauga County Board of Education. Secondly, property taxes go up when you vote them up and I have nothing to do with gas prices. Thirdly, the cable company still hasn't run their fiber-optics out this far."

"Sounds like more excuses," called Crayonella.

"Quiet," said Billy.

"The new businesses pay taxes. They just don't pay the privilege tax. It's only a couple of hundred dollars a year."

"And that's a lot of money," called Marjorie.

"They more than make up for that in the sales tax that they generate for the city."

"Political double-talk," called a voice.

"What about my chickens?"

Pete sighed.

"And why aren't you wearing any drawers?" shouted Arlen Pearl. "You a communist, or something?"

"I am wearing drawers," insisted Pete.

"Let's see!" Arlen hollered.

"I'm not dropping my pants right here," said Pete.

"That's okay," said Arlen. "Let Billy look. I'll take his word for it."

"Fine," said Pete. He grabbed the front of his expando pants, pulled out the front about four inches and faced Billy.

"I'm not lookin' in there," said Billy. "You gotta be crazy."

"Oh, for heaven's sakes," said Cynthia, getting back to her feet.

"Wait!" I shouted, standing up. But Cynthia had already walked up behind Pete and looked over his shoulder.

"Oh, my God!" she shrieked. Pete, startled, let go of his waistband and his pants snapped shut. I sat down heavily.

"This ain't good," I said to Meg.

"You said you were wearing underwear!" Cynthia said, the color draining from her face.

"Well...I...Billy...umm...I didn't think anyone would actually look."

"You were holding open your pants!"

"Yeah...but..."

"But, nothing," said Crayonella, standing up and pointing an accusing finger at Pete. "You were probably the one who invited those Dingle-Dangles into town on Thanksgiving. And now you've gone and flashed Cynthia."

"Not on purpose," said Pete. "And those nudists bought the old camp. I had nothing to do with it. Hey, anybody remember when Cynthia belly-danced for President Clinton?"

"What nudists?" said Noylene. "We got nudists?"

"They're buying Camp Possumtickle," said Cynthia.

"How come we didn't know about this?" asked Carol Sterling.

"Probably because Mayor Moss was keeping it quiet until after the election next week," said Crayonella.

"It was in the paper," said Pete, helplessly. "Last week, in the transfer of deeds."

"No, it wasn't," said Calvin Denton of *The Tattler*. "I left it out. I had to put in the article about Judy Barr coming home to visit her mother."

"It's a gol-danged cover-up!" hollered Arlen.

"What about my chickens?" yelled Marjorie.

"Fergit about chickens," said Noylene, "What about them nudists?"

"I...uh...they're *Christian* nudists!" stuttered Pete, then decided to take a different tack. "Marjorie's chickens cannot be allowed to run around the town square."

"I think they're quaint," said Carol. "And a lot easier to live with than a bunch of nudists, Christian or otherwise."

"The nudists will stay at their camp. If they come into town, they will be wearing clothes," proclaimed Pete. "If they aren't, Chief Konig will arrest them and throw them in jail. Isn't that right, Chief?"

"We don't have a jail," I said. "I guess we could put them in the Beautifery."

"I don't want no nudists in the Beautifery," said Noylene. "How about in the back of your truck?"

"What about those giant rats?" asked Rebecca. "I heard that one of them ate Patricia's poodle."

"We're working on the giant rat problem," I said, wondering how I got into this. "That is, the police department is working on it under the diligent guidance of the mayor."

"Diligent guidance, my Aunt Millie's butt!" said Marjorie.

"That went well," I said to Pete as we walked back to the Slab for a cup of coffee and a piece of pie. The "debate," if it could be so described, had gone on for another hour and consisted mainly of Pete dodging accusations and Cynthia dangling his shortcomings in public. Crayonella was very effective at keeping the chatter focused on Pete.

"Sarcasm does not become you," said Pete, shaking his head. He pulled out his keys and unlocked the front door of the café, then led us in, flipping on the lights as he went.

"Grab some pie and take a seat. I'll make some coffee," he said, walking behind the counter and starting to fill the pot. Billy and Elaine walked in a minute later, followed by Carol, Bev, and Georgia.

"Is the pie free?" Bev asked. "A bribe, perhaps?"

"Sure," sighed Pete. "Why not?"

"What kind of pie do we have?" asked Billy, rubbing his hands together. I was over at the pie case and happy to answer. "Pumpkin, Boston cream, apple," I said, taking each pie out of the case and putting it on the counter. "And rhubarb."

"Pumpkin, please," said Meg, with the rest of the orders following quickly.

The door opened again and Cynthia peeked in. Crayonella was standing behind her.

"No hard feelings?" she said to Pete.

"Nah. C'mon in. Have a piece of pie."

"I do like pie," said Crayonella with a big grin. "Hey, let me ask you something. Why on earth didn't you wear your drawers? Especially tonight?"

"I tried," said Pete. "I just couldn't do it."

# Chapter 18

It was a dark and stormy night, as dark and stormy as the times that try men's souls; the best of times, the worst of times, and all children, except one, grow up. I walked down the street, rain splashing off my hat and running down my back, a walking advertisement for AFLAC, complete with the honking that I suddenly noticed was coming from my own nose. I was cold, I was wet, and I was a gumshoe. Life was good.

I stopped at the corner, dug my hands deep into the pockets of my old trench, the one I'd gotten off my old partner, Sam Manilla, after he'd been snipped, clipped, chilled, and fitted for a Chicago overcoat during the cat milk scare at the local elementary school. There was a clue somewhere in this story. I oughta know—I put it there. It kept gnawing away at my brain like one of those praise-choruses with only one verse, repeating the same words over and over until you either gave your life to Jesus or killed the woman sitting next to you, the one who kept poking you in the eye with her Rexella Van Impe Study Bible.

The clock tower struck twelve. I looked across the street and there she was, draped in mink from her mink umbrella to her mink high heels. I recognized her right away. I wasn't a stranger to the world of opera. In fact, as a liturgical detective and a member of the Bishop's Council on Councils, I knew all the singers in the district. Most paid choir singers were opera wannabes. Not this sheila. She was the real shaloopie.

"Things are heating up, I see," said Meg. "An opera singer. I'll bet she's a mezzo."

"Stop reading ahead."

"How can I read ahead? You haven't written it yet."

"Stop guessing the plot then."

"It's not exactly brain surgery," Meg laughed. "The title is *The Mezzo Wore Mink,* and now a woman shows up draped in mink. Could it be that she's a mezzo?"

"Harrumph!"

"Did you ask the Lemmings about our wedding plans?" Meg asked. She walked over to the leather sofa and flopped onto the down-filled cushions without spilling a drop of her wine. There was a fire in the fireplace and Tchaikovsky on the stereo. I left my hat on the table by the typewriter and joined Meg on the couch.

"I *did* ask Father Lemming and he said it was just a great idea, dontcha know."

131

"And Tony?"

"Yep. I called Tony and he'll be happy to perform the ceremony."

"Then we should tell our friends, I suppose."

"I suppose we should," I said.

"I'd like to schedule a meeting," said Ian Burch, PhD, entering the station two steps behind his prominent nose and announcing his presence in a piercing counter-tenor. He adjusted his glasses and sniffed.

"You're here, aren't you?" said Dave, glancing up from his computer.

"A meeting with Chief Konig."

"Sure," I said, overhearing and coming out of my office. "What's up?"

"I have been contacted by Dr. Adrian Lemming. He'd like to utilize my Early Musik Consort to play for his Thanksgiving show. He told me you were in charge of the musical arrangements."

"Well, I guess I am. I'm playing for some of it and arranging a couple of hymns. What does Dr. Lemming have in mind?"

"He said that was up to me. I told him we had our own costumes."

"Excellent," I said. "Will there be codpieces involved?"

"Oh, yes," said Ian. "We have all the necessary accessories. We also have two people who are well schooled in the Renaissance dance. Do you think that we might include a galliard or perhaps a coranto?"

"I think it *must* be included," chimed in Dave. "It really *must*."

"I have to agree," I said, with a grin. "I'm sure that the Lemmings would welcome a galliard or two."

"Wonderful," said Ian, a discolored smile splitting his face and breath reminiscent of rotten cabbage wafting across the counter. "This will be great fun."

Nancy came through the office door. Ian looked at her without acknowledgement, then turned back to me.

"We also have some English pieces from the 17th century. They would be just the sort of things that the pilgrims might have liked to dance to. Very authentic," he said smugly.

"Pilgrims didn't dance," said Nancy, walking around Ian Burch and sitting in her chair. "They hated all kinds of music."

"You're thinking of the Puritans," squeaked Ian. "The Pilgrims came over from Holland by way of England. They were a good-natured, fun-loving people who loved life and insisted on the freedom of choice. The Puritans, on the other hand, were extremely intolerant of any points of view which conflicted with their own dogma." He looked over his glasses, down his long nose and frowned at Nancy.

"So," said Dave, "dancing it is!"

We were suddenly interrupted by a woman's scream rattling down the street, loud enough to be heard through the plate glass window of the police station. What echoed through the office was not a high-pitched scream of fear, but a scream laden with pain. Nancy, Dave, and I banged out the door, looked across the park in the direction of the commotion, and seeing the crowd gathering in front of Eden Books, took off at a run leaving Ian Burch, PhD, standing in the doorway.

"Oh, my God!" I heard Cynthia say as we ran up. "Don't move. I'll call the ambulance." Cynthia, draped in her Ginger Cat waitress apron, was kneeling down in front of someone, surrounded by seven or eight people who had raced out of the restaurant to see what the uproar was all about. We pushed our way through and found Hyacinth Turnipseed moaning on the sidewalk. Her glasses were askew, her eyes squinched shut and her face a mask of pain. Her back arched and her hands clawed at the unyielding fabric of the sidewalk. The peculiarity that drew every eye, however, was Hyacinth's right leg. At the knee, the leg had discovered a new angle—an angle that gave a whole new meaning to the term "unnatural."

"Jiminy Christmas," said Dave. "That's gotta hurt!"

Nancy was already on her phone calling the ambulance. I squatted down next to Cynthia and looked at Hyacinth. She'd passed out.

"They're already in town," Nancy said, flipping her phone closed. "Asthma attack on Cherry Avenue. They'll be here in two minutes."

"Shouldn't we try to put her leg back?" Cynthia asked.

I shook my head. "The paramedics will be here in a jiffy and they'll get her leg stabilized."

Cynthia shuddered.

"Anyone know what happened?" asked Nancy.

"I know exactly," said Annette Passaglio. "I was having lunch and looking out the window and saw three of those Minquey things eating the flowers in the pots outside the bookstore. Hyacinth came out with a broom to scare them off, I think. She took a whack at one of them and it attacked her. The other ones, too."

I looked skeptical.

"Well, it didn't really attack her," said another patron. "I saw it as well. She was trying to hit one with a broom and the others sort of got tangled in her legs. Then she fell down and screamed."

"They did too attack!" insisted Annette. "And I want to know what you're going to do about it?"

"We're after them," Dave assured her. "They'll all be rounded up before long."

"Hmmph," grunted Annette as the ambulance screamed up to the curb, siren blaring.

133

"I have some news," said Nancy. She came into my office with a big sheaf of papers in her hand. Ian Burch hadn't waited for us.

"Good news?"

"Depends," said Nancy with a shrug. "It's about Davis Boothe."

"Hey, Dave," I called. "C'mon in here and bring the donuts. We seem to have missed lunch."

I sat down behind my desk. Dave came in with the aforementioned consumables and he and Nancy took the two seats across from me.

"I have some news, too," I said. "Payment on the life insurance policy that Upper Womb Ministries took out on Davis was denied. It was a fifty thousand dollar term policy, but it had the standard suicide clause, so no payoff. If it turns out to be murder, though, the Upper Womb can collect. Now, what's your news?"

"We've identified the victim," said Nancy.

"Which one?" said Dave, choosing a chocolate glazed with pink sprinkles.

"Davis Boothe," said Nancy, turning to the first page of her dossier. "Or rather, Josh Kenisaw."

Dave stopped chewing with pink sprinkles still on his lips.

"Davis Boothe is Josh Kenisaw?" I asked.

"Right. Fingerprints confirm it. They even sent his dental records. I'll check with Kent Murphee, but I'm almost positive it's him."

"Do we have a story on Josh Kenisaw?"

"Do we ever!" said Nancy. "Ever hear of Jack DeMille?"

"Sure," I said. "Senator from Iowa or one of those corn states." Dave had resumed eating.

"Kansas," corrected Nancy. I nodded and she continued.

"Oil billionaire from Topeka. His daughter was a freshman at Washburn University and was killed in a drunk driving accident."

"Let me guess," I said. "Josh Kenisaw was the driver."

"Yep. He was a seventeen-year-old freshman at Washburn as well and was coming home from a frat party with Lori DeMille in the car. He flipped the car and hit a tree doing about sixty. She was killed instantly. He broke an arm and had some facial injuries. His blood alcohol level was point-two-four."

"Wow. He was stone-cold drunk. I'm surprised he could get the key in the ignition." I reached for a donut. Glazed. Nancy turned a page.

"He was charged as an adult. No surprise there. Senator DeMille also got the charges changed from vehicular homicide to second-degree murder and the prosecutor indicated they weren't going to accept a plea. They were going to make an example of Josh. Bail was refused. I'm thinking that the judge was a friend of the Senator."

"Probably," I said. "What was Josh looking at?"

"In Kansas, the maximum sentence for second-degree murder is ten years and three months if there's no other criminal history. But Josh had pleaded guilty to shoplifting when he was sixteen and had been given a suspended sentence. In fact, he was still on probation. I guess that's how the prosecutor got it admitted, even though he was a juvenile. He was looking at life with a possibility of parole in nineteen years. They were going for the max."

I let out a slow breath.

"About halfway through the trial, Josh went into the bathroom during a break and disappeared. They don't know how he escaped, but he was gone."

"Did he have a police escort?"

"No, a bailiff. The baliff's excuse was that he was busy talking to a reporter. The judge ordered the trial to continue declaring that 'the defendant has voluntarily absented himself from the court and is deemed to have waived the right to be physically present at the trial.' Josh Kenisaw was found guilty and sentenced to life."

"And never heard from again," said Dave.

"Right," said Nancy. "That was twelve years ago."

"And he shows up here."

"Yep. Somehow got a Social Security card, then a driver's license. I guess it's not that difficult, really."

"He'd be twenty-nine," I said absently. "His driver's license says thirty-two. Nice touch."

"Here's the kicker," said Nancy. "There's a bounty on Josh. Put up by the Senator."

"How much?" Dave asked.

"Two million dollars."

"Holy smokes!" I said.

"Can we...?" Dave started.

"No, we can't," answered Nancy. "We're law enforcement officers."

"I could quit," said Dave.

"You know what this means?" I said.

Nancy nodded. "Bounty hunter."

"Did you two find anything in *The Sketchbook of Geoffrey Crayon?*"

"We went through it page by page," she said. "I didn't see anything out of the ordinary except Washington Irving's autograph. Was he looking at that?"

"I don't know. He was flipping pages, then closed it and took off. I looked through it, too. I didn't see anything."

"Something in one of the stories?" asked Dave. "Legend of Sleepy Hollow? Rip Van Winkle? Those are the only two I know."

I picked up the book, still on Nancy's desk and flipped to the appendix in the back. "I've heard of a few more of these, but there's nothing here that would be considered well known except for those two."

"We can go through it again," suggested Dave.

I shook my head. "I must be missing something. Do the authorities know we have him?"

"Not yet," said Nancy. "All I did was send in the prints and request the FBI file. It won't be long though. I expect some grease has been applied to these particular wheels."

"Hi, Kent," I said. "How're things at the coroner's office?"

"Surprisingly busy. It must be that time of year. Everyone's trying to die before the holidays so they won't get depressed."

"Sounds like a good plan. I will do my best to arrange my demise accordingly."

"See that you do. I hate to get bodies in the summer. They swell up like..."

"I get the picture," I said, cutting him off. "Now, down to business. You still have Davis Boothe in the morgue."

"You need him?"

"I don't know yet, but I expect I will."

"Hang on."

I waited for a couple of minutes and then Kent came back on the line.

"Hmm. Bad news."

"Bad news?"

"I had a tag on him indicating for us to hold him for two weeks. Two weeks was up a couple of days ago. I guess we needed the freezer space. Keith sent him over to the crematorium on Tuesday."

A phone call confirmed our worst suspicions. Davis had been cremated late on Wednesday night, just scant hours ago. I explained, in no uncertain terms, to the crematorium employee—Ruby's employee— that I would be there with a warrant in an hour or two and not to touch anything.

"You don't need a warrant, do you, dear?" asked Ruby. "I'm sure I can give you permission to search the place."

"Then I guess I don't," I replied with a smile. "I just wanted to scare the help. They don't need to be touching anything until we get there."

"May I go along?" asked Ruby. "I've been out there and talked to the boys. Dale gave me a tour. But I don't really know how these things work."

"You sure?" asked Nancy. "It's not for the faint of heart."

"I'm hardly that."

"Let's go," I said. "We'll take the truck."

The crematorium was located about five miles out of town on Old Chambers Road. We rumbled up the dirt driveway and stopped in front of a large, ugly cinderblock building with two large chimneys jutting from the center of the roofline. There was no sign or office that we could see. A set of metal double doors looked to be the only point of egress. I looked at the lock—a heavy deadbolt—as we opened the doors and entered the building.

There were florescent shop lights hanging throughout the large, open room, but about half of the bulbs were out with another two or three flickering desperately. The twelve-foot high walls were flecked with soot and the sunlight tried in vain to break through the dirt-covered panes of the four large windows placed high on the walls. The effect was that of permanent dusk, and it took a moment for our eyes to adjust.

"Maybe I'll get those lights fixed," said Ruby. "And wash those windows."

As our eyes adjusted, we saw two men at the far end of the room. If they knew we were there, they didn't look up from their card game. Just behind them we saw two stainless steel ovens, gleaming modern appliances in the midst of 1950s dereliction.

"Hey there," I called out. "Hayden Konig. Police."

"C'mon in," said one of the men without looking up. "I cain't git up right now. If'n I look away, Panty'll cook the deck. He cheats like a stinkin' weasel."

I knew the two men who worked here. Everyone in town knew them, although they rarely ventured into town. Dale and Panty Patterson were brothers. Some folks said they were twins, but I don't think that even Dale or Panty knew for sure. If they were twins, they weren't identical. Panty was an albino. Dale had a high forehead and fine blonde hair, but he had some color in his skin. Both of them had very small, piggy features. Panty had webbed fingers on his left hand. They were, together, a very disquieting pair. I'd put their ages somewhere between forty-five and dead. It wasn't easy to tell. Both were dressed in overalls, white, collared shirts buttoned all the way up, and work boots.

They'd been working up here at the crematorium since long before I'd come to St. Germaine. I'd heard that they had a house somewhere in the hollers, but no one that I knew had any first hand knowledge of their living arrangements. No one was that curious.

We walked over to the two brothers. They were playing a game of "War," flipping over cards as fast as they could grab them, and Panty was getting the better of Dale.

"Could you boys hold up for a couple minutes?" I asked. "We have to talk to you."

Dale looked up at us and when he did, Panty grabbed a handful of his discards with a whoop.

"See what you did?" Dale said, throwing down a card in disgust. "Now I gotta buy him an ice cream." Panty gave us a gapped grin.

"Well, what'chu want?" Dale spit something unrecognizable onto the floor in front of Nancy.

"We need to see Davis Boothe," said Nancy, her eyes narrowing.

"Like I *tole* you," said Dale, full of venom. "He's already burnt."

"Now, boys," said Ruby gently, "you remember me?"

Dale and Panty both eyeballed her in the dim light, recognition crossing both their squinty visages at the same time.

"Yes'm," they both muttered, hanging their heads.

"I'm the boss, right?"

"Yes'm," came the reply.

"So you help these police officers any way you can, okay?"

"Yes'm."

"So, Dale," I said, "could you show me the ashes?"

Dale nodded and got to his feet. Panty followed his lead. They pushed their chairs under the table and walked the few feet over to the cremators. The two doors were both closed and there didn't seem to be a handle that I could see.

"How do you open it?" I asked.

Dale shrugged. "Panty's in charge of that. He runs the pooter."

I looked over at Panty. He nodded and grinned again.

"I run the computer," he said in a soft southern drawl. "Dale helps me with the rest."

We all blinked. Not one of us had ever heard Panty Patterson speak.

"Would you like me to show you how the crematorium operates?"

We nodded dumbly.

"It's almost all computerized now." Panty pointed to a console beside the ovens. "We had one of the first automated systems in the country. Of course, in the early days, I had to do the programming. When we started, there wasn't any software. Now, all the ovens come with software already installed."

I finally found my voice. "You have some...umm...education," I managed.

"Yessir. I have a Masters in computer science from Georgia Tech."

138

"And Dale?" I asked.

"I been clean through the second grade," said Dale, proudly.

"Forgive the charade. I just don't have much use for people most of the time," said Panty. "And someone has to take care of Dale."

"I understand," I said. And I did. "If you'd show us the operation, we'd appreciate it."

Panty nodded and walked over to the console. He pushed some buttons and the door to the oven slid up revealing a stainless steel tray containing Davis' cremated remains.

"The cremator," explained Panty, "is basically a furnace capable of generating temperatures up to eighteen hundred degrees Fahrenheit. I can monitor the furnace during cremation and, if necessary, control the temperature. The computer won't open the doors until the cremator has reached operating temperature and once the body is in, we can't open it back up until everything has cooled. The entire process usually takes about two hours for cremation and another four hours to cool down."

"Do you cremate the remains in a coffin?" asked Ruby.

"Depends," said Panty. "Usually in a wooden casket, but Davis was in a cardboard box. Most coffin manufacturers provide a line of caskets specially built for cremation."

"What happens next?" asked Nancy.

"We can show you, if you'd like," said Panty. "We were just getting ready to finish up when you called."

Panty and Dale slid the tray out of the oven and moved it onto a stainless steel table with raised edges. They emptied the contents onto the table and Dale spread them out with a metal dustpan. All that was left of Davis was dry bone fragments.

"Where're the ashes?" asked Nancy.

"There aren't any," answered Panty. "During the cremation process, most of the body, especially the organs and other soft tissue, is vaporized and oxidized due to the heat. All that's left is about six pounds of bone."

"What's Dale doing?" Ruby asked.

"I'se lookin' fer metal," said Dale.

"When we get the bodies," Panty explained, "the jewelry's already been removed. Pacemakers, too, if the deceased had one, because they're likely to explode. But sometimes the body contains other metals. Teeth fillings are the most common, but these days we find titanium hips, surgical pins, even bullets. Some of it will have melted."

"And you sift it out?" I said.

"Gots to," said Dale. "Wrecks the grinder."

Panty smiled and put a hand on Dale's shoulder. "After we sift through the bone fragments, we put them into the cremulator. A grinder, really. It pulverizes the bones into powder. What comes out is known as cremains. It has the appearance of ash and sand. If we miss a bit of metal and it gets ground up with the bones, we catch it when we sift the cremains after the process is complete."

"So, it's not really ashes," Ruby said.

"Not really."

"Did you find any metal?" I asked.

"Not a lick," said Dale.

"May I look?"

"Hep yerself."

I motioned to Nancy and we both bent over the table and poked through the remains. I used Dale's dustpan. Nancy used her pen.

"May I ask what you're looking for?" asked Panty, looking over my shoulder.

"Metal," I said.

"Maybe he didn't have any."

"Nancy," I said, "did you bring those medical files?"

"Right over there." Nancy walked over to the card table where she'd laid her folder.

"Get out Davis' x-ray, will you. The one that showed the embolism."

Nancy came back over holding a transparent film in her hand. "There's the embolism," she said. "Kent circled it."

"Look at this though. Seven...no, eight fillings and a whole lot of metal bridge work. Three pins in his jaw and a metal plate in his palate. From the wreck."

Nancy looked confused. "So this isn't Davis?"

"It's Davis, all right," said Panty. "I knew Davis Boothe. I checked him when they brought him in."

"When did they deliver him?" I asked.

"We're here every day at three o'clock. If there's going to be a delivery, we'll get a call by four. Deliveries—including Davis—come by five. We check them in, look for jewelry and get them ready for cremation."

"Then you cremate them?" asked Nancy.

"No, we wait until two a.m. There's a bit of an odor, but no one complains in the middle of the night. We finish up the next afternoon when we come in."

"You stay here all that time?"

"No, we go home after all the deliveries. Around dinner time usually. We come back after midnight. Then we leave again around four a.m. after the cremations. We very rarely have more than a double header and, as you can see, we have two ovens."

140

"Did you check Davis before you cremated him?"

"You mean after we got back?"

"Yes."

Panty shrugged. "No need. The box was already on the trolley ready to be rolled in."

"So someone switched the body?" Ruby asked.

"Maybe," said Nancy. "But if they did, there had to be at least two of them. Davis was a big boy—one hundred and eighty pounds. One person couldn't have done it alone."

"I'm guessing you lock up when you leave," I said.

"Of course."

"And who has a key?"

"Just us," said Panty. "Me, Dale, and Miss Ruby here."

"I don't have a key," said Ruby.

"Oh. I'm sorry. I thought Miss Thelma probably gave you hers."

"No."

"I know who has a key," said Nancy with a smile.

"Me, too," I said.

"What?" said Ruby. "What am I missing?"

"What you're missing," I said, "is a two million dollar head."

# Chapter 19

The old Chevy truck rumbled out of the crematorium driveway and onto Old Chambers Road. Ruby was sandwiched in between Nancy and me in the front seat. There wasn't any chitchat going on. I knew that Nancy was thinking and I was doing the same.

"Okay," Ruby said finally, "who has the other key?"

"This is an ongoing investigation," I said. "So you can't say anything."

"Of course I won't say anything. We're family."

Nancy's head came around quickly. She looked across Ruby and I caught her stare out of the corner of my eye.

"Family?" she said.

"Hmm," I said. "I guess the cat's out of the bag. Meg and I are getting married."

"Really?" said Nancy, just a little too sweetly.

"Meg told you, didn't she?"

"Yep."

"Did she tell you when?"

"She did. The culmination of *The Living Gobbler*. I can hardly wait."

"Back to the key," said Ruby.

"Ah yes, the key," I answered. "Who has the key? That is the question before us."

"It is," said Ruby. "Who has the other key?"

"Nancy, do you know who has the other key?" I asked.

"Yes."

"You're a fine detective," I said.

"Thank you."

"The *key!*" said Ruby. "Dadburnit!"

"Who has the key, Lieutenant Parsky?" I said.

"Why, it's elementary," said Nancy. "The person who has the key is the person who killed Thelma."

"And who is that?" asked Ruby.

I shrugged. "The first question is not 'who.' The first question is 'why.'"

"Why?"

"Because that's the first question," I said. "The second question is 'who.' Or maybe 'what.'"

"Oh, stop it. I mean why did whoever did it, do it?"

"To get the key."

Ruby sighed heavily. "You're not going to tell me, are you?"

"Nope."

Sunday comes early and so does death. It's the motto of the liturgical detective and as Saturday night sloshed over into Sunday like a fat man on a waterbed, the mink-clad heiress to the Polovetsian dancing fortune gave me a twirl and a come-hither look worthy of her reputation.

Her name was Barbara--Barbara Seville--and she was a mezzo. Some said she slid to the top of the opera world on her husband's money: that before she married Aristotle bin Laden, she'd been demoted to seamstress and spent most of her time in the wings tucking up the frills instead of on the stage doing the opposite: that now that she was back, she ate tenors for dinner and baritones for dessert with the occasional bass as a mid-morning snack. She was a Venus, though, and as rich as Turtle Cheese Cake. I wouldn't mind a toss with a world-class looker who could afford to boost a few expenses.

"Miss Seville," I said, tipping my hat.

"Call me Diva," she said with a smile. "Or Mommy. I like it when men call me Mommy."

I heard bells.

Alarm bells.

"I'm enjoying this story," said Rebecca, as the choir gathered in the loft for the Sunday service. "I'm not saying it's good, mind you, but I am enjoying it."

"I heard you and Meg are getting married," said Georgia. "Through the grapevine, of course. It seems that I didn't get an invitation."

"No one got an invitation," I said. "But you'll all be there, dressed up as the four major food groups and singing Thanksgiving hymns."

"Really?" said Phil. "The four major food groups?"

"Beer, chili, garlic and cigars," said Mark Wells.

"I thought chocolate was in there somewhere," said Elaine.

"I don't think so," said Mark. "That would make five. Chocolate is probably in the garlic group."

It was during Father Lemming's sermon on the parable of the Pharisee and the Publican that the first gunshots were heard. Granted, it was deer season, and we were used to hearing shots from time to time echoing through the mountains, but there was a ban on hunting within the city limits and these sounded close. Very close.

"Are you going out there?" asked Meg.

"No. I'll give Nancy a call though."

I walked down the steps and into the narthex, dialing Nancy's number as I went. I wasn't sure, but I figured I still had about ten minutes before Father Lemming finished up and I had to play a chorus of *Seek Ye First* that he had thoughtfully inserted after the sermon. Ten minutes, I figured, if the gunshots didn't unnerve him. Nancy answered her cell on the first ring.

"I'm on it," she said, before I could utter a word. Then she flipped her phone closed and cut me off.

I'd only just reached the bottom of the steps by the time our phone call ended, so I turned around and trudged back up to the choir loft. It was a good thing I did, because the gunshots had spooked Father Lemming and, being somewhat new to the pulpit, he had wrapped his sermon up by wondering aloud who would be shooting outside the church, dontcha know, and whether the vestry had an exigency plan for the safety of the priest in case of terrorist attacks, many of which—he had heard—were directed at the clergy. I arrived back in the loft just as Meg was coming to find me. She pointed to the organ and I scurried onto the bench just as Father Lemming finished announcing the hymn.

The gunshots ceased sometime during the confession, which was a good thing because the choir was getting antsy about Mr. Brahms and Mr. Winchester sharing equal billing. We managed to do Mr. B proud and the rest of the service followed without too much disruption. When I finished the postlude, Meg and I skipped coffee hour and headed out the front doors to find Nancy. I had my phone out to call her, but I needn't have bothered. She met us out front.

"Two kids from the university," Nancy said as we walked up. "Both of them had hunting licenses."

"Not for shooting deer in town," I said. "It sounded like a war out here. How many deer did they get? Or were they just bad shots?"

"They were bad shots all right, but they weren't after deer. They were after Minques."

"Minques?"

Nancy handed me a torn ad from the *Watauga Democrat*. I scanned it quickly.

"So Blueridge Farms has offered a bounty."

"Thirty dollars a Minque. No closed season or bag limit."

"Did they get any?"

"Four," answered Nancy. "Two in the mums in front of the library, one in the park, one behind the church. I explained that there would be no more hunting in the city limits."

"Did you let them keep the Minques?"

Nancy shrugged. "Yeah."

I nodded. "Well, that was a hundred and twenty bucks for a half hour's work. Pretty good pay for a couple of college kids."

A Monday morning meeting of the St. Germaine police force was synonymous with breakfast at the Slab Café. As Monday mornings went, this one wasn't shaping up to be one of the better ones unless you happened to be an otter. The weatherman had predicted cold. Cold and wet. For once, he'd been right. The rain, misting when I arose at about six, was now coming down in buckets. I'd braved the storm, slogged into the Slab, shook off the weather like a sheepdog, and hung my dripping jacket behind the door. A soggy trio of outerwear—Nancy's, Dave's, and mine—dangled on the hooks like dead fish, each contributed to an ever-expanding puddle that was creeping across the floor toward the kitchen.

"All right," I said, pulling out a chair and sitting down at a table across from Nancy and Dave. "Let's figure this out. What do we know?"

"No 'good morning'?" said Dave. "No 'how was your weekend?'"

"Nope," I said. "Coffee."

"I'll bring the pot," said Nancy, getting to her feet. "Noylene's back in the kitchen somewhere getting a mop."

Nancy filled our cups and put the pot on the table.

"I got a report on Hyacinth Turnipseed," she announced. "Cynthia called me this morning."

"Pretty bad?" I asked.

"Her leg is broken in three places. They had to operate. She'll be okay, but she has screws holding her leg together. Cynthia said she'll be in the hospital for three or four days. Then a wheelchair for a month. Then a cast."

"She'll have a nurse?"

"She'll have to," said Nancy. "At least for a while. She won't be able to walk or drive. Also, she's looking for someone to sue."

"Well, I'm glad she'll be okay," I said, "but we've got to get rid of those Minques."

As if in answer to my suggestion, we heard a volley of shots go off somewhere south of town. I gave a heavy sigh.

"Back to work," I said. "Davis Boothe first. Nancy?"

Nancy pulled out her pad. "Davis Boothe killed himself, or so we believe. He had an embolism that he was taking medication for, but he really needed an operation he couldn't afford."

"No health insurance," added Dave.

"His real name," continued Nancy, "was Josh Kenisaw. He was convicted in Kansas of second-degree murder when the car he was driving was involved in an accident and Senator Jack DeMille's daughter was killed. He was sentenced to life with a possibility for parole in

145

nineteen years. But Josh escaped and moved to St. Germaine with a made-up name. This was twelve years ago. He started out working as a waiter in Boone, then got a job at Don's Clothing Store."

"Wow!" said Pete, who'd joined us halfway through Nancy's recitation. "What else?"

"Senator DeMille offered a standing reward for Josh's return. Two million dollars," Dave said. "And now his head is missing."

*"What?"* said Pete.

"I think," I said, "that Davis *did* commit suicide, but not because of the embolism. I think he was afraid to face his prison sentence. He knew that he was about to be caught by someone. But who was it and what tipped him off?"

"Something in the book?" said Dave.

I shrugged. "That's what I remember, but it doesn't make sense."

"What book?" asked Pete.

*"The Sketchbook of Geoffrey Crayon,"* I said. "We were looking at it in Eden Books on the Saturday morning before he killed himself. I remember that he got very quiet, closed the book, made an excuse to leave and took off."

"That's the one you bought?" asked Pete. "By Washington Irving?"

"Yes."

"Did you go through it to see what he might have seen?"

"Sure," said Nancy, "but what could there have been? The book is ancient. It just doesn't add up."

"Okay," I said, "let's leave that for a moment. Here's another interesting fact. Davis Boothe had a life insurance policy with Upper Womb Ministries. If it turns out he was murdered instead of a suicide, and it turns out that they weren't somehow complicit, they get fifty thousand dollars. He was in there on the Saturday afternoon before he died. According to Chad, he was very agitated when he came in, but he calmed down during his massage."

"Back to his missing head," said Pete.

"Yes," I said. "His head. The reward is for Josh Kenisaw, dead or alive. I imagine that the bounty hunter, whoever he is, would rather have brought Davis...er, Josh, back alive. But once he killed himself, the bounty hunter would have to bring back proof that Josh was dead to collect the reward. A death certificate probably wouldn't do it for Senator Jack DeMille."

"So the bounty hunter took the head?" Pete asked.

"What better? Davis was cremated, so there wouldn't be any record of the head being taken," said Nancy. "Once his remains were ground up, there would be no way of identifying anything."

"So the someone went in and stole Davis' head before he was cremated," said Dave.

146

"Someone who had a key," Nancy added.

"And the only people who had keys were Dale and Panty Patterson and Thelma Wingler." I took a sip of coffee. "You beginning to get the picture?"

"No," said Pete.

"Look," I sighed. "You've got to keep up."

Pete nodded.

"Thelma died in the labyrinth on Tuesday. Her purse had been stolen and there had been someone in the garden with her. She'd been talked off her OCD meds by Chad. In addition, she'd left money to Upper Womb Ministries. Five thousand dollars, to be exact."

"Not only that," said Nancy, "her throat was swollen and her vocal cords were paralyzed. She couldn't call for help."

"Poison?" asked Dave.

"Maybe," I said. "I'm thinking rhubarb leaves—maybe in an herbal tea. The leaves contain oxalic acid, a mild poison that causes such inflammation. She may have been drinking it for a few days thinking it was helping her when actually it was causing the problem."

"That's why she bought the krummhorn?" said Nancy.

"Could be. She went to the labyrinth by herself and she knew she couldn't call for help if she got into trouble. Maybe she bought the krummhorn to alert a passerby if she needed to attract some attention."

"But she didn't know she had to put a reed into it first," said Nancy. "Maybe the reason that it was hung up in the bushes was because she was trying to throw it over the hedge to get someone's attention."

I nodded. It felt right. "If all our assumptions are correct," I said, "then someone took Thelma's purse after she was either incapacitated or dead. Thelma had unlocked the gate and entered the garden. At that point, she had Chad's key, her own keys, and her purse. Whoever stole her purse wanted the key to the crematorium, because they needed to be able to get Davis' head sometime after he'd been delivered but before they did the cremation at two a.m."

"And they'd have to know the crematorium's schedule," added Nancy.

"And know the schedule," I agreed. "But that's not difficult to find out."

"So was Thelma murdered?" asked Pete.

"I don't know yet," I said, "but it sure looks like it."

# Chapter 20

The Diva offered me a mink-covered hand and I kissed it diligently, taking time to savor the loose hairs that came away stuck to my gums. Something wasn't right. I smacked my lips. This wasn't mink. I knew the taste of mink the same way I knew my mother's chipped squirrel on toast. This had the minty aftertaste of weasel, or maybe ferret. I took another taste and detected the slightest hint of cumin. Then I knew. It was stoat.

"My," said Barbara Seville, batting her eyes like Nelson Rockefeller in a cabinet meeting. "You certainly do like to kiss a woman's hand. I hope you're equally as passionate in other areas."

"Maybe I am, sweetheart," I said, plucking stoat hairs from my teeth. "But I know your game and the jig is up. You killed AveMaria Gratsyplena and Ginger Snapp. You're not supplying minks to bishops. You're giving them stoat at mink prices and they're too stupid to know the difference."

"Is that any reason not to enjoy the evening?" asked the Diva, as she opened her fur coat extra-sexily. Underneath, she was clad only in a fur bikini obviously made from very small, underprivileged animals with eating disorders; a bikini that was struggling on all edges to maintain its integrity as a piece of clothing. I bent down and looked closely. Maybe it was mink, maybe stoat, but I knew that I was just the flatfoot to handle the investigation.

*The Living Gobbler* rehearsal was in full swing when I arrived. The stage wouldn't be erected until the week of the performance, so the fifty or so participants were being staged on the chancel steps. Fiona was in charge, ordering actors and singers hither and yon. Father Lemming was at the keyboard, providing accompaniment for the rehearsal.

"Hey, Chief!" hollered Moosey, as soon as he saw me. "Look at me! I'm an Indian! And I got a dog!"

I waved to him. Mrs. Lemming snarled "Quiet!" and the cast cowered for a long moment. Then she spotted me.

"Hayden!" she said. "Just the person we need. Do you have *The Living Gobbler* hymn?"

"Hot off the press," I said, holding up a stack of paper that I'd just finished Xeroxing in the church office. "The tune is *Austria*."

Mrs. Lemming looked at me blankly.

"*Glorious Things of Thee Are Spoken*, dontcha know." said Father Lemming, playing the first few bars.

"Perfect," said Fiona, with a big grin. "Let's hear it then." She turned to the cast. "Line up like we'll be for the first number," Fiona Tidball-Lemming commanded. "We don't have the choir yet and I know that not all of you are singers, but let's do the best we can. Then when the choir shows up next week..." She shot me a dirty look. "...we'll really sound great. So let's get in our places."

Ian Burch was sitting on the aisle, three pews back, watching the activities. I gave him a clap on the shoulder as I walked by. I felt him wince.

"How are you, Dr. Burch?"

"Fine, thanks."

"Are you here seeing how the Early Musik Consort will fit into the program?"

"Partly. But Fiona wanted my dog to be in the production. His name's Gamba. She came by the Music Shoppe and saw him, so now he's in the show," he said proudly. "That little boy in the Indian costume is in charge of him."

I looked toward the steps. The only boy in a costume was Moosey. I'd bought it for him over in Cherokee once he told me he'd been assigned the part of "Indian." It was an authentic Cherokee outfit, or at least as close as Jim Thundercloud could make it. Fringed leggings, moccasins, a buckskin shirt with some beaded embroidery and a headband with two eagle feathers didn't come cheap, even if everything *was* in a size eight. But, as Meg pointed out, what good was having money if you never had any fun with it? I knew that Moosey would be wearing the outfit to every rehearsal, for Halloween Trick or Treating, to bed, and if he could talk his mother into it, to school. I wasn't the one that provided him with the tomahawk, however. It was stuck in his belt and looked, from the third pew at least, to be real. I didn't see a dog.

"Is Gamba on a leash?" I asked Ian. "I don't see him."

"Sure." He half stood and peered down his nose and through his thick glasses. Then he smiled. "There he is. The boy hooked the leash on the lectern."

I saw the dog beside the lectern. It was a breed whose markings I recognized. A Rottweiler.

"I hope Gamba's well trained. Rottweilers can be dangerous." I looked carefully at the dog. He seemed relaxed and not at all anxious. "At least he's lying down and looks like he's enjoying himself."

"He's only half-Rottweiler," said Ian, "and he's not lying down."

I looked again. Ian was right, of course. Gamba was a Rottweiler on the shortest legs I'd ever seen.

"His mother was a Rottweiler," explained Ian Burch, "but his father was a Dachshund. He wouldn't hurt anyone. Gamba's a vegan."

"Pass out those song sheets!" commanded Fiona, once the cast was in place. I handed some to the person on the end of each row and every stack made its way across the chancel as Pilgrims, Indians and assorted vegetables each took a copy.

"All right, then," said Fiona. "Let's try it."

"How many verses?" asked Father Lemming.

"Four," I answered. "All in unison. When we add the choir, we'll have parts as well."

Father Lemming nodded and started playing an introduction to the famous hymn.

"You all know the tune," I called over the sound of the keyboard. *"Glorious Things of Thee Are Spoken."*

I saw nods of recognition from the cast. Muffy smiled at me and winked. Then the introduction was over and everyone sang with gusto:

> Lord, we offer our Thanksgiving
> For the vittles that we eat,
> Sweet potato, pumpkin pie, and
> Every kind of fish and meat:
> Lemon Jello—what a wobbler!
> Red-eye gravy, ham and bread.
> Best of all, the Living Gobbler
> May thy food to all be fed.

> Join us as you may be able,
> While we all prepare our food.
> Relishing the growing table,
> As we give our thanks to God.
> Pumpkin pie and apple cobbler,
> Collard greens and cob of corn,
> Celebrate the Living Gobbler,
> With thy blessings to adorn.

> Yea, we sit and share thy bounty,
> Ma and Pa and Junior, too.
> There's Ramelle from out the county,
> With her husband, Elmer Sue.
> Little Bubba—what a squabbler!
> And the twins, Brandine and Clyde,
> Celebrate the Living Gobbler,
> In our stomachs to reside.

Father Lemming modulated up a step for the last stanza. I winced.

> As we stand here, looking perky,
> Let us not our sins forget
> Ere we gorge on deep fried turkey
> While the sun begins to set.
> All our woes and worries probbler-
> -matic that our lives destroy
> Vanish with the Living Gobbler
> Dinner for us to enjoy.

"Good," said Fiona. "That will work just fine."

"Really?" I said, but she'd already singled out Muffy and Varmit to work on the staging of their duet. Marjorie walked up to me shaking her head.

"Kind of forcing that last rhyme, weren't you?" she said, under her breath. "Probbler-matic? I mean, *really.*"

"It was a joke," I whispered. "I thought she'd toss it out immediately."

"Apparently, you don't know the Lemmings as well as you thought."

"So you're in the show?"

"Oh, yes," said Marjorie. "I'll be playing Hiawatha's mother, Nokomis."

I looked at her with my mouth hanging open.

"Don't look so shocked. I'm quite good. Fiona Lemming has suggested I perform several verses of *The Song of Hiawatha* just before your wedding vows. I shall accompany the verse with appropriate sign language." Marjorie demonstrated.

> By the shores of Gitche Gumee,
> By the shining Big-Sea-Water,
> Stood the wigwam of Nokomis,
> Daughter of the Moon, Nokomis.
> Dark behind it rose the forest,
> Rose the black and gloomy pine-trees,
> Rose the firs with cones upon them;
> Bright before it beat the water,
> Beat the clear and sunny water,
> Beat the shining Big-Sea-Water.

Marjorie was getting into the part. She was using some semblance of sign language that wouldn't be understood by either the deaf or the Indians, but might work for deaf Indians if some could be found.

"Okay," I said, quietly. "I get it. You can stop."

> Then the gentle Chibiabos
> Sang in accents sweet and tender,
> Sang in tones of deep emotion,
> Songs of love and songs of longing;

Muffy and Varmit had stopped their staging rehearsal and were now watching Marjorie. In fact, everyone in the church, including the two Lemmings, was watching Marjorie. She gesticulated wildly as her voice rose, sing-songy, her hands painting pictures in the air. Her eyes were closed and she was in a world of her own.

> Thou the wild-flower of the forest!
> Thou the wild-bird of the prairie!
> Thou with eyes so soft and fawn-like!
> If thou only lookest at me,
> I am happy, I am happy,
> As the lilies of the prairie,
> When they feel the dew upon them!

"Marjorie!" yelped Fiona. "Button it up, will you? We're trying to rehearse!"

"Oh. Sorry."

"Amateurs," muttered Fiona under her breath, but loud enough for all the amateurs to hear.

"Do me a favor," I whispered to Marjorie. "Don't tell Meg about this."

"It was her idea," said Marjorie. "*The Song of Hiawatha* is Ruby's favorite poem. Hey, did you see that dog?"

I nodded. "The mother was a Rottweiler and the father was a Dachshund."

"He has a crazed look in his eye," said Marjorie. "His mother was a Rottweiler, eh? His father must have been one tough little wiener dog."

"He's a vegan."

"The Rott-wiener's a vegan? No meat?"

"No meat, no cheese, no eggs. He eats doggie tofu."

"No wonder he looks mean."

"Six more Minques today," announced Dave. "Six that I heard of, anyway. But that still leaves more than a hundred."

"Well, some have probably vamoosed," I said. "They'll be way up in the mountains by now. The rest will turn up. The good thing is, they can't reproduce."

"Are you guys doing anything for Halloween?" Nancy asked.

"Well," I answered, "choir practice is cancelled due to Trick or Treating, so I'm thinking of a quiet night at home."

"You don't get the Trick or Treaters?" said Nancy.

I shook my head. "I'm too far out and besides, everyone knows I don't have any candy. The last kid that bothered to come to the house got a can of soup."

"I'll bet I have six hundred kids come to the door. I have forty-five pounds of candy this year and I'll still probably run out. Dave's coming over to help me hand it out." Nancy looked pointedly in his direction. "Right, Dave?"

Dave nodded enthusiastically.

# Chapter 21

"You can't wear that hat," said Noylene. "Not during the wedding."

Sit down, pal. Breathe quietly, keep your voice down, and remember that a wedding coordinator is to a bridegroom what Toscanini is to an organ grinder's monkey.

I took the hat off. "I wasn't going to wear it during the wedding," I said. "Anyway, I have to be in a Pilgrim outfit."

"I'd like you to wear the hat," said Meg.

"No," said Noylene, decisively. "No hat. He can wear it during the reception."

"What reception?" I asked.

"There's no reception," said Meg.

Noylene sat down at our table, the coffee pot still in her hand. "Look," she said. "This here's the wedding of the year. You have to have a reception."

"No, thanks," I said. "We'll have a big party later on."

Noylene sighed. "Okay. What about bridesmaids?"

"I don't need any bridesmaids," said Meg. "Bev's going to be my Indian Maid of Honor."

"Honey, you're *having* bridesmaids. Noylene Fabergé-Dupont does not put on a wedding without bridesmaids. Not only that, but as my wedding gift, I'm going to give all eight of them…"

"All eight of them?" I said.

"All *eight* of them," continued Noylene, "coupons to the Dip-n-Tan so they can look good for the ceremony."

"Two," said Meg. "Two bridesmaids."

"Seven," countered Noylene.

"Three?" Meg was losing ground quickly.

"Six."

"Four," agreed Meg. "That's it. I'll try to pare my list of potential bridesmaids down to four."

"Okay, four," said Noylene.

Meg sighed. "Okay."

"I'll be a bridesmaid, if you need one."

All three of us turned to see Collette standing behind us.

"Hell, no, Collette," said Noylene. "You're crazier than Tammy Faye's housecat. Meg can find four bridesmaids easy enough."

"Better is a dinner of herbs where love is, than a stalled ox and hatred therewith—Proverbs 15:17." Collette spun on her heel and stomped off.

"That girl just ain't right," said Noylene.

"Hyacinth Turnipseed's out of the hospital," Nancy announced. "Cynthia said she was going back to work even though she's in a wheelchair."

"We should stop by the bookstore," I said. "Things are pretty slow."

"If they were any slower, I'd have to molest Dave in the back room just to keep things interesting," said Nancy. Dave, typing away at his keyboard, perked up.

"Down, boy. Just kidding."

"Aw, jeeze," said Dave, gesturing with a nod toward the window overlooking Sterling Park. "There she is again."

We all looked out and saw Collette, about thirty yards away, standing under a sugar maple afire with reds and oranges. She was wearing her waitress smock and apron, an open Bible in both hands and was staring right back at us.

"She does this every time she gets a break," said Dave. "Walks out of the Slab, stands under that tree, opens up a Bible and stares at me. I tell you, it's starting to creep me out."

"I think it's about time I had a talk with Collette," said Nancy.

"No, I'll do it," said Dave. "I feel bad for her."

"Let's go to the bookstore," I said to Nancy. She grunted.

"I could shoot her, if you want me to, Snookie-Pie," said Nancy.

"Please don't," Dave said. "And if you call me Snookie-Pie again, you'll be the one who gets shot."

I waved at Collette as we exited the police station. She didn't return the gesture, but glared at Nancy without a word. Nancy glared back.

"Maybe I'll just arrest her," said Nancy. "Then shoot her later when she tries to escape."

Eden Books was doing a good business. Hyacinth Turnipseed had hired a college student to come over from Appalachian State three mornings a week, and Wynette Winslow had been helping out while Hyacinth was in the hospital. Nancy and I walked into the little shop and were pleasantly surprised at the number of books that were now lining the shelves. Wynette was busily placing greeting cards in a rack and the college student, a young man identified by his nameplate as Tracy, was helping several customers with their purchases. There were Christmas decorations hanging throughout the store and several holiday book displays prominently crowding the narrow aisles. Hyacinth was in a wheelchair—a narrow, hand-operated model—one leg in a cast sticking straight out, perpendicular to the back, and resting on a pillow supported by a metal shelf. She looked drawn and significantly less jolly than the last time we'd seen her, not counting when she was lying on the sidewalk, one leg pointing south and the other northeast. Her white hair was still tied in a loose bun, but the shine was gone and her blue eyes were sunken. She smiled when she saw us, though, and gave a wave and we walked over to see her.

"I heard you came over to help when I had my accident," she said. "Thank you so much."

"There wasn't much we could do," I said. "Luckily the ambulance was right around the corner. How are you feeling? We got a hospital report from Cynthia."

"I feel okay, but I'll be in this chair for about a month. What a pain. I can't drive, I can't walk. I have to have a nurse with me."

Nancy looked around. "Is your nurse here?"

"I sent her out to do some shopping. She's a very nice woman. I know I'm old, but quite frankly, I'm used to my independence."

"Well, we're glad you're on the mend," I said.

"How are you doing with that murder case?" asked Hyacinth.

I looked over at Nancy and shrugged. "We're still working on it."

"I might be able to help you," Hyacinth said, a twinkle reappearing in her eye. "I'm a clairvoyant. I do psychic readings for the police. Remember?'

"How could I forget?" I said, with a laugh. I looked at Nancy. She shrugged.

"Okay," I said. "Sure. Why not? It's Halloween, after all."

"I'll need something from the scene."

"How about the krummhorn?" Nancy offered. "It's back at the office."

"Perfect," said Hyacinth.

"I'll get it and be right back."

"Don't shoot Collette," I called after her.

I wheeled Hyacinth into the back room off the bookstore as soon as Nancy arrived with the krummhorn. Hyacinth took the instrument in both hands and closed her eyes.

"Don't you have to light some candles, or something?" I asked.

"Maybe draw a pentagram on the floor?" suggested Nancy. "Slaughter a goat?"

"Don't be ridiculous," said Hyacinth. "Now, hush up."

We stood in silence for a couple of minutes, then Hyacinth started talking.

"I've connected with a spirit—a woman. This is a recent spirit. She's new to the Spirit world."

"Probably Thelma," I whispered to Nancy under my breath. Nancy rolled her eyes.

"She wants us to know that she's not happy. Her spirit can't find peace."

"That's Thelma, all right."

"She says she wasn't murdered, but that there was someone present at her death. Also, she wants her money back on this horn. She says it doesn't work."

Nancy and I were paying attention now.

"I'm seeing a large church—a French church. And the initials LP."

I looked over at Nancy as Hyacinth opened her eyes and continued.

"There's a life insurance policy. Not the one for the Upper Womb. Another one. It's somewhere like..." Hyacinth closed her eyes again. "A bank. No. A safety deposit box. I'm seeing the numbers six, three and seven."

We waited for more.

Hyacinth opened her eyes and looked at us with a smile. "That's all I've got. Hope it helps."

"What do you think?" asked Nancy as we wended our way across the park. "Is she for real?"

"There are more things in heaven and earth, Horatio, than are dreamt of in your philosophy."

"Meaning?"

"Meaning let's check out the insurance policy. If it's in a safety deposit box, it's got to be in Boone somewhere."

"What about the French church?"

"An obvious reference to the cathedral in Chartres."

"Not obvious to me!" said Nancy. "Why Chartres?"

"The painted labyrinth on which Thelma expired is a copy of the one in the Chartres Cathedral."

"Would Hyacinth have known that?"

"I don't know. But I wouldn't think that it would be that hard for her to find out."

"The krummhorn?"

"Again, I don't know. We *have* been asking around. Ian Burch knew it didn't work. Pete, Meg, probably some others. We didn't exactly keep the information secret."

"What about the initials LP?"

"That's what's interesting," I said. "How would Hyacinth know about that?"

"About what?"

"About Lacie Peckelsham's real name."

# Chapter 22

Halloween had come and gone without incident and I'd enjoyed a peaceful night at home, safe from the costumed imps that were out in force. Meg had decided that Ruby could use help passing out treats, and elected to stay in town. Nancy went through forty-five pounds of candy in an hour and had to make an emergency run to the Piggly Wiggly. Unfortunately, all the Pig had left were individually wrapped servings of Fig Newtons and, as a result, Nancy's house was the target of some serious toilet-papering. Collette spent the evening across the street from Nancy's house in a parked car, praying diligently, and handing out Bible tracts to kids that stopped and looked in the window hoping for something a little more confectionary than the four-step plan of salvation.

The next morning felt different altogether. A cold front had moved in during the night bringing with it low humidity, a stiff breeze and a seasonal snap that made all the suffering of summer seem worthwhile. I buttoned my coat against the wind as I made my way down the street toward the Upper Womb, keeping a wary eye out for Minques. The two tables on the large, covered front porch of the old house were empty. I suspected that the wind and the temperature drove the coffee and tea drinkers indoors. I walked up the four wide steps, opened the front door, and let myself into the hallway. Cynthia and Crayonella Washington were in the coffee shop sitting at a table for two, deep in conversation. They stopped as soon as they saw me. Cynthia got to her feet.

"Coffee?" she asked.

"Espresso, please. You guys talking politics?"

"Yep," said Crayonella. "We still have a day until the election."

"I've seen your print ads in *The Tattler*. Very nice."

"You should get a circular in the mail this afternoon," Crayonella said.

"I look forward to it," I said, and then turned to Cynthia. She was busying herself behind a large, complicated-looking coffee machine that might have been designed by a NASA scientist. It hissed like a Studebaker as Cynthia turned valves and pulled levers, intent on extracting two ounces of liquid from the gleaming stainless behemoth.

"Is Chad around?" I asked. Cynthia passed me a tiny cup full of espresso.

"He went to the farmer's market in Asheville. He should be back this afternoon. But Lacie's upstairs. You want me to get her?"

"That'd be great."

Cynthia wiped her hands on her apron and disappeared into the hallway and up the staircase.

"What do you think of your chances?" I asked Crayonella.

"I don't know," she said. "Tell you the truth, it's a hard town to read. We can't afford any polling and I'm not sure it'd do any good, anyway."

"Well, you've run a good campaign. I wish you both all the best."

Cynthia interrupted my good wishes.

"Lacie's in the massage room. She says you should go on up."

"Thanks."

I finished up my two ounces of coffee, put the miniature cup on one of the tables and headed up the stairs. The massage room was on the left as I made the second floor landing. I identified it almost immediately by the sign on the door saying "Massage Room." I wasn't a trained detective for nothing. I tried the door, found it unlocked, opened it and walked into the room. It was a room designed to be in perpetual twilight. The windows were covered with blackout drapes and the lighting carefully contrived to show the aromatic candles flickering on the mirrored walls. There was soft, unobtrusive music playing—music with no real melody surrounded by about four chords. Synthesized computer strings. Air pudding. I waited a moment for my eyes to adjust.

Lacie was sitting in a blue leather wingback chair, her long legs crossed and the hem of her skirt just a bit higher on her thigh than was prudent. Her hair tumbled over her shoulders and she looked at me with large eyes.

"Why don't you let me give you a massage?" she offered. "It's on the house."

"No, thanks. I just need to chat, if you don't mind."

"I don't mind at all."

"I just need to clear up a few things about the Thelma Wingler murder." I watched Lacie's posture change at the word 'murder', but just barely. "We have Chad in custody," I lied, "so let's start with what he's already told us. We know all about the rhubarb tea. He admitted that the spa uses tea brewed from the leaves for some of the patients. You know the leaves are poisonous?" Lacie didn't answer.

"He told us that you give the tea to patients and then, when they start to show symptoms—loss of their voice, swelling of the mouth and throat—symptoms brought on by a weak dose of oxalic acid, you simply give them another tea and they're magically cured. They're not really, but since they're not drinking rhubarb tea, the problem clears right up." Lacie was silent.

"I don't know yet if we're going to charge you and Chad in the murder of Thelma Wingler. We know you poisoned her, of course. But, according to Chad, you've done nothing wrong."

Lacie shook her head. "Look, many cultures use rhubarb tea as a remedy for a host of ailments."

"Yes. I looked it up. One part rhubarb to forty-five parts other teas."

159

"We certainly didn't kill Thelma."

"Rhubarb tea was only part of it. Chad also told us that he advised her to abandon her OCD medication. It could be argued that she died as a direct result of your spa treatments."

"Which *may* make us liable in a civil court when *and if* we're sued by her survivors. But you'll never prove anything in criminal court. OCD medication is still in the trial-and-error stage. You'd know that if you read the literature."

"Hmm," I nodded. "Added to that, Upper Womb Ministries will receive five thousand dollars from her will."

"As I said before," said Lacie, "we frequently solicit donations for our ministry. Five thousand dollars is hardly an amount worth killing over."

"But, according to Chad, you didn't actually know the amount before the will was read. It could have been considerably more."

"I'm going to throttle him," said Lacie, in disgust.

I nodded. "Anything else you want to tell me?"

"We didn't kill her."

"I'm not convinced."

I walked out the door and headed down the stairs. Lacie followed me out as far as the landing. Cynthia appeared in the hallway and called up to her.

"Chad just called on his cell. He's on his way home from Asheville and will be back in about an hour. He says he got a great deal on some Burdock root."

I turned and smiled up at Lacie. But it wasn't a nice smile.

"You know what they always say…" I said.

Lacie looked daggers at me. "Never trust the cops?"

"Nope," I said. "Don't leave town."

"For how long?"

I wasn't smiling this time. "I'll let you know."

# Chapter 23

Downtown St. Germaine was bustling with activity. The ladies of the D.A.R. had blanketed the square with red, white and blue bunting, flags were flying proudly outside all the businesses and Pete had set up loudspeakers outside of the Slab to broadcast Sousa marches throughout the day. There were two registration tables on the steps of the courthouse and they were currently being manned by a couple of veterans sporting their medals and wedge-shaped Garrison caps. It was Election Day.

There was only one polling place for local elections in St. Germaine and that was the courthouse. We didn't have electronic voting booths, we weren't computerized, and we certainly weren't bothered by hanging chads. During state and national elections, we traveled over to Banner Elk to vote, but for local voting, we'd long ago decided that paper ballots were just fine. Of the two thousand or so registered voters, we'd have about twelve hundred show up for any given election. Sixty percent. Pretty good.

There were two items on the ballot—the mayoral election, of course, and the bi-yearly attempt by the city council to raise the property taxes. The second item would fail miserably, as it always did, except for that one year Pete snuck it through by running unopposed and no one bothered to check to see what else was on the ballot and consequently, didn't show up to vote. The populace wouldn't make *that* mistake again. Now, Pete always had an opponent, no matter how unlikely, and *The Tattler* always printed a copy of the ballot on the front page two days before the election so everyone could see what those sneaky politicians were up to. This year's ballot had four boxes. In the mayoral race, one box for Cynthia Johnsson, one box for Peter Moss. Choose one. If you happened to choose two, your ballot was thrown away. If there was any doubt about whom you were voting for, your ballot was thrown away.

The second item was a bit more complicated thanks to the verbal gobbledygook, i.e.

> Except as provided in this section, the total amount of municipal tax that can be levied during a fiscal year shall not exceed the total amount approved by the city council for the preceding year by more than a percentage determined by adding the percentage increase in the Federal Consumer Price index for North Carolina from the preceding fiscal year. Etcetera, etcetera.

Once one of the voters had figured out that voting "NO" would increase the property taxes, the word soon spread.

The single person in charge of the whole affair was our election commissioner, Billy Hixon. He'd been election commissioner for twelve years since the last commissioner, Walt Dolittle, ran off to Knoxville with the change girl at the laundromat. Billy would supervise the counting of the votes once the polls closed at six o'clock, then ring the St. Barnabas bell and announce the results from the steps around eight.

Nancy, Dave, and I took turns during the day stomping around the courthouse and looking generally Gestapoesque. I made Dave put on his uniform, but I, being the boss, declined the khaki outfit and dark brown jacket, preferring instead to don the dashing Raymond Chandler hat, a gray, alpaca overcoat, and a red scarf. Meg commented that I looked a bit more Mafioso than law enforcement, but gave me high marks for sex appeal.

"Have you voted yet?" I asked Meg, who was taking a turn helping at the registration table.

"First thing this morning."

"If you get some time off for lunch, I'd be happy to take you out to eat at the establishment of your choice."

"Hmm. How about the library?"

"The library?"

"Rebecca's offering free sandwiches for voters. Well, not free exactly. It's a ploy."

"I'm intrigued. Please go on."

"You can have a free sandwich, but there's a donation basket. She's hoping to make some money for her summer reading program. She gives away books to underprivileged Appalachian kids."

"So," I said, pushing my hat back and rubbing a thoughtful hand across my chin, "free sandwiches that aren't free to pay for a reading program I'm not invited to."

"Exactly."

"I'm in. When do you want to head over?"

Meg looked at her watch. "I have another half hour to do. Can you wait?"

She gave me a smile I could feel in my hip pocket.

"Oh, yes. I can wait."

Supper was Reuben sandwiches for everyone courtesy of Mayor Pete Moss. We were waiting in the Slab Café for the election results. It usually took Billy, Elaine, and two others a couple of hours to count the votes. They divided the ballots amongst themselves and counted them, then switched stacks and counted again. They did this multiple times and when the totals all came up the same, Billy announced the winner. Usually, Pete was so far ahead and the tax measure was so far behind that totaling the votes wasn't that big a deal, but this year, it promised to be close.

Pete had the Reubens stacked high on a tray sitting on one of the tables. Complimenting the sandwiches were bags of potato chips and coleslaw. Plates of pickles and sliced onions completed the feast.

"C'mon in," he said to whoever rang the cowbell as the front door swung open. "Grab a sandwich."

Meg and I were at a table, along with Ruby, Nancy, and Dave. Noylene and Collette were at another table and Wormy was filling his plate with food. Carol Sterling had come in followed by Bev Greene and Georgia Wester. They took a table by the kitchen.

"What if we don't like Reuben sandwiches?" asked Carol.

Pete raised an eyebrow. "Then don't eat one," he said slowly, enunciating every word. I could tell he was getting a little testy.

"I'll just have some chips," muttered Carol.

The door opened again and Cynthia poked her head inside.

"May we join you?"

"Sure," said Pete. "C'mon in. But if you win, you have to pay for the sandwiches."

"What's taking them so long?" Bev asked. "It's already twenty after eight."

Just then the bell in the tower of St. Barnabas began to ring.

"That's it," I said, getting to my feet. "Let's go hear the results."

It was cold. There were about fifty of us gathered around the courthouse steps and our collective breaths hung in the frosty air like the smoke our mountains were named for. Most of us were unmittened and had our hands deep in our pockets. Scarves were pulled tight around necks and hats tugged down over frozen ears as we waited for the announcement.

Billy, clad in an enormous olive green jacket with a fur-lined hood, stepped onto the highest step.

"I have the results," he said in a loud voice. "First of all, I'd like to say that this was the closest election in…"

"Get on with it," Arlen Pearl hollered. "We're freezing out here."

Billy glared at him. "Shut up, Arlen. This here's a sacred duty and I'm going to do it right."

I smiled and took Meg's hand. This was small town America at its finest.

"All right, then," continued Billy. "In the matter of the property tax referendum, the people have voted 'YES.'"

"Does that mean y'all are going to raise taxes?" asked Arlen.

"It means that the people have voted 'YES' to not raising taxes."

"Huh?" said Arlen.

"We're not raising your taxes!" shouted Billy.

"Oh," said Arlen. "Good." He turned on his heel and walked away.

"In the matter of the election of the mayor of St. Germaine—and let me say right now that we counted these votes four times—the results are as follows. Peter Moss, five hundred eighty-three votes. Cynthia Johnsson, five hundred eighty-five votes."

"Whooop!" shouted Crayonella. "You won, girl!" She grabbed Cynthia around the waist and swung her around in a circle.

There were the traditional handshakes and clapping of backs. Pete was pensive, but not dejected. When all was said and done, we walked back to the Slab, Cynthia and Crayonella included.

"It's the end of an era," I said, as we shed our coats and hung them over the backs of any chairs that happened to be handy. "I'm just glad I got one last free Reuben sandwich."

"I'm really sorry, Pete," said Cynthia. "Right now I feel just awful." She brightened. "Tomorrow I'll be fine though."

"That's politics," said Pete with stoic resignation. "I should have worn my drawers."

"Yeah," said Crayonella sympathetically.

"I don't suppose a recount would do any good."

"I doubt it," said Meg. "Billy always counts the votes at least four times."

"Then I guess I have no alternative but to start dating the mayor." He turned to Cynthia. "How about it? Tomorrow night? Dinner and dancing?"

"I'd love to."

"Jes hol' on one second!" said Crayonella. "What the heck's going on here?"

Cynthia giggled. "Well, you might as well know. We've been seeing each other since the debate."

Crayonella's mouth dropped open and she stared at them both. "You mean...after you looked...and then you screamed...and..."

"Yep," said Pete, with a smile. "Sometimes everything just works out."

# Chapter 24

"Isn't that something about Pete and Cynthia?" I sat down at my typewriter, laced my fingers together and gave them a crack. That I was wearing my hat and chomping on an unlit cigar was a given. That I was wearing a velvet smoking jacket was something new.

"What?" said Meg. "You didn't know?"

"How would I know?"

Meg just shook her head. "You men don't notice anything."

"I'm a trained detective. I notice *everything*."

"You didn't mention my haircut."

"I just didn't want to say anything in case you didn't like it," I said smugly. "I learned that in my self-esteem workshop."

"Ah. That explains it then. You know that Dave and Nancy have broken up?"

"*What?* I mean...yes, of course."

Meg laughed. "I haven't had a trim in over a month, Mr. Detective. Dave and Nancy broke up last week."

"Anything else I should know about?"

"I'll let you know."

The sun rose over the squalid city like a giant, orange star of the spectral class G2V, implying a surface temperature of 5780 degrees Kelvin and actually white, although it appeared to be the aforementioned orange due to the scattering of blue photons in the atmosphere and its relative position on the horizon, and it felt like heaven.

Suddenly a shot rang out. A woman screamed. A dog barked, a car honked and a marching band came down the street playing "Moonlight Over Milwaukee." This wasn't heaven. I grabbed my hat, jumped out of bed, put on my hat, then changed my mind, put it back on the nightstand, and reached for my heater. I was a split-second too late. Stretched out on the floor was Barbara Seville, her mink nightie askew and a mink covered sub-machine gun in her lifeless hand. Standing in the doorway were Marilyn and Pedro LaFleur. Marilyn—my ace secretary—was sporting a couple of smoking 38s. Pedro had a gun.

"She was going to ice you," said Pedro. "Marilyn followed you up, but I knew you'd be here." He grinned. "You never could resist a mezzo."

"It's the mellifluous timbre of that middle register," I said wistfully. "The dark sensuousness of musical desire aching for a suspended climax. It's like the call of the siren."

Pedro nodded and holstered his piece. "You and Rossini."

165

"You know the scam?" I asked, mentally tracing the Diva's outline in chalk.

"Yeah. Ginger had me working on it, too."

Marilyn tried on one of the mink coats hanging in the closet. "How does this one look?"

"Looks great," said Pedro, admiring the view. Then he turned back to me. "We'd better cheese it. The bishops will be as steamed as six pounds of mountain oysters when they find out this has gone bad."

"I'm not going to tell them," I said. "I've got no pig in this hunt."

"How about this one?" called Marilyn from the closet.

"Take 'em both," said Pedro. "This case is closed."

"I sense that you're wrapping it up," said Meg. "But I never knew you were attracted to mezzos."

"Not me. The detective."

"One and the same," said Meg.

"Well," I said. "Maybe I am. Actually, *you're* probably a mezzo. Not a soprano."

"I know. Would you like to hear the mellifluous timbre of my middle register? Maybe feel the dark sensuousness of my musical desire aching for a suspended climax?"

"You bet!"

"Well, forget it, Buster. Not till after the wedding."

The leaves had peaked, faded, and were now coming down in bunches, covering the mountains in a soft, multicolored blanket. Billy Hixon had his crews out almost every morning with rakes and leaf blowers, filling giant plastic bags and hauling them somewhere up in the hills. There were still those folks who burned their leaves, and although it was now illegal in town, the smell was delicious and no one bothered the offenders as long as they were careful. The mornings had turned cold, hoarfrost covering the ground and lasting until midmorning— even later in areas that were steeped in shade. It was on one of these white mornings that I got an early call.

"You'd better come on in," said Nancy. "I just got off the phone with Panty Patterson. It seems that Dale's been holding out on us."

"Dale?"

"Panty wants to tell us when we get there. He doesn't want us to bring Dale in. Says it'll terrify him."

I sighed and looked at my watch. 5:30 a.m. "All right. Give me about forty-five minutes. I've still got to shower and feed the boys."

166

"Hurry up. They're waiting for us at the crematorium. They've been up all night."

Baxter was asleep in front of the fireplace taking advantage of the warmth generated by the dying coals from last night's fire. I reached down, patted his shaggy head and then knelt and shook him awake, making sure I scratched his belly in the process. He rolled onto his back in appreciation and let his tongue loll out of his mouth, looking at me through half-closed eyes.

"Get up, old dog! You want to go for a walk?"

The magic words got Baxter immediately to his feet and bounding toward the kitchen door. I wasn't going to take him far—just to the end of the drive and back, but he was always happy to be asked. I took a minute to get a couple of mice out of the refrigerator and leave them on the windowsill for Archimedes. As the weather chilled, he'd spend more time indoors, but for now, the owl was out hunting all night, returning around dawn—still a good hour away this time of year. Baxter and I jogged down to the end of the drive and back and I put his bowl of food down outside the kitchen. He dove into it and I left him to his repast. I still had to shower, grab something to eat and be in town in thirty minutes.

I picked up Nancy at her house and we headed out to the crematorium. It was still dark, but starting to lighten with the first rays of the sun as we pulled up to the main building, the tires of my old truck crunching on the gravel drive. We walked up to the door. It was unlocked and ajar. I pushed it open and we walked into the dimly lit space. As our eyes adjusted, we could see Panty and Dale playing cards at the small table in front of the furnaces. We walked over.

"Hey," said Dale, not looking up. It was another game of War and Dale was concentrating hard. The cards were thrown down and snapped up at a blistering pace. The thing about this particular game, a game we had played as kids when there was nothing else to do, is that it can take *hours*. In fact, as long as both players hold an ace, the game will go on forever. As a kid, I don't think I'd ever played the game out to the end. I just didn't have the patience. Dale and Panty were going at it though, hammer and tongs.

"Okay," said Nancy, finally. "That's enough." She slapped her hand down on the pile of cards in the middle of the table with a smack.

Both men looked up at her, startled.

"I want Dale to talk to us," she said. *"Right now."* There was no mistaking her tone. Dale and Panty didn't move. They sat, dumbfounded, in their matching overalls and white collared shirts, buttoned to the neck.

"Now!" she said.

"Yes," said Panty, relaxing, his white skin glowing eerily in the fluorescent light. "Dale needs to talk to you."

We both looked at Dale. He started chewing on his bottom lip and ran a hand through his fine, blonde hair.

"Dale," I said. "You have something to tell us?"

He nodded.

"Go on, Dale. Tell them what you told me last night," said Panty.

"Well..I..." started Dale. "I didn't tell you before 'cause I fergot."

"It's all right," I said. "Tell us now."

Dale looked over at Panty with a confused look on his face. "What am I tellin' them?"

"About Miss Thelma," Panty said.

"Oh, yeah. The day before Miss Thelma died, she asked me to drive her when she went to that house beside the church."

"The Upper Womb?"

Dale shrugged. "Don't know what it is now. It used to be Miss McCarty's house. Anyway, I picked her up and drove her over."

"Did you drop her off and leave?" asked Nancy.

"She didn't want me to. She says for me to wait in the car right here in the alley beside these bushes. But she cain't talk, you know? She's all whispery-like. And she says 'When I blow this horn, you come runnin' and I says 'Okay, I will.' She says 'If'n you don't hear me blow it after about ten minutes, you go on home.' Then she goes 'round back and I heard her unlock the gate."

"How long did you wait?"

Dale shrugged. "A little while, I guess. So then I hear this other voice—I'm pretty sure it's a woman—and she says 'I'll give you twenty thousand for the head.' And then I don't hear nothin' and then I hear 'Okay, twenty-five.' And then, nothin' again and then I hear 'You're makin' a big mistake,' and then nothin'."

"So what did you do?" asked Nancy.

"Well, I waited and waited and I never did hear no horn, so I came on home."

"How come you didn't tell us this when we discovered Davis' head missing?" Nancy said.

Dale was incredulous and his voice went up about an octave. "I thought they was talking about hogs or cattle or some such thing. Panty only just told me it might be Davis they was talking about."

"Calm down, Dale," I said. "You're not in trouble. Tell me, when you picked Miss Thelma up, did she have her purse with her?"

Dale snorted and his voice returned to normal. "Shore. A big black one."

"Did you recognize the other voice?"

"No, sir. I'm pretty sure it was a woman though. It was sort of high, but she warn't talkin' very loud."

"Did the other person know you were there?"

"Prob'ly heard the car drive off, but she didn't see me if that's what you mean."

168

"A new twist," I said to Nancy as we climbed back into the truck.

"Indeed. A woman. Maybe Lacie?"

"Maybe. She certainly looks good for it. They were poisoning Thelma, that's for sure, but she has an alibi for Sunday night through Tuesday. On Monday, she and Chad were at their naked meeting in Galax, Virginia."

"Well," Nancy admitted, flipping through her notebook, "we didn't actually check that alibi, because, at that point, we thought that Thelma had died of natural causes."

"Time to check," I said.

"It should be easy. All the DANGLs are getting ready for their convention out at Camp Possumtickle. I'll just go have a talk with them."

"Camp Daystar," I corrected.

"Not yet," said Nancy. "They haven't actually signed the papers. I've heard rumblings from some folks in town. The populace is not keen on a Christian nudist colony only three miles from St. Germaine. Why do you think that is?"

"We shall leave that question to the philosophers," I said. "It seems that now we have a murder to solve."

"So what if Lacie's alibi checks out?"

"Then we'll have to look elsewhere."

"Any ideas? Another woman perhaps?"

"Or someone that sounds like one."

"We're sold out!" announced Father Lemming during rehearsal. "Both the Saturday and the Sunday performances!" A cheer went up from the cast.

# Chapter 25

Nancy and I weren't the first to the Slab Café on this frosty morning. There were at least two tables of early risers already enjoying plates of eggs, ham and grits when we showed up, straight from our visit to the crematorium. We spotted the new mayor and the mayor pro tem sitting at a table with two empty chairs and a platter of French toast—a veritable engraved invitation to law enforcement officers. We made a beeline for the table and sat down without comment.

"I'm not even the mayor yet," said Cynthia, "and they're after me."

"Welcome to my world," said Pete. "Well, my ex-world."

"You're still the mayor for another two months. They should be bothering you with this."

"I guess they should," said Pete, "but I told them I didn't care."

"Good morning," I said. "Pass the French toast, please."

"Morning," said Cynthia, passing the platter across the table. Nancy managed to skewer a couple of pieces on the way by.

"Did you know," said Cynthia, "that there is a new organization in town headed up by Shea Maxwell? The Society of Decency. They want the city council to stop the sale of Camp Possumtickle to the DANGLs. They're threatening a lawsuit and a court order to halt the proceedings."

"I don't think they could stop it, even if they wanted to," I said. "Camp Possumtickle is outside the city limits."

"Actually," said Pete, sipping on his coffee, "it is and it isn't. We annexed that parcel last year. The camp was all for it because it gave them some fire protection, but the other neighbors are still fighting it in court. It hasn't been decided."

"You mean the city council *could* stop the sale?"

"I don't know," said Pete. "The parcel isn't legally in the city limits, but we've been taxing the residents, letting them vote, and affording them fire protection until the courts decide whether the city annexed the parcel legally. Either way, I'm not going to any more council meetings. Cynthia can go if she wants. As future mayor, she's encouraged to attend."

"I don't like meetings," said Cynthia.

"You're in the wrong biz, now, Sweetheart," said Pete. "Oh, by the way..." He gave a sly grin. "I gave Wormy permission to put his Ferris wheel in Sterling Park on Thanksgiving weekend. He's going to bring it in and set it up on Saturday morning."

"Is it a big one?" asked Nancy.

"Big enough," said Pete. "It's a twelve-seater, thirty feet tall."

"Is there room in the park?" I asked.

"Sure," said Pete. "We stepped it off, although the only place it can go is right in front of St. Barnabas. You know, where the Kiwanis Club sets up the Christmas Crèche. The rest of the park has too many trees."

"You won't get to ride it, you know," I said. "You're my best man. And someone has to dress as the turkey."

"I talked to them," said Nancy, coming in to the police station just after lunch. "I went out to Camp Possumtickle. Luckily, they all had their clothes on when I showed up. Every last one of them said that Chad and Lacie were at the DANGL meeting in Galax from Sunday night until Tuesday morning when they all left. There was even a video of their "Christian Karaoke Night" they showed me—dated-stamped Monday night. Lacie and Chad do a mean duet rendition of *The Prayer*. I watched a bit of it."

"They could have changed the date on the camera," I pointed out.

"Except it wasn't their camera. I don't get the feeling that these people would lie to protect a murderer."

"Were they naked?" asked Dave. "On the tape, I mean."

"Naked as jaybirds," said Nancy. "Except for their microphones."

"Can we get a copy?" asked Dave hopefully, as a fleeting vision of Lacie Ravencroft leapt into his frontal lobe. "Just for archival purposes?"

"No, you may not," said Nancy. "Oh, one more thing. Those DANGLs are pretty mad about the people in town trying to stop the sale of the camp. They told me that if the 'so-called Society of Decency' keeps up this policy of discrimination, they'll be forced to come into town to hold a demonstration."

"Lacie, too?" asked Dave.

Nancy glared at him.

"I've been busy, as well," I said. "I called Jack DeMille's office in Topeka. He's out of the country, so they transferred me to his lawyer. I asked if the reward on Josh Kenisaw had been collected. He told me that it hadn't."

"That's interesting," said Nancy. "If I were that bounty hunter, I would have turned in Davis' head by now."

That afternoon Nancy arrested Collette for shooting at a Minque that she had cornered under the gazebo in the middle of Sterling Park.

"You can't arrest me, you Jezebel! You Athaliah! You dirty Rahab!" screamed Collette, face down on the ground, her hands cuffed behind her back. "I have a hunting license!"

"Call me one more name," said Nancy calmly, "and I'll lock you up in the old outhouse. You can't shoot in town. Where did you get a pistol, anyway?"

"Dr. Ken's Gun Emporium," Collette grumbled. "He's having a Minque sale."

# Chapter 26

Noylene had called a wedding powwow at the Beautifery and invited, or rather required, all parties involved to be present. Meg, thinking that I'd be very interested in the proceedings, had "invited" me to come along also. Meg was mistaken. I wasn't interested. But Noylene had promised that pie would be served, so I was in. Pete, too.

"Now," said Noylene, "are all eight bridesmaids here?"

"Four," said Meg. "Four bridesmaids. That's what we agreed on."

Noylene sighed. "Okay. Four. Are they all here?"

"I have three," said Meg. "Bev, Elaine, and Cynthia."

"You can't have just three," Noylene explained patiently. "It'll be unbalanced. The chop suey will be all wrong."

"Feng shui," I corrected.

"Whatever," said Noylene.

"I asked Georgia, but she's serving communion," said Meg. "Nancy's going to be on duty, so she can't do it, either."

"Collette said she'd do it," I said.

"Collette's crazy," said Noylene. "How about Crayonella? She was in here yesterday for a manicure."

"That would add a little local color," I said, garnering an amused look from Bev and Elaine.

"Crayonella will be just fine, if she'll do it," said Meg.

"I'm sure she will," said Cynthia. "I'll give her a call right now." Cynthia pulled out her cell phone and excused herself.

"Now," said Noylene, "the actual wedding ceremony is at the end of the performance. That should give everyone time to change into their bridesmaid outfits."

"What bridesmaid outfits?" asked Bev. "I thought we were wearing our Indian costumes."

"That's the plan," said Meg. "My wedding dress was made by Jim Thundercloud. It's quite lovely. White fringed and beaded doeskin with matching moccasins."

"You mean y'all aren't wearing matching bridesmaid outfits?" Noylene was appalled. "You're at least getting your hair and nails done, aren't you?"

Noylene was spared her latest disappointment by Cynthia's interruption.

"Good news," Cynthia announced. "Crayonella says she'll be happy to do it. She's honored to be asked."

"Are you wearing an Indian outfit as well?" Noylene asked.

"Nope. I'll be a belly dancer. I have my own costume."

"Well, one thing's for sure," said Noylene in disgust. "We're getting you three in the Dip 'n Tan. Y'all look like a trio of Pillsbury Dough Girls."

I was practicing on Friday morning—a voluntary by John Stanley, the hymns for Sunday, and the accompaniment for the communion anthem—and was almost finished when I was interrupted by a half dozen children scampering loudly into the choir loft, followed doggedly up the narrow stairs by a huffing and puffing Mrs. Tidball-Lemming.

"You kids get back here," she wheezed, without much vigor. She'd gotten to the top of the stairs and three steps into the loft when the children, screeching like howler monkeys, dodged her clumsy attempts to corral them and shot back down the stairs. I watched from my perch at the organ console as they tore through the nave and banged open the door to the sacristy, finally disappearing to wreak whatever havoc they could find. Fiona looked at me, defeat etching her face.

"They're Adrian's from his first marriage," she said. "Seven of those little brats. His first wife thinks it's funny to tell them to do anything they want when they get here. She's knows Adrian won't discipline them. He's got too much paternal abandonment guilt."

"Hmm," I managed. "And how long will the little Lemmings be with us?"

"We were supposed to have them for Christmas this year, but the ex found true love and decided to go to the Bahamas for Thanksgiving. Adrian told her we'd be *happy* to take them."

"So they'll be here for *The Living Gobbler*?"

"I guess I'll have to write them a part," said Fiona, her shoulders slumping. "I wonder what they're doing now?"

In response, a huge crash came from the sacristy followed by the sound of breaking glass. A lot of glass.

I didn't go down to the sacristy, preferring to let the Lemmings clean up after themselves. I did hear quite a lot of screaming going on behind the closed door, but eventually the furor died down and I resolved to play through the voluntary at least once more before heading back to the office.

"Hayden?" said a low voice from the back of the loft. I recognized the voice immediately.

"Hi, Carmel. Come on up."

"I've got some friends with me. May I introduce them?"

"Of course."

The Reverend Carmel Bottoms came into the loft followed by four others, three middle-aged women and a young man, all wearing open academic gowns with an embroidered red cross on the left breast.

"We are the Exorkizein. It's the name we've given ourselves. From the Greek."

I nodded. "Pleased to meet you, Exorkizein. I'm Hayden Konig the organist. I thought you guys were coming weeks ago."

"We had to wait until Thanksgiving holiday break," said the pimply young man. "We're still in seminary. All except Carmel."

"Well, what do you think?" I asked, gesturing around. "Demons? Yes or no?"

"Yes," said Carmel. "Demons. I sense at least five of them. I would name them for you, but that would give them more power."

"Absolutely," said the others. "It certainly would. No question."

"Then do what you have to do," I said. "Do you have your... umm... equipment? Bells? Books?"

"We have our wands," said one of the middle-aged women.

"And candles," added another.

"This may take some time," said the third. "Our last exorcism took two weeks."

"Take as much time as you need," I said. "But could you start downstairs? I've got to practice a bit more."

"Hey, Nancy, you watching the game?" I flipped through the channels looking for the football game.

"Of course. Like Denver's going to play and I'm *not* going to watch."

"What channel?"

"Forty-two."

I clicked over and settled back onto the leather-covered down cushions of the sofa. I had a big bag of Pete's Barabba-que flavored Communion Fish, a bottle of ice-cold Imperial stout called Surly Darkness, and a willingness to finish them both before halftime.

"Let me ask you something," I said into the phone. "You remember that day we were in the bookstore with Davis Boothe?"

"Yep."

"And he was looking through the *Sketchbook of Geoffrey Crayon?*"

"Yep."

"I keep trying to replay that conversation. Maybe he said something that we're missing. I just can't remember."

"I was over looking at the books in the best-seller section."

"But you were listening, right?"

"Well, sure, but....oh, no! Tennessee just scored!" Nancy screamed at the television. "You idiots! A 3-4 defense on fourth and one? What are you thinking?"

I leaned back, listened to Nancy's tirade, and gobbled down a handful of Communion Fish.

"Sorry," said Nancy, when she'd calmed down. "What was the question?"

"I was asking whether you remember the conversation in the bookstore right before Davis left."

"Hmm. You guys were talking about that book. Meg said that she liked *Rip Van Winkle*. You said that you liked *The Legend of Sleepy Hollow* and that you had a dog named Iggy."

"Not Iggy. Icky. After Ichabod Crane."

"Oh, for heaven's sake! Catch the stupid ball!" Nancy hollered. "Don't let those Oilers score again!"

"Oilers?"

"What? Oh, yeah. I meant the Titans. Tennessee used to be the Oilers. Now they're the Titans. I hate it when they change mascots."

"Huh," I said, feeling something small and mousy nibbling at the edges of my brain-pan. "Hey, Nancy, can you check something on the internet for me?"

"Sure."

"Google 'Ichabod' and 'mascot' and see if anything comes up."

"Hang on."

I had a sip of my Surly Darkness and waited for a moment.

Nancy came back on the line. "Well, blow me down a rathole. Washburn University."

I laughed. "Now I know why Davis Boothe's head never got turned in for the reward."

"You going to tell me?"

"Yep."

And I did.

# Chapter 27

Dave brought the donuts into the police station promptly at nine, being exactly one hour late for work. It didn't really matter to Nancy and me. We'd arrived at the station at seven to meet with Judge Adams and Todd McCay, the new Watauga County Sheriff. Judge Adams signed the warrant and the three of us made short work of the search and subsequent arrest. Meg came through the door two minutes after Dave carrying a box with five steaming pumpkin spice lattes from the Holy Grounds Coffee Shop.

"I thought you could use a treat," said Meg. "You solved the case! Why didn't you call me?"

"I did call you," I said. "That's why you came by, right? Anyway, we had to get a warrant, then go over and find Davis' head and finally make the arrest. First things first."

"Hey," said Dave. "Why didn't you call *me*?"

"You didn't have your phone on, Dave," said Nancy quietly.

"Oh. Sorry. I must have forgot."

"We went by your house to pick you up."

"Uh...I wasn't home."

"You were at Collette's?"

Dave hung his head. "Yeah."

"She's crazy, Dave," said Nancy. "I like you a lot, so as your friend, I'm telling you. She's certifiable."

"Who's certifiable?" asked Pete, coming through the door. "Collette? Hey! I heard you solved the case!"

"We did," said Dave. "All thanks to me." Nancy snorted.

"So where was Davis Boothe's head?" asked Meg.

"It was in Hyacinth Turnipseed's freezer," I answered. Meg blinked and looked shocked.

"Not the Upper Womb?"

"Nope. I finally remembered what I couldn't remember..."

"With a little help," added Nancy.

"With a *lot* of help," I added. "Think back to when we were in Eden Books the day before Davis killed himself. We were talking about *The Sketchbook of Geoffrey Crayon* and Davis was thumbing through the book. I said I liked *The Legend of Sleepy Hollow*."

"And I said I liked *Rip Van Winkle*," said Meg. "I remember."

"And I mentioned that I had a dog named Icky for Ichabod Crane." Everyone nodded.

"And then Hyacinth said 'Where I'm from, the college mascot is the Ichabods.'"

Everyone nodded again.

"That's it," I said.

"That's what?" said Pete.

"That's the part I couldn't remember—the part about the college mascot. Nancy looked it up. The only college in the country that has a mascot called the Ichabods is Washburn University in Topeka, Kansas. Davis Boothe, or rather, Josh Kenisaw, was a freshman at Washburn when he was convicted of killing Senator DeMille's daughter in a drunk driving accident."

"And when he heard Hyacinth Turnipseed mention the Ichabods, he knew she'd found him," added Nancy. "And that she now had his fingerprints on the book."

"And he killed himself rather than go to prison," said Meg. "How sad. What did Hyacinth say?"

"What could she say?" I said. "Davis' head was underneath some frozen pizzas in the freezer in her basement. She did claim she'd broken no laws."

"Has she?" Pete said.

"Oh, yeah," said Nancy. "When we searched Hyacinth's house, we found Thelma's purse and keys. They were in the basement as well. We know that she was in the garden when Thelma died. At the very least we can get her on depraved indifference murder and theft."

I nodded. "Hyacinth met Thelma there and offered her money for Davis' head. She was probably amazed when Thelma refused. But then Thelma had an OCD attack in the maze and all Hyacinth had to do was wait. She didn't know that Dale Patterson was waiting on the other side of the hedge."

"And when the krummhorn didn't work, Thelma tried to get his attention by throwing it over the hedge," added Nancy.

"But why didn't she collect the reward?" asked Pete. "After she had Davis' head?"

"I'm sure she was planning on it," I said. "But she fell and broke her leg. She was in the hospital for a few days, and then she was in a wheelchair with a full-time nurse. She couldn't get back down into the basement, so she called us over to give us a fake reading to throw suspicion on Lacie Ravencroft."

"And the life insurance policy in the safety deposit box? The numbers she saw during her reading?" asked Meg.

"Made up to throw us off the track and keep us busy."

Nancy nodded in agreement. "By the way, Senator DeMille's office is denying all knowledge of any Hyacinth Turnipseed."

"There's a surprise," said Pete.

"Where's Hyacinth now?" asked Meg.

"Todd McCay took her over to Boone for booking."

"What about Chad Parker and Lacie Ravencroft? Surely they're not innocent in all of this?" said Dave.

"We don't have any real evidence except Lacie's so-called confession, and I'm afraid that won't hold up in any court," I said. "I was just fishing for information. She wouldn't have said anything if I'd Mirandized her. I expect we'll be asking them to leave town though."

"Oh, my GOD!" screeched Bev, as she was hoisted out of the Dip 'n Tan. "Just look at us!"

Crayonella Washington gave a tremendous whoop. "Y'all look great! Couldn't be better!"

"What's the matter?" said Noylene, "I put in a triple dose, no extra charge. Y'all want to match, don't you?"

"Noylene!" wailed Elaine, looking down at her chocolaty skin. "Crayonella is *black!* Of course we don't want to match!"

"Well," said Cynthia, "I guess I can be an Arabian belly dancer."

"Nubian is more like it," said Bev, with a sob. "How long till this stuff wears off?"

"Well, you'll get darker for a day or two, then start to fade in a couple of weeks," said Noylene.

"Darker?" gasped Elaine in horror. "*Darker? How much darker?*"

"Oh, just a bit," said Noylene with a dismissive wave of her hand. "I think y'all look fabulous! Now, let's talk about your hair."

# Chapter 28

The Saturday after Thanksgiving started out like no other day in the history of St. Germaine. It wasn't the weather—the weather was perfect. Warmer than usual and perfect for shopping, perfect for hiking, perfect for everything you could imagine. It wasn't the Ferris wheel that Wormy and his step-son, D'Artagnan Fabergé-Dupont, had hauled over from Wormy Acres and set up in the corner of Sterling Park. It wasn't the five members of the Exorkizein, all dressed in their gowns with red embroidered crosses and wielding their exorcism wands as they marched around the square, having decided that at least one of the demons had taken refuge in the park. It wasn't the occasional Minque racing for its life through town, being chased by teenagers with baseball bats. It wasn't even the air of expectancy that hadn't been experienced by St. Germainians since the Crèche Wars of ought-two, a palpable feeling of anticipation brought on by the inaugural performance of *The Living Gobbler* at St. Barnabas Church.

It was the culmination of all of these things, plus the largest Thanksgiving weekend shopping crowd in ten years. And it was still only nine o'clock. Wormy and D'Artagnan made quite a pair: Wormy, a short, stocky man with a big grin; D'Artagnan, about six and a half feet tall and as big around as a knitting needle. He still had his trademark "mullet" but had changed the color of his hairdo from lime green with pink highlights to a horrific blondish-orange. He sported rimless, round glasses and under his nose hung a wispy mustache like a piece of colorless, limp seaweed. They hadn't begun offering rides yet, Wormy being content to send the unoccupied Ferris wheel around and around, demonstrating its safety to the onlookers before opening for business at ten.

As the Exorkizein made their way around the square, single file, wands waving, people moved amiably out of their way and watched them as one might watch an impromptu parade in downtown Asheville. Every so often, Carmel Bottoms would point at a tree, or sundial, or even the statue of Harrison Sterling himself, and the group would surround the landmark, join hands and chant together in Latin:

Exorcizo te, omnis spiritus immunde,
in nomine Dei Patris omnipotentis.

I couldn't tell if it was working, but the crowds going from store to store appreciated the show, and several folks even tossed a few coins as a tip into the smoking brazier that was being carried aloft by the young man.

I was in town early because I'd received a phone call from Pete informing me that the DANGLs were indeed planning on demonstrating against the City Council who, two days before, had decided they'd try to block the sale of Camp Possumtickle, citing family values and the St. Germaine decency law of 1903. Pete had not been present. Nancy, Dave, and I were in town to escort any naked DANGLs to the Police Station, after which we had no idea what we'd do with them. Luckily, by noon, none had shown up.

Ian Burch, PhD, took the opportunity to bring his Early Musik Consort to the park as a preview for the evening's performance. Ten of them had taken up places in the gazebo and sat behind stands on wooden stools. Two others were performing intricate and extremely boring dances on the lawn. I waved at Kent Murphee as I walked by and watched him redden. He was clad, much like the others, in a bright blue tunic, red tights, pointy shoes and a great floppy hat adorned with an ostrich feather. Nancy spotted him and laughed out loud, but then, Nancy has always had a cruel streak. I just waved, tipped my hat and smiled. Gamba, Ian Burch's vegan dog, was on a leash and tied to the gazebo. He looked hungry, but then, he always looked hungry. During one of the Consort's frequent breaks, I saw a Minque shoot out from under the gazebo, give the dog a vicious nip and take off toward the library. Gamba was apoplectic, but tied securely. His barking ceased once Ian gave him a bacon flavored lentil chip.

Bud McCollough spent the afternoon sitting at a table with Anne Cooke in front of the Ginger Cat. Anne decided that Bud was a model salesman for her new line of local wines. There were at least seven wineries in the tri-county area and the Ginger Cat was a perfect distribution point, having both a liquor license and a cute little shop featuring local arts and crafts. Bud was still too young to sell the wine directly, but he could give the customers a bit of his wine-speak and some recommendations. Then Anne would give them a taste and send them inside to the cash register. It was brilliant.

Pete had let Ardine set up a table outside the Slab to sell her quilts. Cash only. No checks. She brought ten. All were gone by noon.

As the afternoon wore on, the Ferris wheel business began to wane and the crowds that had been thronging the stores started to disperse. By five, it was getting dark and Wormy wanted to close it down, but D'Artagnan said that since the park was well lighted, he'd man the wheel till the end of *The Living Gobbler*, just in case some of the kids wanted rides after the show. This was fine with Wormy. He was beat and wanted to get home before Noylene left for the church. Also, he suspected there might be tuna loaf and collards for supper.

And so, with a seven o'clock curtain, the stage was set.

"I thought you were kidding about the turkey outfit," grumbled Pete. "What about my dignity?"

The cast, according to the Lemmings' instructions, had gathered to costume in the Parish Hall while the audience was being herded to their seats.

"Pete," I laughed, "you flashed Cynthia during the debate in front of everyone. You have no dignity. Anyway, that'll teach you to skip dress rehearsal."

"I was checking Cynthia's tan," said Pete, grinning beneath the beak and comb that made up his turkey headdress. "I must say that I find her chocolate hue disturbingly prurient." He flopped his arms, now concealed in two massive brown, feathered wings. "Shouldn't a woman be playing the turkey? What about their giant breasts?"

"What about them?" said Meg, coming up behind us.

We turned and caught our collective breaths. "Holy smokes!" I said. "You look..." Words failed me.

"Breathtaking? Stunning? Stupefying?" asked Meg, with a giggle.

"All that and more," I answered. "Wow!"

Meg was wearing her Indian outfit, an off-the-shoulder, form-fitting, white doe-skin dress with fringe in all the right places and Cherokee bead-work that would feel at home in any art gallery in the country. Her black hair, crowned with a wreath of baby's breath, settled softly around her shoulders, and her gray eyes sparkled like diamonds.

"If he won't marry you," said Pete, "I will."

"I can't marry you, Pete," said Meg. "You're a real turkey."

"Oh, ha ha," said Pete. "Like I haven't heard that one twenty times already. Listen, could you straighten out my tail feathers? I can't reach back there."

It was true enough. He couldn't reach his tail feathers. Not only did they fan out a good five feet in all directions, but his torso had been padded to give him that well-fed, butterball look. The whole package, including his spindly legs clad in yellow tights and giant orange shoes, looked very turkey-esque indeed. Meg straightened out his tail and spun him back around.

"You remember your line?" I asked.

"Gobble-gobble," said Pete. "Gobble-gobble? Who the hell wrote that?"

"Not me. That's one of Fiona's," I laughed.

"Hey!" yelled Noylene from across the room. "Meg, you get away from there. He's not allowed to see the bride."

Meg gave my hand a squeeze and disappeared though the crowd to the other side of the hall.

"I'd rather be a pilgrim," said Pete. "Wormy could have been the turkey. Or Billy."

"Nope. You have to be the best man, and therefore, the turkey."

"But why?"

"I have no idea," I said, "but you must embrace the way of the Gobbler. You think this is any better?" I gestured to my own costume—black pants, a black coat, a black stovepipe hat with a buckle on it and shoes to match.

"Hell, yes!" said Pete, straining his neck to see over his shoulder. "Look at me. My butt's a Technicolor nightmare."

*The Living Gobbler*, as conceived by Fiona Tidball-Lemming, was a loose collection of skits and songs all tied together with narration and poetry that she'd written for the occasion. I had gladly relinquished creative control early on in the project, just happy to have my *Hymn to the Living Gobbler* included in the festivities. Since I was to be in the production, Father Lemming was conscripted to play the keyboard and Ian Burch's Early Musik Consort instructed to accompany wherever they could. Father Lemming had written down some lead sheets for the Consort, but the recorder and cornamuse players were having a hard time playing from the charts. They were used to actual notes.

Christopher Lloyd, an interior designer from Boone, had been conscripted by Fiona to be the narrator. Fiona had met him when, upon consultation with Annette Passaglio, she had hired him to help her redo the rectory. The vestry had since squelched her redecorating ambitions, but a deep bond had been formed, and now Mr. Christopher, dressed in black spandex pilgrim eveningwear with just a few sequins, was the MC for the evening.

We began with a hymn, the whole congregation—from Buffet seating all the way to the Gourmet section—standing and singing *We Gather Together To Ask The Lord's Blessing*. During the hymn, the vegetables and side dishes made their way to the front of the church where the Lemmings had constructed a stage to resemble a giant dining room table complete with an eight-foot tall candelabra. What followed was nothing short of fantastic.

Broccoli and squash, apple and cauliflower, corn and dinner rolls, all put aside their ancient animosity and did a square-dance to a Virginia reel played by the Consort and culminating with Christopher Lloyd in the middle of the group doing a fair impression of Michael Flatley in *Lord of the Harvest*. The applause was tremendous as Mr. Christopher ended up on one knee, his arms outstretched, one side of his headband drooping over an eye thanks to the weight of the pilgrim's buckle he had hot-glued to the black satin.

Moosey made an impressive debut as Little Feather, The Wampanoag Indian boy, as he and his faithful vegan dog, Pequot, told the story of hunting the mighty Gobbler for the first Thanksgiving.

"Me hunt-um mighty gobble-gobble," said Little Feather. "Me heap big brave. This Pequot, heap big dog."

"Brilliant writing," mumbled Pete. "She heap big idiot."

"Quiet," I whispered. "You're almost on."

"Me see-um gobble-gobble, me shoot-um," said Little Feather, leading Pequot on a stealthy stalk around the front of the sanctuary. He had a bow and arrow in one hand and Pequot's leash in the other. Then, suddenly, he dropped the leash, put his hand to his mouth, and gave a great war-whoop.

"That's your cue," I said, giving Pete a light shove.

Pete waddled out onto the table. A huge laugh and a round of applause greeted his appearance.

"Little Feather see-um gobble-gobble," yelled Moosey. "Pequot see-um gobble-gobble."

Pequot not only see-um gobble-gobble, Pequot recognize gobble-gobble from vegan dreams. His wiener-dog legs weren't long enough to get him onto the stage, but he ran around the outside, growling and barking like he was an actual Rottweiler and Pete was a walking, talking Tofurkey. Pete's eyes grew wide, not knowing if this was actually part of the show or not. It didn't pay to skip dress rehearsal.

"Say your line," hissed Moosey.

Pete looked at him in alarm. Ian was now trying to corral his dog and trying to make himself as inconspicuous as possible by walking bent over at the waist, his head tucked into his shoulders, and scurrying with tiny steps, in the time honored belief that walking like a duck makes a person invisible.

"Say your line!" insisted Moosey.

Ian grabbed hold of Pequot and hauled him over to the door. Pequot was still growling.

"Your line!" said Moosey, baring his teeth.

"Gooble-gobble," said Pete.

"Thwang!" sang Moosey's bow. The arrow, mercifully devoid of an actual arrowhead, hit Pete right in the chest with a resounding "thwack!"

"Son of a bitch!" yelped Pete. "You shot me! Is this in the script?"

"Whoop-whoop-whoop," hollered Moosey, leaping onto the stage, wielding his tomahawk in his free hand.

Pete gave a girlish scream, turned tail feathers and hopped off the table quicker than you could say "Little Feather scalp-um gobble-gobble." Moosey chased him all the way to the sacristy to great applause and general hilarity.

"I think he would have killed me!" Pete puffed. "Was that a real tomahawk?"

"Yeah," I said. "But he probably wouldn't have killed you. I think it was just method acting."

"Sure," said Pete, glaring at me. "That's probably it."

Cynthia's belly dance to *Over the River and Through the Woods* was especially moving, especially when she got to the part that went "Oh, hear the bell ring, Ting-a-ling-ling!" Her Nubian hips rang every bell on her girdle and then some. The Little Lemmings, all seven of them, dressed as cranberries, were on their best behavior as they sang along with their father's nightclub stylings.

Following Cynthia's galloping gyrations, Muffy and Varmit Lemieux, Pocahontas and John Smith respectively, performed the *Indian Love Call*, complete with lute and sacbut accompaniment.

"When I'm calling you...ooo...ooo," sang Varmit.

"I will answer too...ooo...ooo," answered Muffy, batting her eyes.

The vegetables and side dishes came wandering onto the table two-by-two and hand-in-hand, providing choral backup. The cranberries swayed back and forth in rhythm.

"When I call, our love will come true," sang Muffy and Varmit.

"You'll belong to me," answered the vegetables.

"I'll belong to youuuuu."

We were treated to a dramatic reenactment of the *First Thanksgiving* with Billy Hixon as Miles Standish, Beaver Jergenson as Squanto, and Bootsie Watson as Priscilla Mullins. Mr. Christopher provided the narration and many other Indians and pilgrims had one-liners to spice up the story.

"Ugh!" said Beaver. "Me show-um how to plant-um corn."

"Thank thee, gentle Squanto," said Billy.

The *Hymn to the Living Gobbler* was the finale, of course, and I was looking forward to it, but before that I had to get married.

After the Thanksgiving dramatization, Marjorie struck a chord with her spoken and signed version of *Hiawatha's Wedding Feast*, and then, as the Consort began to play, Meg's bridesmaids began the short walk down the aisle. I was standing by the side door at the front of the north transept with Father Tony, also dressed in pilgrim garb.

"Who's that?" said Tony, nodding toward the balcony.

"That's the Exorkizein," I said.

"Exorcists?"

"Your Greek is pretty good," I said with a grin. "I hope they're just here to watch."

"Too late now," said Tony, giving me a nudge. "Time to go."

Tony and I went to our positions on the table. The vegetables, side dishes, Indians and pilgrims moved back and gave us room. Pete waddled in from the other side, his tail feathers resplendent in the spotlight. He took his place beside me.

"Lookin' good," I whispered.

"Thank thee, gentle Squanto," he said under his breath.

Bev was the first maid-of-honor, followed by Crayonella, Elaine and Cynthia. They were all dressed the same—dark yellow dresses made of a material suggestive of buckskin, with a design that conveyed the impression of Indian princesses. They all had yellow flowers in their hair and carried bouquets of yellow flowers. Four black women. Very pretty. Very PC. I tried to look past them but couldn't see Meg.

Then, the music changed and there she was, walking by herself, a vision of loveliness. She didn't carry any flowers, but walked down the aisle, head high, hands at her side, and took her place by my side. She reached down and took my hand.

"Dearly beloved," began Father Tony, "we are gathered together here in the sight of God, and in the face of this congregation, to join together this man and this woman in holy matrimony; which is an honorable estate, instituted of God in the time of man's innocency, signifying unto us the mystical union that is betwixt Christ and his Church."

Meg and I had chosen the 1662 service with a few changes, it being the closest to the one that real pilgrims might have used.

"I require and charge you both, as ye will answer at the dreadful day of judgement when the secrets of all hearts shall be disclosed, that if either of you know any impediment, why ye may not be lawfully joined together in Matrimony, ye do now confess it."

We didn't answer, but looked at each other and smiled. Then my nose twitched and I smelled something burning.

"Hayden Konig, wilt thou have this woman to thy wedded wife, to live together after God's ordinance in the holy estate of Matrimony? Wilt thou love her and serve her, comfort and honor her, and keep her in sickness and in health; and, forsaking all others, keep thee only unto her, so long as ye both shall live?"

"I will." The odor was stronger now.

"Megan Farthing, wilt thou have this man to thy wedded husband, to live together after God's ordinance in the holy estate of Matrimony? Wilt thou love him and serve him, comfort and honor him, and keep him in sickness and in health; and, forsaking all others, keep thee only unto him, so long as ye both shall live?"

"I will." Meg smelled it now. I could see her eyes dart toward the back of the church.

"Then repeat after me. I, Hayden..."

I repeated the vows, trying to keep my mind on the task at hand.

"I, Megan," began Father Tony, leading Meg through the same ritual. I could now see other people looking around from the corner of my eye. I didn't see any smoke, but the smell was pervasive.

"You may place the ring on her finger and repeat after me. With this ring, I thee wed..." I followed his lead.

"With my body, I thee worship," I pledged, "and with all my worldly goods I thee endow: In the Name of the Father, and of the Son, and of the Holy Ghost. Amen."

"Let us pray," said Father Tony, oblivious to the smell. Then I heard a low growl come from under the platform where we were standing.

"Those whom God hath joined together let no man put asunder. For as much as Hayden and Megan have consented together in holy wedlock, and have witnessed the same before God and this company, and thereto have given and pledged their troth either to other, I now pronounce you..."

It was at that moment that all hell broke loose.

Gamba, the vegan dog, had followed his nose under the giant dining table and found a nest of Minques taking refuge behind the orange material draping the front of the platform. He was not amused. Gamba was easily the match for one Minque, maybe two. But there were more. A lot more. The odds weren't good. Still, he had quite a pedigree—half Rottweiler and half Dachshund, a tough little dog bred to hunt badgers. Added to that, he'd never tasted meat and seemed quite anxious to do so. All this may not have been the exact analysis of the situation that went through his little canine brain at that moment, but was probably a better explanation than his actual thought process, a process that went something like this:

*"Roooowwwwwwrrr!"*

Minques shot from under stage like brown, furry bullets out of a scattergun. Crayonella screamed and tried unsuccessfully to climb up the nearest pilgrim. Bev bent over and smacked one of the creatures on the snout with her flowers.

"Get out of here!" she screeched. "You...you...Minque!"

Elaine and Cynthia had taken refuge by standing on the front pew, a position taken by most of the women (and some of the men) in the congregation as fifteen or twenty Minques beat a panicked exit toward the front doors with a mad Rott-wiener in hot pursuit.

Dave and Nancy had their hands full. They'd planned to come into the church and watch the wedding ceremony, but the DANGLs had marched into town to protest the halting of the sale of Camp Possumtickle.

The DANGLs had arrived in the park, bought Ferris wheel tickets from D'Artagnan, and subsequently disrobed, timing their demonstration so they'd be very visible, riding atop the Ferris wheel, just as *The Living Gobbler* came to a close. They had all twelve bucket seats filled with thirty-six DANGLs when Dave and Nancy, sitting in the office having a cup of coffee, spotted them and came running.

Dave and Nancy rounded up the ones on the ground, three and four at a time, and took them over to the Police Station. When the station filled up, they took them to the Slab. Dave called for help from the Boone PD, but Appalachian State had a home football game and they couldn't spare the manpower for a bunch of Christian nudists.

Collette had been walking into town from her basement apartment, determined not to have anything to do with the wedding, but curious nevertheless. She planned to stand outside and watch as the wedding party exited the church, but, upon reaching the square, found the town deserted, most of the occupants either out of town visiting relatives, inside relaxing, or at *The Living Gobbler* performance. Adding to her confusion were piles of clothes in the park. Lots of them. She grabbed her cell phone and tried to call Dave. Imagine her surprise and subsequent panic when she heard Dave's ring coming from a phone sitting on top of a pair of khaki pants. She never bothered to look up into the Ferris wheel but ran screeching toward St. Barnabas.

Collette flung wide the doors of the church. The Minques didn't even slow as they raced past her. "It's the Rapture!" she wailed, bursting into the confluence of panicked Minques, vegetables, Indians, ticket-holders, assorted pilgrims, and one enthusiastic Rott-wiener. "We who are alive shall be caught up in the clouds, to meet the Lord in the air— First Thessalopians 4:17! It's the Rapture! It's the Rapture *and I've been left behind!*"

The Exorkizein, not content to wait until *The Living Gobbler* performance finished, had taken the occasion to light some candles in the choir loft and do a bit of wand waving while Marjorie was bewitching the audience with her rendition of *Hiawatha*. While the Exorkizein were busy watching the performance, one of the lit candles fell into the organ pipe case. They didn't think much about it until they smelled the smoke. They tried, in vain, to open the case, but it was locked and they were far too late. All five of them had snuck down the stairs and were standing by the front doors just as Collette came in screaming.

"Fire!" yelled Father Lemming, being the first to spot the flames. "Nobody move! You kids get out of here!" he shouted to his children. The cranberries headed for the front doors in a bunch. "Follow the Lemmings!" Father Lemming yelled over the panic, pushing people aside in his effort to get to the front doors. His wife, Fiona, was left on the stage along with most of the cast.

"We can go out the side door," I said calmly to the folks in the front. "No problem. We have plenty of time. Father Tony will lead you out."

Tony led the cast off the stage, into the transept and out the side door. Pete, Billy, and I hung back surveying the impending doom. The fire had now engulfed the organ loft and was licking at the roof. This building was built in 1904. We knew it wouldn't last long.

"It's a sad day," said Billy. Pete and I nodded.

"Everybody out?" Billy asked.

I squinted down the nave and saw the last of the crowd disappear out the front door. "Looks like it."

"Anyone call the fire department?" Pete said. "I don't have a phone in this stupid turkey outfit."

"I'm sure someone has," I said. "Most of the department was here anyway. They've all got to go home and get their gear, then get the truck and make their way back. Could be a while."

"What about your gun?" asked Pete. "In the organ bench?"

I shrugged. "You guys head around front. There's no telling what's going on out there. I'll go make sure the Parish Hall is clear."

The park in front of the church was bedlam. The audience and cast members who had rushed out the front of the church were watching in horror as the flames burst through the roof of the narthex and started engulfing the bell tower. The supply of power to the Ferris wheel, coming from St. Barnabas Church, suddenly shut down as the breakers shorted out leaving thirty-six naked DANGLs swinging back and forth in the glowing firelight of the burning church. Three of them, occupying the lowest swing, slid under the safety bar and dropped to the ground. The rest of the folks on the Ferris wheel could do nothing but sit and watch.

The other DANGLs, the ones who had been locked up, simply turned the deadbolts and came back into the park. Both the police station and the Slab Café could be easily unlocked from the inside, not having been built to restrain prisoners. The DANGLs all stood there—naked as jaybirds— watching the church burn. I saw Lacie and asked her if I could get her a blanket. She declined with a shake of her head. A couple of feet away, Mr. Christopher was talking to Chad, but didn't offer to get him a blanket.

Gamba, no longer a vegan, had caught four of the Minques, killed each of them, and was piling the parts of them he didn't eat in front of the church steps. Once he dropped his Minque remains onto the pile, he headed back into the park after yet another one.

Once everyone was safe, there wasn't anything Dave, Nancy, or I could do except wait, like the others, for the fire department. The members of Ian's Early Musik Consort had gathered on the front lawn and were counting their instruments. I waved to Kent and he gave me a wave in return. The Lemmings, father and cranberries, were huddled under an oak tree. Fiona was there too, giving Adrian a very large piece of her mind.

The St. Germaine Volunteer Fire Department was on the scene quickly, all things considered. Their main job, as the fire chief explained to me, was to confine the fire to the sanctuary and try to save the Parish Hall and the surrounding buildings. I found Moosey trying to talk to a fireman and sent him over to the gazebo. Then I went searching for Meg.

"Has anyone seen Collette?" asked a frantic Dave. "Someone said she went into the church! I need to call her, but I can't find my cell phone. I must have dropped it."

I shook my head and gave a quick look around and pointed to the front steps. "Nancy has her phone. She's over with the firemen. Use her's." I caught his arm as he started to run off. "I'm sure Collette came back out, Dave. I didn't see anyone in there and I was the last one to leave."

Meg and Father Tony were standing together across the street in front of the Slab. I made my way across the park, weaving through the clumps of people: some huddled together sobbing: others, shaking their heads in disbelief: still others, watching the fire stoically.

Meg had a blanket around her shoulders. I thought she'd be crying, but she wasn't. She watched as the fire engulfed the bell tower, tilting her head as it collapsed inward in a shower of sparks. We heard the bell crash to the floor. She gave a small, sad smile.

"It's the end of something, isn't it?" she said.

"And the beginning," I said. "We'll build it back."

"Hey," she said, suddenly looking at me. "Are we married or not?"

I thought for a moment. "No. No, I don't think so. We never got to that part."

"Of course, you're married, you nitwits!" said Father Tony. He waved his hand absently in front of him in the sign of the cross. "I now pronounce you man and wife, blah, blah, blah. You may kiss the bride."

And I did.

# Postlude

No one in St. Germaine, including Dave, ever saw Collette again. The firemen sifted through the wreckage during the next few days looking for her body, but it wasn't to be found. There was some talk from folks in her church about putting up a monument in the park. They even designed a triptych and commissioned Beaver Jergenson to carve it out of a giant stump with his chainsaw. It portrayed the three saints who had never experienced death, but were taken directly to heaven—Elijah, Enoch, and Collette. Cynthia Johnsson, the new mayor, declined the offer of a permanent installation.

There were two other miracles that night, people would later say. The first was that nothing but the church had burned. The fire department, working far into the night, couldn't save the parish hall, but even with the proximity of St. Barnabas to the other buildings on Main Street, the flames were confined to the church. The second miracle was the one they still talk about. The congregation came to the square the next morning, intent on having a service of Thanksgiving in the park in front of the charred ruins. There, sitting amongst fallen leaves of gold, orange and red, was the St. Barnabas altar, the communion elements set in their place.

"Marilyn," I said, "how about some java?" I tugged my hat down over my eyes, kicked back in my chair, and lit up a stogie. Marilyn came in with a cup of joe, wearing a mink, high heels and a smile.

It was good to be a detective.


The End

# About the Author

Mark Schweizer lives and works in Hopkinsville, Kentucky, where he composes music, writes books, and directs a church choir.

In the field of bad writing, he had the distinction of receiving a Dishonorable Mention in the 2006 Bulwer-Lytton Fiction Contest (www.bulwer-lytton.com), an annual contest in which the entrants compete for the dubious honor of having composed the worst opening sentence to an imaginary novel. In 2007, his sentence found on page 17 (the one about the rosary) was runner-up in the Detective Category.

# The Liturgical Mysteries

**The Alto Wore Tweed**
*Independent Mystery Booksellers Association*
*"Killer Books" selection, 2004*

**The Baritone Wore Chiffon**

**The Tenor Wore Tapshoes**
*IMBA 2006 Dilys Award nominee*

**The Soprano Wore Falsettos**
*Southern Independent Booksellers Alliance*
*2007 Book Award Nominee*

**The Bass Wore Scales**

**The Mezzo Wore Mink**

*Just A Note*

If you've enjoyed this book—or any of the other mysteries in this series—please drop me a line. My e-mail address is mark@sjmp.com. Also, don't forget to visit the website (www.sjmpbooks.com) for lots of great stuff! You'll find recordings and "downloadable" music for many of the great works mentioned in the Liturgical Mysteries including *The Pirate Eucharist, The Weasel Cantata, The Mouldy Cheese Madrigal, The Banjo Kyrie* and a lot more.

Cheers,
Mark